Smolder

Sam E. Kraemer

Kaye Klub Publishing

ROAD TO ROCKTOBERFEST 2024

COPYRIGHT

This book is an original work of fiction. Names, characters, places, incidents, and events are the product of the author's imagination and are used fictitiously. Any resemblance to actual persons, living or dead, business establishments, events, or locales is entirely coincidental.

Copyright ©2024 by Sam E. Kraemer

Cover Designer: Jo Clement, Covers by Jo

Formatter: TL Travis

Editor: Abbie Nicole, ASP

Proofreaders: Mildred Jordan, I Love Books Proofreading

Published by Kaye Klub Publishing

These characters are the author's original creations, and the events herein are the author's sole intellectual property. The novel has been edited and recovered for this rerelease. No rights to the content of this story are forfeited due to the previous versions of the manuscript.

All products/brand names mentioned in this work of fiction are registered trademarks owned by their respective holders/corporations/owners. No trademark infringement intended.

No part of this book may be reproduced, scanned, or distributed in any form, printed or electronic, without the express permission of the author. Please do not participate in or encourage piracy of copyrighted materials in violation of the author's rights. Purchase only authorized editions.

Note: NO AI/NO BOT. The author does not consent to any Artificial Intelligence (AI), generative AI, large language model, machine learning, chatbot, or other automated analysis, generative process, or replication program to reproduce, mimic, remix, summarize, or otherwise replicate any part of this creative work, via any means: print, graphic, sculpture, multimedia, audio, or other medium without express permission from the author. I support the right of humans to control their artistic works.

Their Story—

Skyler Ashe, a mild-mannered band teacher, hates the spotlight. His father is the drummer and lead singer for From the Ashes, a hard-partying eighties hair band on the brink of a comeback—until Skyler's father has a cardiac event during a scandalous liaison. Enter Skyler, who gets guilted into picking up the sticks until his father is up to performing again.

Sanders "Sandy" Kensington, former defensive tackle for the Chicago Breeze, doesn't have much going on since being pressured to retire from football. His little brother is the manager of a washed-up late-eighties hair band, and when one of their gold records is solicited for use in an action-movie blockbuster, Sandy gets goaded into helping his brother keep the band members out of trouble.

After a series of unlucky events, it's clear to Sandy someone is trying to keep From the Ashes off the stage. Sandy vows to protect Skyler and the band while struggling with his attraction to the young drummer.

Will Skyler's kindness and innocence hurt the band's rock-star image, or will Sandy introduce Skyler to the ways of the world? Will the looks that Smolder between them go unnoticed, or will they become the stars of the show?

Smolder is a book in the multi-author Road to Rocktoberfest 2024 series. Each book can be read as a stand-alone, but why not read them all and see what antics our bands get into next? Hot rock stars and the men who love them, what more could you ask for? Kick back, load up your Kindle, and enjoy the men of Rocktoberfest!

CONTENTS

Prologue		IX
1.	Chapter One	1
2.	Chapter Two	11
3.	Chapter Three	25
4.	Chapter Four	38
5.	Chapter Five	50
6.	Chapter Six	61
7.	Chapter Seven	73
8.	Chapter Eight	92
9.	Chapter Nine	103
10.	Chapter Ten	115
11.	Chapter Eleven	125
12.	Chapter Twelve	137
13.	Chapter Thirteen	148
14.	Chapter Fourteen	160

15.	Chapter Fifteen	171
16.	Chapter Sixteen	184
17.	Chapter Seventeen	198
18.	Chapter Eighteen	214
19.	Chapter Nineteen	227
20.	Chapter Twenty	238
21.	Chapter Twenty-one	249
22.	Chapter Twenty-two	261
23.	Chapter Twenty-three	273
24.	Chapter Twenty-four	285
25.	Chapter Twenty-five	301
26.	Chapter Twenty-six	317
27.	Chapter Twenty-seven	330
28.	Chapter Twenty-eight	343
29.	Chapter Twenty-nine	358
30.	Chapter Thirty	376
31.	Epilogue	393
	About Sam E. Kraemer	400
	Other Books by Sam E. Kramer/L.A. Kaye	401

Prologue

Skyler Ashe

"One. Two. Three. Four."

I swung my right hand holding the baton to count off the beat for my middle school band members. The drummer began pounding the concert bass in time with me before I lifted my left hand to bring in the woodwinds.

The middle school band members were preparing for the end-of-school concert, and I was beyond proud of their progress. We were practicing "Go Tell Aunt Rhody," which I was planning to have the kids who weren't in the band sing along to as a finale. We had three songs at the concert, and my kids had been working hard to impress their parents. I was busting my buttons at how far they'd come since the beginning of the school year.

My cell phone vibrated in my shirt pocket, but I ignored it. It was a Friday, and it was likely my softball friends wanting to make plans for the evening. I was exhausted from a long week of preparing for the end of the school year, so going out wasn't on my to-do list.

After glancing at the clock over my office door, I rotated my wrist while folding my hand into a fist to signal the band members to stop. "Okay, let's call it a day. You guys are doing great. Monday, we'll invite your classmates into the gym to practice the song for the finale. I'm proud of you guys. Get ready for the bell, and no roughhousing. We only have two weeks left of school, and you don't want to spend it in detention."

I gathered my music folder and baton, stepping off the podium as the kids began storing their music stands at the back of the room and putting away their instruments, which reminded me. "Don't forget—two hours of practice over the weekend with a signed note from your parent or guardian, please. The concert is next Thursday."

I unlocked my office door and went inside, placing my notebook on my desk and the conducting baton in my pencil holder. I retrieved my phone from my pocket to check the messages, seeing a text from my mother, Hope, and a missed call and voice message from Dusty Carson, one of my dad's bandmates in From the Ashes.

With Mom, it could be anything from a leaking pipe to a question about her computer to something my little brother had done to piss her off. Dusty's voicemail would be more to the point, though I couldn't begin to imagine what he could want.

When the dismissal bell rang, I walked back into the band room. "Have a great weekend, everyone. See you Monday!"

I opened the door and stood in the hallway to attempt to keep things orderly as the kids went to their lockers to gather their things. The library was across from my music room, and I could see Mrs. Maroney through the open door, likely boxing up the books she'd banned for the next school year.

It never failed to amaze me the things people believed would harm children. They were a lot more resilient than they were given credit for. If we wanted them to grow into well-rounded adults, they needed to learn things that people like Mrs. Maroney wanted to keep from them. It made no sense to me.

Rumor had it she'd removed all the books that mentioned anything to do with the differences between boys and girls from the school library before the year started, and then she went after the local library. Thankfully, the librarian at the West Peoria Public Library was younger than forty, and she refused to kowtow to Mrs. Maroney's demands.

Once the hallway was clear, I returned to the band room and straightened the chairs, picked up a few pieces of trash, and set the garbage can by the door to help the custodian. West Peoria Middle School was like a family—a very conservative family, but there were a few people at the school who weren't homophobes. Nonetheless, I kept my sexuality to myself.

I returned to my office and tapped the voicemail icon from the earlier call. "Sky, this is Dusty. I wanted to give you a heads-up before someone else reaches out. Regal's in El Camino Hospital in Mountain View. He had a heart attack, and the docs found his arteries were ninety percent blocked. He's in surgery right now, and they say he'll be okay, but I thought you should know. Call me back."

A heart attack? Hell, I believed Reginald Regal Ashe was bulletproof. He was a hell-raising son of a bitch who had a long list of sins to his credit. A heart attack had to be anticlimactic as far as Regal was concerned.

I sighed and gathered my messenger bag to go home before I turned off the lights. I lived within walking distance of the school, so I could call Mom as I walked home.

I stopped to fill my water bottle at the drinking fountain and headed out the front door, waving to the school secretary, Mrs. Brownlee. She was a nice woman who tried to fix me up with her daughter, Natalie. I stayed out of her way as much as possible.

I opened the text from Mom to see it just said, "Call me, honey," so I did.

"Sky? Thank you for calling me back. Have you talked to anyone?"

Obviously, she knew about Regal, which was a surprise. I knew she didn't get along with wife number two, Jeanne, and I didn't know if she knew fiancée number three. There were so many nameless women in between that I'd given up keeping track.

"I haven't talked to anyone, but Dusty left me a voicemail earlier. He said Regal had a heart attack. Something about surgery?"

Mom released a huge sigh. "It's not what you think."

I heard a loudspeaker in the background but couldn't determine what was said. "Mom, where are you?"

"I'm in Mountain View at the hospital, Sky. It's complicated, sweetheart. Can you come out? Your father wants to see you, and I know River would love to spend time with you. Can you come?"

"What's going on, Mom?"

"Just come, please. I need you, Sky." I heard the tears in her voice, and they crumbled my resolve.

"Mom, it's the second to last week of school, and we have the end-of-the-year concert next—"

"Sky, Jeanne and I were with your father when it happened. The three of us are in a polyamorous relationship, and we were having sex when your father had the heart attack."

I stopped on the sidewalk and sat on a bench. How the hell would I ever get that out of my head?

Chapter One

Skyler

Friday morning, after the Thursday night concert, I stepped off the plane in San Jose. Regal was still in the hospital. After speaking with the school district administrator, I stayed in West Peoria until after the end-of-year concert and skipped the last week of school to go check on Regal, not that I thought he deserved my care or concern after all the crap he'd pulled.

I'd tried like heck to block the idea out of my mind that my mother was part of a ménage à trois because I didn't want to know anything of the sort. Why was my mother so set on telling me the dirty details of what happened behind closed doors?

I walked out of security to see a man—a very handsome man—holding a tablet with my name on the screen. I approached and offered a smile. "I'm Skyler Ashe."

The driver was unbelievably handsome in a familiar way, but I hadn't spent time in California since before I went to college in Carbondale, Illinois. He was either a model or a celebrity moonlighting as a driver.

He took my large duffel. "Do you have a checked bag?"

"I, uh... No. I only brought this. Should I have brought more?" I'd brought enough clean clothes for five days because I wasn't planning to stay longer. I had a summer job working at Mindy's Botanicals in Peoria. It paid the bills, and I loved plants. I'd been fortunate to land the spot and planned to return by my start date.

The driver shrugged and led us out the door to the parking garage. He opened the back door of a black Suburban SUV, and I got inside while he tossed my duffel in the cargo area. He hopped into the front seat and started the vehicle, heading out of the parking garage of San Jose Mineta International Airport.

He turned onto I-280 and headed west toward Cupertino, where Mom lived, or so I thought. "You drive this route a lot?" There was no music to get lost in, and I had no idea who the guy was in the front seat. I was nervous, unsure of how I would handle myself when we arrived at my mother's place.

"No."

Obviously, that wasn't a conversation opener. "I'm Skyler."

His eyes met mine in the rearview mirror. "Yeah, uh, I got that from when you told me inside the airport. Plus, I can read." He lifted the tablet and shook it before dropping it back into the passenger seat.

I decided not to attempt to talk to him, so I slid in my wireless earbuds and listened to some rock music, my all-time favorite genre. My dad's band, From the Ashes, was secretly my first pick for a sing-along. I used to listen to their music all the time because my father was never around, even after the band stopped being invited on big tours. Their music was dated, or so critics always said. Though I supposed they'd be considered vintage now.

From the Ashes were always trying to find their way back into the spotlight, playing county fairs and some small clubs on the West Coast during the summer to relive their youth. As far as I could tell from infrequent conversations with my little brother, River, they were only playing throwback concerts, which I guessed wasn't flattering in their opinions.

I never told my father how much I loved the band because we didn't talk much after he left us for Jeanne, but I knew every beat, accent, rimshot, and attack of every song From the Ashes ever played.

My old drum kit from my youth was in storage at my mom's place. As a teenager, when Regal backed out of something he and I were supposed to do, I'd go into the garage where Mom let me have my kit, turn on one of From the Ashes five albums, and beat the heck out of those skins with thoughts of my father's head being the pedal drum.

Every cymbal crash, choke, swell, and bark helped relieve the anger from my father's abandonment, but it was never completely gone. I might have been a huge fan of From the Ashes, but I wasn't a fan of Regal Ashe in the least.

I also mimicked every tone and note that came out of his mouth, though not always as well as my father. When I was having a bad day, I'd turn on their music and sing as loud as I could while the tears rolled down my teenage cheeks. I'd forgiven him for my own peace of mind, but I darn well hadn't forgotten any of it.

My favorite From the Ashes song was "'Bury Me'." It'd been their first gold record, and Regal swore he wrote it for my mom. Regal should have won an award for his ability to lie while staring into someone's eyes. He had the capacity to make anyone believe he was being honest while he crossed his fingers behind his back…figuratively.

I was humming "Man for the Job," one of their last hits, as we turned down my mother's street, Henderson Lane. At the end of the drive was the animal rescue farm Regal had bought Mom when they got their first record deal. I guessed he believed the animal rescue would keep her busy so she wouldn't realize he wasn't sleeping next to her at least five nights a week.

The driver stopped the SUV in front of the white Rambler ranch house with black trim. It was the same as I remembered from my childhood, including the tire swing I fell off and broke my arm when I was seven. There was something to be said about going home.

I braced myself when Mom hurried out of the house because I knew the drill. She'd throw herself into my arms and start crying because I only made the trip to Cupertino twice a year: for her birthday in July and around Christmastime. This trip in mid-May was an anomaly.

"Sky, my sweet boy. I'm so glad you came." She hugged me, and I hugged her back, happy to have a moment to reconnect before I heard the story of what happened with Regal.

The front screen door slammed, and I glanced in that direction to see my little brother, River, step onto the porch with his mom, Jeanne. They both looked worried, but I didn't know why. Did they live at the house now? Had Regal talked Mom into taking them in?

"Mom, what's going on?"

She pulled away and put her hands on my face. "Holy shit, Sky. You get more and more handsome every time I see you. Thank you for coming. Come say hi to Jeanne and your brother."

I liked River a lot. He was a sweet kid and hadn't let Regal's earlier successes or fortune go to his head. He cut the neighbors' grass for spending money because Regal didn't give any of us a cent the court didn't force him to provide.

"Wow, Riv! Look at you." The kid had grown a foot since I'd seen him a year ago when I visited for Mom's birthday and she invited him and Jeanne over. He was now taller than me with Regal's brown hair, while I had Mom's blonde.

River hugged me, slapping me on the back harder than I expected. "Dude, you're getting flabby." He pushed away, popped me on the stomach, and laughed.

"Brat. How're things going? You decide whether to go to college yet?"

River smirked. "Still weighing my options, bro. You hear this shit about my mom and your mom both fuckin' Regal?"

"Not in such detail, but I heard something about it. What do you think?"

River shrugged, which was exactly what I'd been doing since I agreed to come to Cupertino. I couldn't imagine what Mom saw in Regal after all his antics.

"I think it's bullshit, Sky. Does this guy have a fucking magic dick?"

I chuckled. "God, I hope not. I don't even like to think about that."

The driver carried my duffel over and dropped it beside me. "I'll be taking off now. Good luck." Without waiting for me to tip him, he returned to the Suburban and left.

"Wow, how the fuck do you know Sandy Kensington?" River had a look on his face I didn't understand.

"Who?"

"Sandy Kensington. He's the former defensive tackle for the Chicago Breeze. He retired last year under mysterious circumstances. Rumor has it he was dating the owner's barely legal daughter. The owner threatened to have him killed unless he disappeared. I saw a post that said the other thing was just a story told by the club to embarrass him."

I stared at River. "Where do you see this crap? Stop scrolling TikTok and open a book, Riv."

Was that true? Once River said it, I put the face to a name. I remembered the story on the news about Sanders Kensington, a former fifth-round draft choice from San Francisco, retiring at the end of February from the Chicago Breeze. He'd had a successful career, and there was talk of him turning down a job doing color commentary for Sports News Network.

I barely cared, but several teachers had discussed it at school. I wasn't a sports guy, but it had stuck with me. Now that I'd seen Sandy Kensington in person, I understood why all the females on staff had been bummed he was retiring. He was gorgeous.

"Grab my duffel and let's go inside. Is there any food in there?"

River picked up my duffel, and we headed into the house to face whatever fresh hell Regal Ashe had conjured for us.

As I let River in ahead of me, I glanced down the gravel driveway to see the dust hadn't settled yet from Sandy's departure. Would there be an opportunity for me to run into Sandy Kensington again? Was a chauffeur job the best he could get after retiring from football?

"He really wants to see you, Sky. Please come with us." I was in the kitchen with Mom. I was starving, having been up since before dawn, and Mom was trying to talk me into going with her and Jeanne to visit Regal. I was here. What more did they want from me?

"Mom, I highly doubt he wants to see me. He clearly didn't give a crap about me after River was born, and he didn't give a crap about River after he started seeing the next woman in line.

"Sky, honey, your father loves you and River. He wouldn't trade you boys for anything."

I sat across from her and sipped my coffee. "Mom, I love you, and I know you wish that was true, but I don't think Regal has given it that much thought. I don't think he loves anyone but himself and the next notch on his bedpost."

Mom sighed. "Just come with us. Talk to him, Sky. He paid for your education and made sure you never did without."

I laughed at her comment. "No, he didn't. Don't rewrite history, Mom. I got a scholarship to college in Illinois, and Regal gave me ten grand for expenses until I could find a job in Carbondale. He also told me he wanted me to pay him back, which is why I sent you money every month until my debt was paid. Did you forget that?"

Rewriting history in her mind was how my mother coped, but it didn't change a damn thing for me.

Chapter Two

Sanders "Sandy" Kensington

"I need a simple favor."

Famous last words from my little brother, Marshall. It was never *a* favor, and it was never simple.

"No."

I hooked the barbell on the weight bench clips and sat up. He'd been spotting me in my basement gym, and I needed to get rid of the guy before he talked me into something I would never want to do.

"You don't even know what it is, Sandy."

I didn't have to. I'd known the kid for thirty-five years—his whole life—and he was a pain in the ass. Always had been, always would be.

"How's Tina?" I stood and went to the linen closet by the stairs to get two towels.

It was hot in my basement because when Marsh came downstairs to work out with me, he started bitching that the place smelled like a cantina, so we opened the doors. I was sweating out a lot of tequila from a night out I didn't want to talk about because there wasn't anything to tell, and Marsh was a whiny asshole.

"Her name is Juliana, and she's history. I swear to fuck, Sandy, do you ever listen when I talk?"

"Close enough. What happened?" I didn't give a shit, really, but if we were talking about him, we weren't talking about me and my epically fucked-up life.

"She wanted me to introduce her to Ross Wilson from Begging for Trouble, another band CEA represents, so I did. Now she's fucking *him* instead of me. How long are you planning to wallow in self-pity?"

I handed him a towel and opened the fridge, grabbing two water bottles. I tossed one at him, and he barely caught it, making me laugh. "I see why you quit playing with any balls other than your own."

"Ha-fucking-ha. I got all the good looks and charm in the family, you fucking shit-house."

That made both of us laugh. My lovely granny gave me that nickname when I hit a growth spurt at thirteen and shot up almost a foot from one Christmas to the next when we visited her in Michigan. The next semester, the football coach at my junior high school in Cupertino started harassing me to train so I could play varsity football during my freshman year of high school.

"I do miss old Maude. She was a ballsy gal. Anyway, have you talked to Mom and Dad lately?"

Our parents moved to Stanford, California, when Dad got a job teaching at the university the year I went to college on a football scholarship. Marsh was just starting high school, and our parents had some grand idea that he would go to Stanford Law. Dad hoped he could get a break on the tuition, which was exactly what happened.

The only flaw in the plan was Marsh got his MBA and went into entertainment law instead of corporate. He lived in Los Angeles most of the time but came to visit me when he wanted something—like now.

"Talked to Mom on Thursday. Dad's up for department head next year. She doesn't want him to get it. She wants him to retire, but of course, he doesn't want to. You can call them, you know."

I guzzled the water and tossed the bottle into the recycling bin. "Leave it alone, Marsh."

My brother sat on the weight bench and stared at me. "Why won't you tell me what happened? Mom and Dad don't care that you're gay, Sandy."

I put my hands on top of my head, twining my fingers. "I beg to differ. Look, it's been a year, and they haven't tried to get in touch with me after everything happened. Leave it alone."

Marsh was silent for a moment before he glanced at the bench. "Dude, seriously? That stupid story about you dating the owner' teen daughter was ridiculous. It was all over the papers about you getting arrested for soliciting an undercover cop at a gay sex club in Albany when you were there for a game. It was a members-only club, Sandy. How the hell did you get in?"

I was ready to crawl out of my skin, so I changed the subject. "What's the favor?"

Marsh's face lit up. "Fine, don't tell me. I'm representing From the Ashes as a favor to Alicia. Her dad represented them back in the late eighties, early nineties. They were a hair band, which was popular then—they were signed by

RayCom, and when John, Alicia's father, left the company, he took them with him. They were his first clients."

One thing about Marsh—he liked to ramble like a narrator in a historical movie. "Marsh, cut to the chase. How do I come into this?"

"The drummer and lead singer had a heart episode yesterday. He had an emergency angioplasty. He was in the middle of having sex with his two ex-wives, if you can believe that shit."

"How old is he?" I laughed along with Marsh.

"Sixty-five. Fucker has had more tail than I've ever seen in my life. Anyway, he's engaged to a twenty-five-year-old girl, who is stirring up a whole lot of shit."

"I swear to god, Marsh—"

"Okay, okay. Harmon Studio is currently in post-production for a big action movie to be released next summer, and they want one of the band's old songs for it. They want the song re-recorded, and we have studio time booked for the end of June. I'm trying to set up a summer tour schedule. It'll only be five cities from San Diego to San Francisco to road test the updated song before we send it to the studio. Regal Ashe, the frontman, wants his oldest son to collaborate on the rewrite, but the two of them don't get along at all."

"So, what do you want me to do? Lock them in a room together until they kiss and make up?"

That was a load of bullshit. Some relationships just weren't meant to be—even between parents and their children, as I'd learned the hard way after my arrest.

The fucking owner of the club—Hot Sauce on the Side—got in trouble with local law enforcement over a drunk driving charge, and he allowed the cops to stake out the club and arrest people for lude and lascivious behaviors, me for propositioning a police officer for sex.

The guy had been eyeing my junk all night, and I was riding a high because I'd caught an interception and got a sack that night, so I was down to at least get my dick sucked. I was arrested before the guy pulled down the zipper of my pants.

It was ruled as entrapment when the prosecutor reviewed the case, and all charges were dropped against everyone caught up that night, but not before the news about me being arrested in a sting at a gay club spread like wildfire.

I embarrassed myself, my team, and my family. I resigned from the Chicago Breeze after a heart-to-heart discussion with the general manager, who strongly urged me to talk to a former teammate, Jackson Delacroix, who had been plagued by bad press after he got caught with his then-boyfriend on a tropical vacation.

I decided to save the Breeze from another scandal, and I "retired" after my phone call with Delacroix. The fucker was damn happy now—not one, but two gorgeous husbands, kids on the way, and the world by the ass. Last I heard, he was opening his own gym in Chicago.

How the hell had the Cajun gotten himself out of his mess and into such a great life when I couldn't get out of my own fucking way? My indiscretion had cost me nearly everything, but most of all, it cost me my parents. I'd been spinning my wheels for a year. I was sick of it. Hell, I was sick of myself.

"No. All I want is for you to pick the son up at the airport on Friday. He's coming to town to see his father, and I want you to make sure he doesn't change his mind. He lives in Peoria, as a matter of fact." Marsh laid back on the weight bench and braced his hands on the bar, so I moved over to spot him.

"You think you can lift this?" I'd been working out like it was still my job, and I could bench three-fifty, which was currently loaded on the bar. Marsh was nowhere near my size.

"What's on it?" He sat up and started adding up the weight I'd just finished lifting. I waited for him to take off his shoes to get a final count.

"Fuck you, Sandy. I'd die if I tried to lift that." He stomped over to the fridge and grabbed a beer.

"Hey, you just plopped your ass down on the bench. I didn't know if maybe you had some skills you've been keeping secret." I unloaded the weights and put them on the stand before I sprayed and wiped down the equipment, grabbing a beer for myself.

"You need me to be sure the guy gets to his parents' place? I don't have to make sure he stays, do I? How big is the fucker?" I sat at the bar in my mancave just outside the gym and stared at him.

"Nope. Just pick him up at the airport and take him to his mother's animal rescue in Cupertino. His mom, Hope Ashe, will take it from there. She's going to talk him into working with his father, she thinks. I don't know the guy. He's probably thirty, and judging by Regal Ashe, he's probably not too big. If you can bench three-fifty, I'm sure you can handle him."

I took a gulp of my beer. "Fine. I'm not taking my car." I had recently purchased a Maserati MC20. I wasn't risking my baby on some guy with daddy issues.

"Fine. He'll probably have luggage anyway. I'll rent an SUV and have it delivered here on Friday morning. You pick him up and take him to his mom's place." Marsh pulled out his phone and pecked in something before he put it on the bar.

My stomach growled, echoing off the walls of the basement. "You hungry? Let's get cleaned up, and I'll let you buy me a steak."

Marsh nodded, and we each grabbed a beer to go upstairs and shower. I enjoyed having my brother visit, though I didn't tell him so. I didn't want him to come and go as if he lived with me. No matter—I was sure he wouldn't have shown up if his client hadn't had a heart attack.

I didn't like getting roped into a favor, but it wouldn't kill me. Marsh was my kid brother, and I loved him. I'd do anything for him—I just didn't want him to know that.

Friday morning, I went for a run before the sun came up, having snapped awake from what I wished had been a nightmare but was, unfortunately, a bad memory from my last days with the team.

That October morning, my phone had rung as I stepped out of the shower to rinse off the stench from my night in jail. "Kensington, get your ass up to my room right now." It was the coach, Beau Richelieu. I'd known I was in fucking trouble.

"I'll be right up, Coach."

We had returned from the Albany County jail at three in the morning after I was released into Beau's custody. The front office had promised to square it so I didn't have to return to Albany to go to court. I'd been charged with solicitation of a police officer, but in my own defense, he'd been a hot fucker and was in the club, so I'd assumed he was available. Why would I expect anything different?

When I arrived at Beau's room, he had a plane ticket for me to fly commercial back to Chicago—not with the team for the next game. "What's this?"

"We're going to Denver instead of back to Chicago so the guys can get acclimated before the game on Thursday night. You're going back to Chicago to meet with the GM. He'll probably tell you to clean out your locker and turn in your keys and pass to the front office. I believe they're gonna cut you, Sandy. They'll concoct some story to try to cover for you getting arrested for soliciting a cop, but the team can't go through another scandal like we did with Delacroix. I'm sorry, son. I don't give a good goddamn who you fuck, but the backlash from Delacroix was hard on the club's morale."

"Does it matter that the cop approached me?" I'd been standing at the bar when the hot cop had come up to me, not identifying himself as an undercover police officer, though I guess that was the motivation behind the undercover part.

"I'm sure the lawyers will be in touch with you. For your sake, I hope they can get the charge dismissed without much fanfare. Hell, son, you're thirty-seven. You're about at the end of your career anyway. Hopefully, the press has a short memory." With that, I'd been bounced on my ass like a rubber ball.

In the end, the lawyers got the charges dismissed and the arrest removed from my record. Mr. Orr paid out my contract, and my football career was over.

The sight of my house pushed away the memories I couldn't shed the previous night, and as I walked up the driveway, I saw a black Suburban parked in front of my house. I hurried up the steps and onto the front porch, sliding off my running shoes before I made my way inside, down the hallway, and into the kitchen.

Marsh was at the breakfast bar, sipping coffee as he read shit on his phone. "You eat already?"

He glanced up and pointed to the microwave. "I made scrambled eggs. There's toast in the toaster oven. Do you always run so damn early in the morning?"

I filled a glass with water from the front of the fridge and gulped it down. "Gets too fucking hot to run later. How'd you get the SUV here so fast?"

Marsh smirked. "I've got people, big brother. Anyway, the flight comes in at eight on Southwest. Here's the information and my tablet. I have no idea what the guy looks like, so use the tablet with this graphic I made." He handed me the tablet with "Skyler Ashe" on the screen.

"Sure. Look, I'm sorry I was such a prick yesterday. I'm sorry I embarrassed the whole family, Marsh. I just wanted to have a good time. The charges were dismissed because it was a dirty sting, but I still did something that violated the morals clause in my contract. I gotta get over it."

Marsh stood and walked over to the microwave, taking out my plate and reaching into the toaster oven to grab two pieces of wheat toast. He set them on the counter in front of me, along with a cup of coffee.

"Thanks."

I reached for the fork, but Marsh pulled it away. "You didn't do anything wrong, Sandy. You were trying to live a double life, and I hate that you felt it necessary. I love you, bro. I want you to find your happiness."

He handed me the fork, but he grabbed my hand. "I want you to be happy, Sandy. Don't ever forget that."

I cleaned my plate like a good boy and hurried upstairs to shower and get ready to pick up Skyler Ashe. I hoped he wasn't an asshole.

I stood at the security exit with Marshall's tablet in hand. I was dressed in a suit with a white shirt unbuttoned—portraying the professionalism my brother wanted—and watched everyone leaving the Southwest security exit.

I saw all kinds of men walk out of the exit—old, young, tall, short. None of them were my type. I was just about to leave because being a fucking chauffeur wasn't my gig, but I remembered I was doing this for Marsh and turned back around.

A gorgeous guy walked up to me with a nervous grin. "I'm Skyler Ashe."

I sucked in too much air for a second. He was fucking stunning with blond hair and golden-brown eyes, but knowing his father was a rock star, I was sure the pretty boy was a stuck-up brat. I decided not to engage but not be rude. "Do you have a checked bag?"

"I, uh... No. I only brought this. Should I have brought more?"

He seemed quite unsure of himself, and why the fuck was that so sexy? His short blond hair and beautiful smoldering eyes had me dumbstruck—which wasn't as hard to do as one might think. Too many tackles during my time on the field.

Skyler asked questions, and I nodded or shook my head in response because I wasn't sure how my voice would sound if I tried to speak. I couldn't take my eyes off the guy in the back seat, and I'd much rather imagine him as a sexy mute than a spoiled rich boy.

I drove Skyler Ashe to his mother's strange little rescue farm. I hadn't spoken more than three words aloud. After I dropped his duffel at the door and returned to the SUV, I drove away, vowing to never think about Skyler Ashe again.

Chapter Three

Skyler

I was determined to storm out of Mom's house because I didn't want to hear her defend Regal, which she was prone to do. It had happened far too often, and I was tired of it. Then, my mom spoke up.

"Please, Sky. We need you. You don't understand what's going on, and I'd like the chance to explain it to you."

God, the pleading in her voice had me anchored to the spot. I knew in my gut I should have left because she was going to guilt me into doing something I didn't want to do.

I sat at the table again. "Mom, you know how much I don't give a crap about Regal. He never gave a care about me, so why should I try to help him now?"

Mom sat forward and grabbed my hand. "Sky, he didn't know how to be a good father, okay? He loves you, and he wants to see you. Please, son, come with me to talk to him."

I sighed. "Will that make you happy? He's been a real jerk to me since I can remember, Mom. Tell me why he wants to see me."

"He needs you to help with 'Bury Me'. The movie studio wants to hear an updated recording of the song with more heavy metal influences, and Regal can't write it by himself. He needs you, Sky."

Why did I have to deal with this crap? I was a schoolteacher, and a darn good one. I tried to be a resource and support system for my students and the members of my school community, and I found a lot of satisfaction in my job. I'd seen too much of my father's world as a kid and wanted no part of it. I'd walked as far away from Regal Ashe as I could get—all the way to West Peoria, Illinois.

Now, Regal wanted to use me as if we'd had a relationship all along? *Nope!*

"No. He never gave a crap about me, Mom. Why should I help him now?"

Hope stared at me for a moment. "I've never asked you for anything. This is me asking you for one favor. This is me asking you to help your father, not for him, but for me."

I stared at my mother. At forty-seven, she was still beautiful with her long blonde hair and bright smile. She was right. She'd never asked me for anything, but now she was asking me for something I didn't believe my father deserved. She would always be my Achilles heel.

"Mom… Fine, I'll go with you to the hospital to talk to Regal, but I'm not making any promises."

My mother nodded and tried to hide her smile, the dirty dealer. She'd won, and she knew it.

I went upstairs to my room to shower the airplane off me. I was fucking exhausted and only wanted to sleep, but instead, I was going to the hospital to see a man I cared nothing about.

What a fun trip this was turning out to be…

I stood in the hallway of El Camino Hospital outside of Regal's room, where he was recovering from surgery. Mom went inside to talk to the doctor, and I waited for her to flag me in.

After a few minutes, the doctor came out and offered a tight smile, Mom hot on his trail. "Will you come in now, Sky?"

I blew out a huge breath as if I were preparing to walk across hot coals. "Sure, Mom."

I followed her into the hospital room, where Regal was propped up in his bed. He had a nasal cannula in place and was pale, but he still had that cocky smile I remembered.

"Regal." His eyes were closed, but I knew he was awake and wanted to hear what was said about him.

His eyes opened and he turned in my direction. "Son, it's great to see you."

"*Is it*? Is it *really*, Regal? Why? Give me one reason why it's good to see me other than you need something and put Mom up to talking me into it." My words were harsh, but with everything he'd put our family through over the years, I believed he'd earned my disdain.

"Sky! Don't talk to your father like that! He just had heart surgery." Of course Mom would stick up for the jerk.

"It's okay, Hope." He took her hand and kissed it before he turned to me. "Sky, you know I love you. That's why I asked your mom to get you to come. I need you to help me with the song because I don't trust anyone else to do it right."

Was I supposed to be grateful for that crumb of praise? Why did it feel so flippin' good to hear?

"What do you want me to do?" And now, I was the pushover I always believed my mother to be.

As Regal was about to answer, Dusty Carson walked in. "Regal, man, you scared the shit out of us." He walked over to the bed and grabbed my dad's hand, half-hugging him.

Regal gave him a cocky smile. "This is what I get for trying to take care of my women at the same time." He then reached around my mom and smacked her ass, which I didn't appreciate.

"Where's Jeanne?" Dusty glanced around the room, his eyes settling on me for the first time in a long time.

From the Ashes didn't tour much anymore, and Dusty lived in New Mexico, so I hadn't seen him in a few years. I remembered him always being with Regal when he'd come get me at the farm—the few times he bothered to show up. Dusty was there when I went on tour with Regal a few times, looking out for me more than my own father.

"There he is! How you doin', kid?" Dusty took two long strides and hugged me tightly. I still felt like a kid in his long arms.

Dusty Carson was fifty-five—ten years younger than the rest of the band. He wasn't a big talker, but when he spoke, it was smart to listen, or so I'd gotten the impression from the rest of the guys. I looked up to him far more than I ever did to Regal.

"I'm good, Dusty. It's great to see you." I stepped out of his grasp and leaned back against the windowsill where I'd been standing.

"How's Illinois?" Dusty had been supportive of my decision to teach band and music at a small school in West Peoria, while Regal wanted me to join their band. After everything I'd seen the few times Regal had taken me out with the band when they went on tour, I wanted nothing to do with that lifestyle.

"Things are great. We had our end-of-year concert last night, which was fantastic. I have a job lined up to work at the nursery in town for the summer, and then marching band camp starts in August."

"You didn't ask him?" Dusty's head swung in Regal's direction.

"Didn't have a chance. All I asked—" Mom cleared her throat. "All Hope asked was that he help with 'Bury Me'."

Dusty turned to me. "Did you say yes?"

"Not yet. What's it need? That was one of your number ones."

"The film producers asked that we give it the heavy metal treatment. They wanted to license it and get another band to sing it, but your dad and I don't trust it with anyone outside the family. Regal and I were rewriting the music—or at least trying. We were planning to lean heavily on guitar riffs and add in a metal break, but then this idiot thought he was twenty-five again and could fuck two women at the same time."

I winced at Dusty's choice of words. The dude was talking about my mom.

"Sorry, kid. Anyway, I think we can rewrite it, perform it, and get it in the movie. He's"—Dusty pointed to Regal—"worthless at this point, so will you work with me and the guys to get it up to what the studio is looking for?"

I'd double majored in music education and composition, so it wasn't like I couldn't do it. I did it for the kids in my classes all the time, usually to simplify the orchestration for their skill level or to write parts for instruments not included in the original compositions. I also played piano, which was what got me into my music program in the first place.

I lifted my eyes to meet Mom's. "It'll take more than a few days, and I didn't pack for that. I have a job waiting for me, and I'd need a place to work and a piano. I need the money I'd make over the summer to live on. I have my own life and responsibilities in Illinois."

Mom mouthed, "*I know. Please.*" She then placed her palms together like she was begging.

I sucked in a calming breath through my nose and blew it out, just as I'd learned in the Saturday morning yoga class sponsored by the school district. It helped after a long week of teaching band to kids between the ages of eleven and eighteen, though my high schoolers gave me a rougher time than the middle schoolers.

Regal stared at me. "Please, Sky. I know you'll do it justice and give it the treatment—"

"I don't listen to metal music, and what you guys played back in the day was nothing like the music metalheads today. How do you know the studio will like what I come up with?" I was teetering, which I didn't like in the least. I was usually stronger in my resolve not to allow Regal's crap to seep into my life. Why was I even considering this?

Dusty stepped forward and put his hand on my shoulder. "We need something more than just rewriting the music, Skyler. We need you to sit in and record the new track with us. I'm asking you to take Regal's place as the drummer and lead singer for the band until he's back in fighting shape."

I stared at Dusty with my mouth open, then swung around to my mom. "You knew this? You knew they were going to ask me to—"

"And they'll need you to tour with them so they can try out the song at a few venues their manager is setting up." Mom's cheeks flushed as her eyes scanned the room, not meeting mine at all.

"Wait. You dragged me out here under the pretense that Regal might die—when you knew he was going to be fine—all because you want me to score 'Bury Me' and tour with the band?" I put my hands on my hips and stared at my mother.

I respected Dusty because he was just trying to do what was best for the band. I didn't give a damn about Regal because he only thought of himself. But my mom? I'd have never thought she'd stoop so low as to manipulate me in such a fashion.

"Walk with me, Sky." Mom crossed the room and took my arm, leading me out to the elevator. "Let's get some coffee."

We stepped into the box and she pressed the button for the second floor where the cafeteria was located. There were other people with us, so we didn't speak.

Mom found a table away from anyone before she went to get our coffee, returning with a tray and a couple of sweet rolls. She set it in front of me and sat in the chair to my left.

"We're broke."

I nearly dropped my coffee cup at her confession. *How had this happened?*

During their heyday, From the Ashes made money hand over fist. Their concerts were sold out in every US city, and after 'Bury Me' hit number one on the charts and stayed there for ten weeks, they had three successful international tours.

John Cordell, their manager back then, made the guys invest their money, always saying, "You need to plan for the future." I thought my father had enough sense to listen. Clearly, I was wrong.

"How? What happened to the money?"

Mom sighed and began shredding a beverage napkin. "Child support. Alimony for me and Jeanne. My farm. Her house. A lot of it went up his nose, and then there was rehab—three times. After he overcame his addictions, the idiot met Cassie, and they had a whirlwind romance, which is Regal's favorite thing. The first part of a relationship is his favorite, but the follow-up is where he messes it up every time.

"Your dad asked Cassie to marry him because that's his go-to when he thinks he's about to be caught doing something he shouldn't, and when Cassie found out he was still seeing Jeanne and me, she drained his bank account. He was stupid enough to put her name on it and give her a credit card with an unlimited line of credit.

"Regal's made a lot of mistakes over his lifetime, but Jeanne and I still love him. I wanted to help him, but the grants I get for taking care of rescue animals can only pay the few bills *I* have. Regal needs more than I can give him, and Jeanne's job doesn't pay much either. We don't have enough to cover the bills Cassie racked up."

"Mom, you shouldn't be giving him anything. He walked out on us." My teeth were gritted so tightly that I was afraid they would shatter.

"Honey, just because he left doesn't mean I stopped loving him. I'm sorry for the shitty way he treated you as a kid, but I know he wasn't purposely trying to hurt you. He wasn't deliberately trying to hurt me, Jeanne, or River either. His actions are a by-product of the lifestyle he got sucked into. The band became a success too quickly, and none of us knew how to handle it."

I shook my head and pushed the tray of pastries away, having lost my appetite. "Mom, I love you more than anything, but I can't sit back and watch Regal weasel his way back into your life. He leaves a wake of destruction everywhere he goes. When did all this crap go down?"

Mom gave me a tender smile. "You don't curse anymore, do you?"

It struck me as funny that she would focus on my lack of swearing instead of the cesspool that had become her life. "Teacher, remember? Shaping young minds is what I do."

"We sold Jeanne's house last year, and she moved in with me at my invitation before Thanksgiving when your father couldn't afford to pay the mortgage in Santa Clara. It was nice having River in the house. Made me miss you a little less.

"Anyway, Regal told Cassie he was taking River to see your dead grandmother's grave in Pasadena so he could spend the holiday with us, but she had him followed and confronted him at the farm. She threw him out of the condo, but thankfully, they were just leasing it. She'll get the boot from it at the end of June.

"Look, Sky, I didn't tell you because I knew you wouldn't approve, but Jeanne and I still love your dad. River's been doing much better by having Regal around, and I wish you'd had the same opportunity. Riv had been hanging with a crowd that could be problematic, but things have become more stable with all of us now. We're trying to figure out how to pay for River's college if he decides to go, but that's not certain. I'm not sure if college is best for him, but it's a place to start for him to build a future."

"Except there's no money for him to go, right? You kept all this from me? Is that why you said you weren't hosting Christmas last year because you were going camping instead? You were hiding Regal, Jeanne, and River from me?" I was boiling mad, and keeping my voice down was hard.

"No, no. It wasn't designed that way. I planned to tell you what was happening, but I didn't know how to do it without upsetting you. I'm sorry I didn't invite you to come with us. I've been trying to figure out how to get you and your father in the same room so you could talk, but then this happened."

I finished my coffee and stood. "I need to think. I'll meet you back home."

I walked out of the hospital cafeteria, took the stairs to the lobby area, and exited through the emergency room.

What a disaster!

Chapter Four

Sandy

Grocery shopping wasn't my favorite thing, but Marsh and I were in dire need of sustenance at my place, so I was wandering around my local market when my cell phone rang. I slid it out of my pocket and checked the screen, seeing my brother was calling. "Yeah?"

"Hey, where are you? I got off the phone, and you were gone?"

"I'm at the grocery store so we don't starve. Anything special you want?" I grabbed a tub of protein powder and tossed it in the cart.

"I need you to take me to Hope Ashe's farm so I can talk to Skyler. You know where she lives, right?"

I rolled my eyes, though Marsh couldn't see it. "Yeah, uh, as you know, I dropped him off there very early this morning. What's up?"

"I'll explain on the way, and after my meeting, I'll take you out. We can go food shopping later."

Oh fuck. I can't be around that guy again. He scrambled my fucking brain last time!

"Uh, I can give you the address, and you can drive yourself there in that Suburban. I really need to run some other errands."

Liar!

"Look, I need to talk to you about something important. We can discuss it on the way. Come get me, asshole." Marsh hung up on me before I could say no again.

I went to the self-checkout and bagged the groceries before carrying them to the car. I put them in the passenger's seat because the stupid car only had five cubic feet of cargo space. Why the fuck did I think I needed that expensive piece of shit, anyway?

I hurried home and parked in the driveway, carrying the cloth grocery bags inside with me. Marshall rushed into the foyer wearing a suit I didn't know he'd brought. "What's with the straight jacket?"

Marsh took the bags. "Go put on something else. I can't believe you left the house in basketball shorts and a tank top. No wonder you're still single."

"Why do I need to change? Who do I gotta impress?" I followed Marsh into the kitchen, where he put away the groceries.

"I need you to look professional because I've got a job lined up for you. Go change. I'll tell you about it on the way."

Figuring I wouldn't be able to get out of it and not wanting to listen to him bitch for the rest of his stay, I trudged up the stairs to my bedroom and changed. It was almost five, so traffic was going to be horrible. Marsh didn't know it, but he was taking me out for a very expensive meal and driving us back home because I was going to order the best tequila that Hi-Life, a fancy steakhouse in San Jose, stocked.

I pulled on a navy suit and a white dress shirt sans tie and put some product in my hair. After slipping on a pair of Ferragamo double monk strap dress shoes, I hurried downstairs. "Ready."

"You clean up pretty well, big brother. Let's go." Marshall grabbed his suit coat and slid his arms into it, adjusting his cuffs as we walked through the house and out the front door.

We got into the car, and I turned to my brother. "Okay, what are you trying to talk me into?" I started the car and waited.

"I told you about the band and the movie deal. Well, Harmon Studio wants the song to be edgier than the original. The band wouldn't agree to license it to the studio and allow someone to rewrite it and have another band sing it for the movie. They want to do it themselves." Marsh glanced at his phone and pecked away before he slid it into the breast pocket of his jacket.

"Wait a minute. Are you confused and think I can write music? I'm good with balls, remember?" I merged onto I-280 and hit the gas.

"Not hardly. You couldn't carry a tune in a bucket. Anyway, it seems Skyler Ashe is a musical savant. They need him to rewrite the melody and orchestrate the other parts of the song. Whoever does the soundtrack will use the song's theme to write the background score for the movie, so it has to be done right. That's why they need the kid."

Marsh could have been reciting the preamble to The Constitution for all the attention I was paying. All that kept circling my brain was how gorgeous the blond was and how I'd acted like a real prick to him.

I had no desire to get entangled with anyone. I'd already fucked up my career by letting my dick lead the way. I didn't want to be stupid again. I had a life to straighten out, and falling for a band teacher from the Midwest wasn't on my Bingo card.

"Why *won't* you come in?" Marsh stood outside the Maserati, and I was about ready to shut the door and leave his ass there.

"I'm not needed for this. You wanted a ride, and I have a podcast I want to listen to while I wait for you. Go do your job. I'll give you thirty minutes, and then I'm going to get dinner at Hi-Life. You can find your own way there." I sounded like an asshole, but I needed to get the hell away before that sexy blond walked out and fucked with my common sense again.

"Come on, Sandy. I need the moral support. It's very important I get this deal made. I need you."

God, I was a sucker for a guilt trip, and Marshall had learned how to traverse the road from Mom. I picked up my keys and phone and stepped out to follow him. Going inside was against my better judgment, but I wouldn't be accused of letting Marsh down.

We went up on the front porch, where three dogs, two little goats, and a goddamn chicken greeted us. "What the hell is this? Doctor Doolittle's house?"

Marshall laughed. "Hope runs a rescue farm, asshole. These animals are so happy to have somewhere safe to be, they won't hurt your candy ass."

I wasn't afraid of the animals, at least until a fucking goose came at me, flapping its wings and squawking. I wasn't stupid. I pulled Marsh in front of me, and when the goose went after his nuts, I pushed him at the crazy fucking bird.

The front door opened and Skyler Ashe hurried out, waving his arms and chasing the demented thing away. "Matilda, what the heck?"

Skyler grabbed the goose and tossed it into the air at the end of the porch. I was stuck to my spot as I stared at the guy wearing red running shorts and a tank top. I was sure my tongue was hanging out. The fates were mocking me.

He walked over and helped Marshall up. "Sorry about that. She's usually harmless. Can I help you?"

"I'm Marshall Kensington. I'm the manager for From the Ashes. You're Skyler, right?" Marshall was too busy dusting off his expensive suit pants to notice Skyler Ashe staring at me. I winked.

"My dad's in the hospital. Didn't anyone notify you?" Skyler scowled at me, which made me laugh. He was a fiery little guy. Sadly, that revved my motor.

"I was with your mother when Regal had his surgery. How's he doing today?" Marshall was much more diplomatic than I'd have been.

Skyler sighed. "He's supposed to come home in a couple of days. What can I do for you?"

"I'm here to talk to *you*. You got a few minutes?" Marshall stepped forward and extended his hand. Thankfully, Skyler accepted the handshake.

He turned to me, but I shoved my hands in my pockets. He wasn't the friendliest guy in the world, and I wasn't going to get wrapped around the axle to suck up.

"Sure. Come inside. Pay no attention to the snakes."

"S-Snakes? Are you fucking kidding me?" No goddamn way was I going into a house with snakes.

I didn't expect the sexy blond to crack up. "I'm joking. No snakes, but that's just because nobody's brought any recently. My mother would have taken them in if they showed up." That made me laugh. I hadn't met his mother, but even hearing him say it and the snarl in his voice was fucking sexy.

"Come in. Can I get you something to drink? Why are you here? Shouldn't you be at the hospital with Regal?" Thankfully, the sexy blond was looking at Marsh.

"I'm here because Dusty called me. The band needs you. They need you to help them—"

"Mr. Kensington, let's not kid ourselves and don't try to blow smoke where the sun don't shine. It's not me they need. It's my songwriting and orchestration skills. They just want me to help them rewrite 'Bury Me' and record the revised song because Regal can't play right now. Oh, and the tour they mentioned so they can get the song in a stupid movie. They don't give a dang about me. They just want to use me."

"I don't think it's that way at all, Skyler. Can I call you Skyler?"

I chuckled. "Marsh, don't bullshit him, man. You and I both know that's exactly what they want with him. If they can't do this shit for themselves, then they don't deserve his help."

Marsh looked at me as if he wanted to slit my throat, but I was trying to be fair to the blond.

"Seriously? You think they're not gonna try to fuck him over? They'll get what they want, and then they'll kiss his ass goodbye, and that's it."

"You're a shitty wingman." Marsh clearly wanted to deck me, but he knew that would be a mistake.

I laughed. "You never asked me to be your wingman before. I don't know what you expect from me."

Marsh stared at me. "Do you even know how to be a human?"

I shrugged and sat on one of the rockers on the large front porch. I wasn't there to speak with the hot guy. I was there to make sure my brother didn't get his ass kicked.

"Look, Skyler, after Hope relayed their current, uh, financial challenges, shall we say, I reached out to Harmon Studio to see how much they'd pay for the song. It wouldn't be worth the fight if it was just a hundred grand because that won't help your parents. I tried to talk the band into licensing the song to the studio and allowing them to change it to suit their needs, but your father and Dusty were adamant they wouldn't allow it, to the point Harmon nearly took a pass.

"Your mother was instrumental in changing their minds by promising you'd rewrite the song and give it the treatment the studio wants for the movie. She showed them family videos on her phone of you playing original music, and there's a chance they might want you to score the whole soundtrack. You can't tell me that a nice check like that wouldn't go far for a schoolteacher."

There was my brother, spouting bullshit to schmooze someone into doing what he wanted. He was good at that—clearly, he'd chosen the perfect profession.

I glanced in Skyler's direction to see his brow scrunched as he stared at the ground. Finally, his eyes met Marshall's. "How much?"

"I can only make a guess, but I'd say high six figures, plus whatever deal you can get with the band for a cut of the royalties from sales of the updated single."

"Is he officially joining the band?" Yeah, I spoke up because the kid was about to get screwed, and not in the way my dick was thinking.

Marsh shot me a pissed-off snarl. "Sandy, what are you doing?"

"No, I'm not joining the band, so I want to be paid for the recording time and whatever else I have to do. I was on the road with the band when I was a kid, and I see no reason to relive that hell. Plus, all of this has to be wrapped up before school preparation begins in August."

Skyler gave a cute nod as if he believed he'd made his point, and then he sat on the porch steps to pet the two mutts that flopped all over him. The goats came back around after the goose was scared off. The chicken was in the yard doing whatever chickens do.

Marshall stared at Skyler for a good minute—to the point I was about ready to slap him in the back of the head. Finally... "You'll need a makeover. Lot less teacher. More rock star."

He then stared at me. "That'll be your job. He'll need the stamina to be able to play a hard-rocking hour-and-a-half. His hair needs to look less Poindexter and more rocker. How fast does your hair grow, kid?"

Skyler appeared to be amused with my brother's babbling, based on the big smile on his face, but I was caught on his comment, "That'll be your job."

"Whoa, whoa. What the hell are you talking about, *my job*?" I glanced at the gorgeous blond and thought, *that's not the job I had in mind.*

"I have no idea how fast my hair grows. Pretty fast, I guess. I just got a cut before our end-of-year concert. If I let it go, it'll probably be to my shoulders in a few months." Skyler absentmindedly ran his hand through his blond hair. It wasn't curly, but there was a lot of it. The sides were shorter, but the top was long enough that someone could get a handful while getting a blowjob. *Just sayin'...*

"That won't work. I need it photoshoot ready in a week so we can do publicity for the five shows I have lined up.

We need to announce that Regal Ashe's son will be sitting in with the band until Regal's ready to take the sticks again." Marsh already had his phone in his hand, pecking into it before he walked away.

I glanced at Skyler. "I don't guess you work out or anything?" My voice sounded really fucking judgmental, but I wasn't the diplomat in the family. That was my little brother.

Skyler stood and put his hands on his hips, giving me an evil eye that nearly had me attached to his plump, kissable lips. No doubt he was pissed.

"I do cardio, lift weights, and do yoga, I'll have you know." He flexed his arms, and I had to admit, the guns were impressive. I had to remember he was a band teacher, which wouldn't require him to tackle anyone, though he could try to tackle me anytime he wanted.

"That's good. Then it'll just be building up your stamina, I guess. Arms and core, maybe?" Wait, had I agreed to help Marsh with his fucked-up mission to make Skyler Ashe—who was perfect, in my opinion—into a rock star. Was I up to the task?

Chapter Five

Skyler

As I was considering whether I needed to show Sandy Kensington that I could take care of myself and didn't need him to train me, Marshall returned to the front porch with a cocky smile.

"Okay, guys. Skyler, you'll need to pack up your stuff. Hope said you're riding the couch in your brother's room, but I've got a better idea. You'll need somewhere to work and—what do you use when you compose?"

"Piano or guitar are my preferred. I can get by with a keyboard, but I'd rather use an actual piano. A six-string guitar works in a pinch." I had use of the upright piano at school, but that was back in West Peoria, and I was definitely *not*.

"Okay. Hope said the garage has been converted into a recording studio, but it hasn't been used for a while. I'll get someone to come check it out on Monday to ensure all the equipment is functioning. I think it would be better to record here rather than take everyone to Los Angeles. I'll have the piano delivered to Sandy's place in San Jose on Monday." Marshall's phone rang just as I was about to complain.

"Does he think I'm going to stay with you?" My eyes met Sandy Kensington's. No way was I staying with such a Grumpy Gus.

I appreciated a much calmer lifestyle than I was sure the large football player enjoyed. He was a jock, and my mind kept replaying movies I'd seen with athletes and what they liked to get up to when they all turned their caps backward and hung out, drinking beer and burping.

Sure, it was a stereotype, but the jocks at West Peoria High only served to reinforce it, based on what I witnessed when my band kids were pushed off the field by the football team as we tried to practice for halftime shows. The team, led by the vicious Coach Sutter, made so much fun of my kids that I wanted to pummel them.

I wasn't a fighter, believing harmony was always the answer, but I could defend myself, and I would defend my kids. However, I firmly believed nothing ever came of violence.

Sandy's expression was one of pure confusion. He stared at me for a few seconds before jogging around the side of the house, chasing his brother. I walked to the corner and watched him, laughing as he kept yelling "Marsh!" and his brother stuck his finger in his other ear so he could hear whoever had called him.

The football player did have a nice, tight...rear end, especially in the navy linen suit pants that had to have been tailored to his form. He was wearing a white dress shirt without a tie or suit coat. The long sleeves on his shirt were rolled up to his elbows, showing off strong forearms covered in ink. My first thought was how I wanted to be closer so I could thoroughly inspect each one. Maybe trace them with my tongue?

When he'd picked me up at the airport before dawn, he'd been wearing a gray suit my foggy mind barely remembered. I was sure the guy could wear a burlap bag and be attractive.

Marshall was leaning against the wooden fence that separated the yard from the paddock where Mom kept larger rescue animals. Currently, there was a miniature donkey eating hay from a haybox nearby.

Once Marshall ended his call, he and Sandy began shouting at each other. The donkey glanced up, seemingly unhappy about having his dinner interrupted. It was all quite comical.

The sound of crunching gravel caught my attention, and I turned to see Mom getting out of her pickup truck with Jeanne and River following behind in Jeanne's small SUV.

"You don't get to invite people to stay with me, Marshall. It's my house, and you haven't started paying part of the mortgage, as far as I know. Find somewhere else for him to stay. Not with me." Sandy stomped by me and hopped into his fancy car, not waiting for Marshall, who stopped to talk to Mom and Jeanne.

It was all too much for me. I'd been up nearly twenty-four hours, so I went to my duffel and grabbed clean shorts and a T-shirt. After I changed, I went to the hallway closet to get a blanket and pillow. There was an old couch on the back porch where Mom and I used to sit when I was young. We'd listen to the band practice in the garage, and I'd fall asleep there every time.

Those were the memories I wanted to focus on, not the times when Regal was nowhere to be found.

Something was licking my face. "Bess, please stop!" The stupid mutt didn't listen. I opened my eyes to see it wasn't one of my mother's two rescue dogs—a golden retriever and pit bull mix named Bess and a brown collie mix named Midnight.

What was licking my face was one of the disgusting goats, which was just cringeworthy. "Get away, you big gross-out."

I got up and walked into the kitchen to find Marshall Kensington sitting at the table with Mom, Jeanne, and Dusty. They were having coffee and chatting with a batch of warm everything cookies my mother must have made that morning. They had any kind of seed that could be consumed by humans mixed into an oatmeal base.

Sometime during her life, my mother got on a health kick and became vegan, but I knew she snuck a cheeseburger on occasion. I wasn't vegan—not even close—though Mom had tried her best.

"Good morning." I went to the cabinet and pulled down a mug, filling it from the old-fashioned percolator that had been my grandmother's.

I turned to the group. "What are we talking about?" Obviously, it had something to do with me because they all clammed up when I walked into the room.

"Sandy and I came to an agreement regarding his assistance with getting you ready to play the five concerts coming up in late summer. He's also agreed to give you space in his basement to work on 'Bury Me'. Harmon Pictures wants to hear the intro by Monday. I realize this is short notice, but—"

"But your dad and I have been working on it, and it's not right. I'm not sure how we take an eighties hair band anthem and make it into a screaming, headbanging song worthy of mosh pits and busting guitars," Dusty said.

I chuckled because that had been my same concern.

River came into the kitchen in his boxers, scratching his right butt cheek and scrolling on his phone. His dark-brown hair looked as if he never combed it.

"River!" Jeanne hissed at him.

The poor kid glanced up from his phone and gasped. "Shit. Sorry. I didn't know anyone was in the house. What's going on? Is Dad all right?"

It was weird to hear River refer to Regal as Dad, but then again, it was probably stranger for *me* to refer to him as Dad. I wasn't jealous of River because he was a kind, decent young man. It wasn't that I didn't want to know him. But my mother hadn't kept me up on the changes that led Regal, Jeanne, River, and Mom to live in the same house because they were broke.

"Yes, River, your dad is fine. We are trying to figure out how to help Skyler with the work he needs to do on 'Bury Me'," Jeanne said.

All of them were helping me? That was new information.

"Wait? What's going on? Dusty, you and the guys are going to help, right?"

Dusty turned to me, his face red. *Why?*

He cleared his throat. "We'll help as much as we can, but like I said, we don't think we can get it right. We need you, River, and JD Horn, Ripper's son, to work on it together. You young guys write it, and we'll perform it for the movie."

I drank my coffee, staring at the rest of them. "That's a great idea. Get JD and River to help." Mom offered her placating smile, which upset me. Heavens, I hadn't even agreed to actually rewrite the dang song.

"Can JD play an instrument?" I glanced at Dusty.

"River sings and plays guitar, and JD does too. He's hell on the bass. Maybe the three of you will understand what it needs better than us old farts?"

Dusty had never had children. Based on how kind he'd been to me, I was sure he'd have been a great father.

"Wait... We only agreed to pay Skyler. These other two..." Everyone turned to look at Marshall, whose eyebrows were somewhere in his hairline. I could imagine he was about to swallow his tongue regarding two more people being added to the payroll.

"I don't need money—" River's eyes darted to Marshall and back to me. "I wanna help."

"Yes, you do need money," Mom and Jeanne said in unison.

"How about I write the new melody, and after that, I'll meet JD and River here so we can go into the studio and work out the rough edges." I looked at River. "You got a six-string?"

"Sure." He left the room and returned a few minutes later with clothes on, which was good, and an old six-string guitar that had seen better days. If it worked, I'd be fine.

"I'll be ready to go to your brother's house in half an hour." I held out my phone to River. "Put your number in. Do you know JD Horn?"

"Sure." River took the phone and tapped in his number. The device on the counter rang, and he shut it off, took a selfie, and then pecked in something else before handing it to me. I looked at the screen and laughed. *Younger, Smarter, & Better-Looking Bro.*

I chuckled. "Yeah, well, I'll reserve judgment until I hear you play. You got access to an electric guitar?"

"He can use one of mine." Dusty stood and hugged us both. "I'll call JD and give him a heads-up. Thank you, guys."

Dusty left, and I went to River's room to grab my stuff, changing into jeans and a T-shirt with West Peoria All-Star Band on the front. It was part of a fundraiser we'd held the previous fall so band members from each grade could travel to Carbondale to perform at a Saluki football game during halftime. I was so proud of my kids. They competed for the spots and went through tryouts to win their place in the band, which wasn't easy for the younger kids. They worked hard and were proud of themselves for the great show they put on. I missed them.

Once I was dressed and had my duffel and River's six-string, I went to find Marshall. Mom was standing on the back porch, so I walked over and put my things down. "I'll be in touch. I just need a little time to get this started, and then I'll come back and work in Regal's studio. Call me if anything happens." I hugged Mom and then Jeanne. She was a nice woman who got caught up with my father. It wasn't her fault she'd succumbed to Regal Ashe. Many had.

After goodbyes, I went outside to find Marshall still on his phone. I stopped beside the SUV he was driving and put my things in the back seat before I got into the front passenger seat.

Marshall got in and gave me a fake smile. "I need to return to LA tomorrow for a meeting at the office, so I'm going to leave my rental for you so you're not stuck. Pay absolutely no attention to Sandy. He's been in a bad mood since he left the Breeze. I hope he'll snap out of it eventually."

"Forced change is hard to accept—just like what you're forcing me to do." I hated to be so angry, but I had a life, and here I was, being bullied into doing something I really didn't care about. I needed to quit whining about it, but I'd had a nice, calm summer planned, and now everything was going down the drain.

"Look, Skyler, I know you may not want to do this, but your family needs you. The record label is building a whole thing around this song that could relaunch From the Ashes. Your parents need the money, and I'm sorry to say if this doesn't happen, the label will drop the band and my management company will be forced to do the same. Then where will they be?"

If Marshall Kensington thought he was good at a guilt trip, he'd never had the pleasure of having Hope Ashe on his trail. I laughed. "I said I'd do it, and I don't go back on my word, Mr. Kensington."

Marshall nodded as he kept his eyes forward. Hopefully, I'd be able to get the rewrite done relatively fast, refine it with JD and River, and then get the whole band together for practice for a couple weeks. That should put me back in West Peoria in late July if Regal took care of himself and was able to play for the tour. That was the goal.

Chapter Six

Sandy

I wanted to beat the life out of my brother for bringing Skyler Ashe over to my place to stay against my wishes, but as much as my parents didn't talk to me now, if I killed Marsh, I'd never get back into the family. Not that I really thought I would, queer as I was. Life was certainly a first-class bitch.

Marsh's rental SUV stopped in front of the house, so I went to the door and peeked through the sidelight, not happy to see Skyler Ashe step out of the passenger side. As easy as Skyler was on the eyes, I had to wonder how the next few weeks would work between us. Could I keep my cock locked in my pants while being around the man every day? That was the question.

I opened the door and stepped onto the porch. Skyler had his duffel and a guitar case as he walked around the corner of Marsh's SUV. Marsh was in the vehicle on his phone, as usual, so I walked down the stairs and banged on the window. It was satisfying when Marsh jumped like I'd shot him.

"Get the fuck out of the vehicle, Marshall, and tell me what the hell you've gotten me into."

Without an invitation, Skyler went in through the front door, but I'd figure that shit out later. I turned to my brother and fought the urge to sucker-punch him in the throat as he got out of the vehicle.

"Look, Sandy, I need him to rewrite the song. He's got some guys to help him out, and they'll be done in a couple of weeks, tops. The piano will come on Monday, and you can put it in the basement or maybe the living room. He can work in either space. Once he has it figured out, he'll go back to his mom's rescue farm because that's where the studio is. He'll work there to finish up, and then he'll be out of your hair." Something about the look in his eyes told me he was bullshitting me.

"What's in it for him, Marsh? I get what you and the band are getting out of this deal, but what about the teacher?" I hitched my thumb over my shoulder toward the house.

Where those feelings came from, I didn't know, but I couldn't keep them inside. It was clear that Marshall and the band were setting Skyler up to be used, and I didn't like it one bit. I didn't give a damn about Skyler Ashe—except to watch his round ass in motion—but I wasn't fond of those who took advantage of others.

"Skyler will get paid, though it will be split into three shares since he insisted on bringing in other musicians. If it all works out, everyone will make a lot of money. I have a feeling this song will be fantastic, and the kid might get the chance to write the movie score and make a lot of money."

I stared at Marsh. "What about me? What about the shit I gotta endure to help you? What the fuck, Marsh? What do I get out of it?"

My brother sighed. "You know, Sandy, *I* wasn't the one who got a contract with the NFL. I wasn't good at sports like you, so I had to figure out another way to make a living. I'm sorry you got screwed for being yourself. That was a rotten thing for the team to do, and I wish I could make it up to you. I love you, Sandy. I won't ask you for another favor as long as I live if you help me with this."

I chuckled as I pointed toward the house. "Do you fucking know what you're doing to me? This guy? God, he's beautiful. How the fuck am I supposed to...?" I couldn't finish the sentence.

Marsh touched my arm. "Why on earth would you hold back? If you like him, why not try to make something of it while he's here? He's legal, and he's nice. Fuck, he's a teacher and works with kids, so he must be a good guy. I hate that Regal Ashe pushed me to rope him into this shit, but Regal blew through his money, and now, he's got nothing. Please help Skyler help his family."

I stared at Marsh for a full minute. "Get your shit and leave. I'm not taking you to the airport, so call a fucking cab. You better do right by them, Marsh, or I'll kick your ass."

He nodded, went into the house, and returned a few minutes later with his suitcase. "I'll be back in a week. Thank you for this, big brother." He hugged me before he walked down to the end of the driveway, where a car was waiting for him.

Marsh turned before he got into the car and waved, which I returned. He slid inside, and it drove away. I hoped to hell he really came through for them as promised.

I climbed the stairs and let myself inside the house, going to the kitchen where I found Skyler staring out the bay windows. He didn't look back, just stood there. "I'm sorry I've been foisted on you. I don't plan to be a problem. I just need some solitude to do this, and then I'll be gone. I swear."

My heart wanted me to wrap him in my arms and tell him he could stay forever. Of course, that was a stupid impulse. My gut reminded me I'd just met the guy. I didn't know him at all, did I?

"Hey. No, okay? You're welcome to hang around. I'll try to stay out of your way." I sounded like a pussy, but I'd figured out that what he'd been tasked with wouldn't be easy.

I marveled at anyone who could make something as beautiful as music, though I doubted I'd ever tell Skyler. It was a talent I didn't have, but it was inspiring.

I glanced up to see his beautiful grin. "I appreciate you letting me come here. Where can I write? You tell me where to go so I won't be in your way, and I'll respect your privacy."

Respect was the last thing I wanted from him. I wanted him to disrespect me. Disrespect me all over my fucking body.

"Yeah, sure. There are a couple of bedrooms upstairs, so pick one. I'd say the best place for you would be in the living room. When your piano comes on Monday, it can go in front of the windows. The kitchen isn't far, and there's a powder room down the hall. I'm usually downstairs working out or in the pool, so no worries."

Skyler smiled, which was the best thing I'd ever seen, though I told myself he was off-limits. *Nothing permanent, right?*

I scowled. "Don't get all fucked up about this. I'm doing this as a favor for Marsh." I stomped away.

What the fuck was I going to do? How would I survive even two days with Skyler Ashe under my roof?

Sunday morning, I went out for my run at seven, just as Skyler returned from his. "I left the door through the garage open so I could get back in. I hope I didn't wake you when I left. Enjoy your run."

Mr. Nice went inside, and I went out. When I returned, I followed my nose to the kitchen to find a sticky note.

> Food in the microwave.
> Thanks for letting me stay.

I opened the microwave to find an egg-white omelet. It smelled incredible and reminded me of my days on the road with the team. I had a limited cooking repertoire, but I would damn well eat what he'd made. I just hope he didn't thank me for letting him live with me every time I saw him.

After I changed, I walked down to the first floor before going to the basement. I heard the echo of guitar strings being plucked from the living room, so I hid by the stairs to listen.

The chords started in one key and then changed to another, moving up the scale, but that was about as much musical knowledge as I had. What was he looking for? No clue, but the sounds he produced were melodic.

He began toying with the melody of 'Bury Me'. I didn't know the song well, having only listened to it after Marshall explained what the guy was trying to do. Whatever he had planned, what he was doing right then sounded incredible to my ears.

I pulled myself away, went downstairs, and headed outside. I dropped my phone on the glass table by a lounger before diving into the pool. My head was as fucked up as it used to be when I'd fumble a play or we'd lose a game because of a stupid mistake.

For years, football was my life. The guys on the defensive line were my brothers, and then, one day, they were just gone. For an unguarded moment, I lived my truth with what I thought was a faceless partner who had the same goal as me—getting off—and I got caught in a hugely humiliating way. Those I thought I could turn to for support under any circumstances turned their backs, including my own parents, and I was completely alone.

I thought I had a thick skin before I left football. Trash-talking was a staple of the game, and my teammates were champions at it. It was done to hype us up on the field, and it worked. We all talked smack, but we loved and supported each other.

Going from that comradery to being completely cut off was like being struck by lightning. I was in a dark and lonely place—had been for a year. Swimming laps in the pool was a twisted metaphor for how hard I was trying to find my way back to the surface of my life. I was trying to find what was next for me because, right now, I had nothing that gave me any hope and certainly nothing that made me happy.

The pity party was too fucking much, so I slid out of the pool and went to sit on a lounger to dry off. I picked up my phone to check messages, and when I found none, I touched the icon for the cameras I had set up around the outside and inside of the house, cycling through them until I found the one for the living room.

I touched the screen and turned up the sound. The camera showed Skyler sitting on the floor by the glass cocktail table with his legs stretched out in front of him and the guitar across his lap. A notebook was in front of him, and he'd play a few chords a couple of times before he grabbed a pencil and scratched out something I couldn't read.

I relaxed on my chair, slid my sunglasses on, and watched the live feed from the living room for at least an hour. I couldn't move my eyes away from the screen.

Watching him was beautiful. Much like I imagined it would be to see a master at work.

He put the guitar on the couch behind him and stood to stretch. His shirt raised enough to show muscled abs I hadn't expected. Clearly, I'd misjudged Skyler's physique.

He was well-toned, which wasn't a surprise, but as I studied him, I could see he was much fitter than I first assessed. He was a short guy, about five-nine, if I were to guess.

God, the idea of him riding my cock had me steel-rod hard in my trunks. There wasn't a lot I could do, so I went into the basement through the patio doors and into the bathroom. I slid off my trunks and turned on the shower before reaching into the cabinet under the sink and grabbing a bottle of lube I kept there. I placed it on the shelf in the shower.

I stood under the spray for a few minutes, trying to decide how I'd like to have Skyler. Those muscular legs wrapped around my ass was a good place to start. As I pounded into him without mercy, him saying my name like a prayer. Would that be the way I wanted to take him the first time?

I reached for my hard cock, giving it a couple of slow tugs before I reached for the lube. After a squirt into my right palm, I turned my back to the spray and slid my hand down my cock to the base.

The water pounding on my back made a river down my crack, and as I spread my legs, it slid over my hole, tickling the nerves. That brought a scenario to mind that I hadn't entertained for a long time.

"*I wanna—*"

No, that wasn't right. He was more articulate.

"*I need to be inside you, Sandy.*"

Sandy? Would he call me Sandy? Would I want him to call me Sandy?

"*Sanders, baby, I need to be inside you.*"

That sounded a little too fucking formal.

"*Baby, please let me fuck you?*"

Yeah, that was exactly what he'd say.

The whole thing played out in my head while I fucked my fist. I reached around and shoved my middle finger in my ass, imagining it was Skyler, who I was guessing had a big dick. Feeling him inside me would be incredible.

A few more strokes, and I blew all over the tiled wall. I stood under the spray for another minute to clean the sheen of sweat and jizz off me and catch my breath. Water dripped in my eyes from my wet hair as I tried to push the images out of my head.

It would never happen, Skyler and me, but something inside me believed it would be amazing.

Chapter Seven

Skyler

I needed to relax and get rid of some excess energy. I'd been working for five hours and had only gotten through six bars of the intro. The original music was in my head, and I couldn't get it out to hear it any other way. I needed to do something to work off the tension.

Hearing feet on the stairs, I glanced up to see Sandy emerge from the basement as I stretched. He was drying his hair with a small towel and had a large towel draped across his hips and tied on the left. I almost swallowed my tongue with all that gleaming flesh on display.

"You, uh… The pool's out there. Feel free to use it." He pointed toward the back of the house before he went upstairs. A door slammed, and I exhaled.

Without waiting for Sandy to return, I hurried downstairs, sliding off my T-shirt as I went out to the pool deck. I slid off my jeans and dove into the pool in my boxer briefs, coming up for air after gliding halfway toward the other end. I held on to the side and stared at the large house casting a shadow over the warm water before lying back to float as I stared into the sky. I thought back to when I settled on a career in teaching.

Deciding what to do after college was important to me, and I'd vowed that whatever I chose would be so far removed from my father's profession that people would never link us as family. Through my first two years of college, I was stymied when it came to the next steps, even though I was majoring in music composition. I had a song in my soul and knew I'd never be happy unless I was doing something with music, though I didn't know what.

During high school, I'd given piano lessons after school and on Saturdays to make spending money, and I'd loved teaching, especially younger kids. The excitement on their faces when they learned their first song fed my soul, and the amount of money I made ended up being a secondary consideration.

The summer between my junior and senior years of college, I worked as a camp counselor at a theater camp in Murphysboro, near Carbondale. I had the time of my life, though I pissed off my mom by not returning to California. At the end of camp, my mind was made up. I stayed in school, got a second degree in music education, and never looked back.

When I got my first job—which happened to be with the West Peoria school district—I was excited and anxious. I'd gotten over most of my shyness in college, thanks to music. And while giving piano lessons and working at the theater camp, I'd learned I was good with kids.

The Friday before school officially started, we had a teacher meet-and-greet. I noticed a teacher sort of hanging back, much as I tended to do, so I grabbed a cup of coffee and a cruller, slowly making my way over. "I'm Skyler Ashe. New music and band teacher."

"I'm the new eighth-grade science teacher, Brendan Wray." We shook hands, and I suspected he was scared to death, much like me.

I'd done some student teaching during the last semester of my master's requirements while I worked toward my teaching certification. Brendan told me he'd worked as a teacher in Chicago for two years at an inner-city school.

He was cute, with flaming red hair and pink cheeks, and he had a love for teaching I believed I mirrored.

Brendan also had a deep-seated fear of interacting with strangers—except students—due to being assaulted on his way home from school while living in Chicago. He'd been so traumatized by the attack that he had to take medication just to get through the day.

Despite all our insecurities and nerves, Brendan and I bonded, mostly over the stench of tuna salad in the teacher's lounge. He had the most incredible laugh, and we'd become fast friends.

Brendan helped me with the all-school Christmas concert that year, which was a great success. We went out for pizza after the event, and when I drove him home—he didn't drive—he gave me a kiss on the lips.

It was a sweet, though awkward, moment. There was no great spark of passion, but I welcomed the intimacy. I'd missed being affectionate with someone. I'd thought maybe when we returned from the holiday break, Branden and I might have been able to pursue something more than friendship. That had been my hope, anyway.

Brendan went home to Chicago for the holidays, and we chatted a couple of times during the break. On the first day of school after Christmas vacation, the teachers received a text message from the principal to meet in the teachers' lounge fifteen minutes before the start of the school day that January morning.

"I'm sorry to announce that Brendan Wray passed away over the holiday break. His family has asked that we respect their privacy at this time, but I thought we could take up a collection for a memorial donation in his name to a charity of the family's choosing. He will be missed."

Rumors had swirled around the school regarding the many ways Brendan had died—from him committing suicide to a shootout with the cops—but I couldn't see Brendan doing any of those things.

At Easter break, I received a nice letter from Brendan's mother. She told me Brendan had been in a snowmobile accident in Colorado, where the Wray family gathered for Christmas. He hadn't survived the accident, having hit a large tree, but he'd spoken highly of me when they'd all been together. She was sorry she hadn't reached out to Brendan's *boyfriend* sooner. That threw me for a loop.

I spent the following weekend locked in my shitty apartment, mourning the loss of my friend and wondering why Brendan had told his parents we were boyfriends. Was there more to the attack he'd suffered in Chicago that his family didn't know? Did he want them not to worry about him being alone in West Peoria, so he told them he had a boyfriend? Had I done something to make him think we were boyfriends?

My biggest question: did he intentionally run his snowmobile into that tree because he believed he could never find anyone to love him? I knew that fear far too well.

Anytime I allowed myself to think of Brendan, those same questions plagued me. I hadn't been looking for Mr. Right, but now that thirty was in the rearview mirror, I wondered if the easiest way to make it through life was alone. If I settled my mind that I was fine by myself, could I avoid the heartache I'd witnessed my mother suffer at Regal's hands? I had a good life, didn't I? Couldn't I be just as happy on my own as I could as part of a couple?

When I climbed out of the pool, I found a large towel and a bottle of water on the patio table. I hadn't noticed Sandy coming out, but the towel and water didn't miraculously appear. At some point, I must have been so lost in my thoughts that I didn't notice.

I sat on the side of the pool to dry a little before wrapping the towel around my waist and dropping into a chair. The view was incredible. There was a bit of land before the privacy fence, and I thought I saw some flowering bushes there. Maybe I'd walk down there to see what they were?

I finished the water and carried the empty bottle and my clothes while still wearing the towel. When I climbed the stairs, I didn't expect to see Sandy standing at the counter.

"I made some burgers that I'm going to grill if you're interested. Go ahead and shower. If I'm not in here, I'll be downstairs on the patio if you'd like to join me." Sandy wasn't rude, but he wasn't exactly inviting. His face held no care regarding whether I joined him or not.

"Thanks. I'll be back in twenty minutes. I'll help if you want."

Sandy nodded, so I went upstairs to the bedroom I'd chosen at the far end of the hall. It was tan...everywhere. There was an upholstered headboard the same color as the walls, so much so that it blended in. I guess if that was what he liked...

After a quick shower, I dressed in shorts and a T-shirt, knowing the amount of clothes I'd brought along wouldn't last a week, much less however long it would take me to finish the project. I could do laundry, but I'd have to check with Sandy whether he wanted me to do it at my mother's or if it was okay to use his machines.

I gathered my stuff and shoved it into my duffel before going downstairs. I put the bag by the front door to take to my mother's house in the morning and wandered into the kitchen.

Tomatoes, a head of lettuce, a red onion, and a few packages of cheese were on a cutting board on the counter, along with a plate of uncooked burgers and a package of buns. "Need help?"

Sandy glanced up from where he was buttering the buns. "What's with the duffel bag? You already going back to your mom's to begin recording?" His face was emotionless, and I wondered if he hoped I was.

"I'm going over in the morning to do laundry. What would you like me to do?" I pointed to the vegetables on the counter.

Sandy cockily walked over to the door next to the refrigerator and opened it. "There's a washer and dryer right in there."

I already knew that from when I'd looked around, but I hadn't been sure how to ask if I could use it. I was fine around kids, even the seniors at my high school. It was the adults I encountered that threw me for a loop.

My face heated as I walked over to the counter. "I, uh, I didn't want to assume anything. May I use your washer? I'll happily pay you what I'd pay at the laundromat." There, that was polite.

Sandy chuckled. "No payment necessary. What's mine is yours." He put a cutting board, a chef's knife, a tomato, and a red onion in front of me. "Slice." I did as he said.

Once I had the tomatoes and onions sliced, Sandy handed me a platter before he put the head of lettuce in front of me. "Tear off some leaves, please."

I nodded and proceeded to tear off a few leaves before rinsing them and placing them on a paper towel to dry. "Next?"

"You drink alcohol?" I glanced to my left to see Sandy staring at me.

"Uh, not a lot, but I like a beer now and then."

Sandy nodded and went to the fridge, pulling out two pale ales, popping off the caps, and handing one to me. It was ice cold and smooth going down. I only had beer during the summer at cookouts with friends, but since it was almost summer and we were cooking outside, I considered it as keeping up with my regular routine. The only difference—I was with a drop-dead gorgeous football player instead of the school staff and the folks I played summer softball with back in Peoria.

"Did this impromptu trip cancel any plans you had for a vacation? School's out, right?"

I glanced up from where I was staring at the packages of cheese he'd put on the counter to see the man was studying me closely as he waited for my answer.

"School's not out until next Friday. I had to leave a week early because of Regal's surgery. My middle school band had their concert on Thursday night, so our year was pretty much over after that. The high school band had a competition in April, so their work was already over. The concert choir is singing at the graduation, but one of my colleagues is handling that in my absence."

Sandy nodded. "That didn't answer my question about vacation plans."

He was blunt. I'd give him that. "Oh, sorry. No, I had no plans for vacation. I have—rather I had—a job lined up at a nursery in Peoria for the summer, but that's out the window now. I play on a summer softball league and volunteer at the animal shelter in town, but I won't be doing any of that now."

Being unable to work at the West Peoria Animal Adoption Center for the summer was a letdown. I enjoyed helping with the love and care of the animals during the summer, especially the big dogs. I could take them running with me and not worry about them keeping up. Was that more of my mother rubbing off on me?

"I couldn't do that. They kill those animals if they don't get adopted, right?" Sandy stared at me.

It was a harsh reality of the rescue animal world, but thankfully, not at WPAAC. "Uh, some do, but I volunteer at a no-kill shelter. They collaborate with other no-kill shelters around the country. If an animal isn't adopted within six months at one place, they rotate them through another shelter. Just because the animal isn't a fit for a family in West Peoria doesn't mean it won't find a forever family in Iowa or Kentucky."

I then pointed to the cheeses. "You want me to open all of these? Are you expecting company? I can make myself scarce if you have a date." If he had a date, I could eat really quick and disappear.

Sandy chuckled. "No dating for me. Once burned, twice shy. I planned to put the extra burgers in the freezer. How many do you want? I always eat two. Pick a cheese. I like the jalapeño cheddar."

I looked at the size of the patties to see they were probably eight ounces. I'd be fine with one, but I wasn't nearly as tall or muscular as the football player. "One's fine for me."

When Sandy's eyes scanned my body, I shivered. The heat from his sage-green stare could set me on fire in a heartbeat. "Mm-hmm. You're a lot fitter than I thought. Sorry for judging a book by its title—well, if that makes sense. I remember my teachers from high school, and our band teacher got winded when he walked across the room."

"Oh, were you in band?" I picked up the jalapeño cheddar and opened it, removing several slices and putting them on a small plate on the counter.

Sandy handed me a walnut tray. "Can you put all of that here? It's a nice evening, and I thought we could eat outside. I'll bring out a bucket of beer and meet you there. The table's already set."

That was a surprise. He seemed to be going to a lot of trouble for me, which I wanted to assure him wasn't necessary. I truly needed to chip in on the food. I wasn't a freeloader. I'd paid my own way for a long time.

I carried the tray downstairs and out the French doors, where a glass-topped dining table was set for two and lighted citronella torches flanked the ends of the patio not covered by the large awning near the pool. There were two grills at the uncovered end. One was gas and the other charcoal. Sandy seemed to have a perfectly stocked home for someone who lived alone.

I walked over to the enormous gas grill, lifting the lid to see it was immaculate. It was large enough that a whole suckling pig could be cooked on it—not that I was a fan of suckling pigs.

The French door squeaked open, and I turned to see Sandy with a small, galvanized bucket with a few bottlenecks sticking out of the ice. There was also a green-and-tan canvas bag over his shoulder. His eyes stayed trained on me as he approached his large grill. "I'm heating the charcoal grill. Unless you don't like charcoal flavor?"

I hurriedly closed the lid like I'd been caught doing something wrong. "I'm fine with charcoal. It sounds delicious. What's in the bag?" *Man, I sound nosy.* "I mean, what can I help you with?"

My host opened the tote and produced two kinds of chips and a condiment caddy complete with napkins and barbecue tools. "It's easier to bring things down in the tote. I've thought about putting a deck upstairs and making the bay window into a walkout, but I don't think I want the grills up there. I like having the outdoor kitchen by the pool. I spend a lot of time down here, and this is convenient, especially with the refrigerator over there." He pointed to a large stainless drawer under the kitchen counter. I had no idea it was a refrigerator.

Sandy had an entire kitchen built in the grill area. It was a cool setup, absolutely nothing like my little concrete slab and two chairs behind my rental house in Peoria, where my mini charcoal grill sat.

"I see what you mean. You could build a small balcony where you could sit outside up there, maybe have your morning coffee. You could also add a dumbwaiter somewhere so you could load everything on it and move it from the kitchen upstairs to the patio downstairs a lot easier."

Sandy turned to give me a glare, so I shut my mouth. Clearly, my opinion was of no importance, and he didn't appreciate it.

"Sorry."

He picked up the tray of burgers and put it on the counter of the large gas grill. "What are you sorry for? I'm kicking my own ass for not thinking about adding those things."

I swallowed my nerves. "I thought maybe I spoke out of turn. You have a beautiful pool. Was it here when you moved in?" I glanced around to see how well everything went together. It was obviously designed by someone who knew what they were doing.

There were rattan loungers with aqua cushions. All the chairs matched, and it made quite an incredible visual. The pool tiles were shades of blue with a sunburst in the center of the pool floor, and small solar lights surrounded the ledge. It was quite impressive, like nothing I'd ever seen.

"It was here. I bought the place furnished. Only replaced the mattresses. I could never put this together myself." Sandy then went about putting four burgers on the grill and four sets of buns on the rack above to brown.

He turned to me. "You want your onion grilled or do you take it raw."

The way he said *raw* had me thinking of something else, but I pulled my mind out of the gutter quickly. If I thought I had a chance in Hades of kissing the man, I'd skip the onion, but... "Grilled sounds good." I put raw onion slices on my plate and carried them to the charcoal grill.

"Thanks." Sandy used a set of tongs to place the onions on the grill next to the burgers and closed the lid.

"Do you have any siblings besides Marshall?" He hadn't said anything for a minute, and the silence was daunting. I imagined my attempt at small talk was probably way worse.

"Nope, there's just me and Marsh. Oh, I'm sure Mom and Dad wish they could have another, but they're too old now. They thought Marsh was a girl because the sonogram was unclear. He came out with a penis, which surprised them. Funnily enough, I called my parents after I got fired from the Breeze, and do you know what my father said when I called back after Mom hung up on me? 'I guess your mom actually got the girl she always wanted, only it was our oldest child. Don't call us again. You're dead to us now.' Nice, huh?"

My heart squeezed at his words. Who could do that to a child? I started to open my mouth, though I wasn't sure if I had anything to say that would be consoling or appreciated. Thankfully, Sandy waved me off.

"It's done. All water under a very ugly bridge. Anyway, how do you like your burger?"

"Medium, please."

Sandy nodded and flipped the patties. A few minutes later, he carried over a clean plate with the meat, buns, and onions. We each dressed our burgers before Sandy took my empty beer bottle and replaced it with a full one.

"Thank you. I want to pitch in on the food you're providing. I'll go to an ATM tomorrow and draw out more cash. I can go grocery shopping if you want to make a list. I know you didn't get much of a choice in this matter, so I don't want to be a burden." I meant every word.

"It's fine. I look forward to collecting a few favors from my brother over this. Tell me about your school."

I could talk about my school and my students all day long. "It's a smaller school system in West Peoria, a sister city to Peoria. I teach middle and high school band classes, which I love. I have about ten middle schoolers in the concert band and thirty-two high schoolers in the marching and concert bands.

"I also sponsor the jazz band, which is open to every student, whether they're in band or choir, and I teach music to the middle schoolers. I'm the director of the high school concert and acapella choirs, too, but I have a co-director who helps with those, Christine Quinton. She's working part-time at the elementary school right now, but she's hoping to get something full-time soon." I was downplaying how much I loved teaching. I didn't imagine someone like Sandy Kensington would really find my gushing over my students very entertaining.

"She your girlfriend?" He was studying me to the point I was fidgeting like the younger kids in my classes.

I couldn't hold back the laugh. "Gosh, no. Gold-star gay here. Christine is a sweet young woman who is engaged to be married next spring. Her fiancé, Rich Sohn, works for the West Peoria police department. Super nice guy. He holds the active-shooter drills at our schools."

Sandy flinched. "God, I hate to fuck that's even a thing kids need to know."

I reached for a bag of chips and opened it, extending it to him. "Since 2000, there have been over sixteen hundred casualties from school shootings. It's better to teach kids what to do if, God forbid, it should happen at their school than to leave them as sitting ducks. I hate it as much as the next teacher, but it's a necessary evil."

"Are you worried about it?" Sandy took a sip of his beer.

"Every day." That was no lie.

"On a much lighter note, how's the song coming along?"

I groaned. "You think that's a lighter subject?" We both laughed. "I hate to tell you, but I'm just as worried about the song. I'm having trouble not hearing the original melody in my head. It's my favorite song the band ever made. Regal said he wrote it when Mom left him the first time after she caught him fooling around with a groupie while she was pregnant with me. They broke up and got back together more times than I could count after that.

"From the Ashes started playing gigs in 1985. They had a few songs chart but no big successes over the ten years before 'Bury Me' came out. Hair bands gave way to the grunge movement in the nineties, but the guys couldn't let go of their love of rocking out. They weren't as hardcore as the other bands, but they were trying."

In my mind, From the Ashes was never meant to be a metal band. They had a unique sound at the time, but until 'Bury Me', they were just another hair band without a place to fit in.

"'Bury Me' doesn't sound like a rock song." Sandy fixed himself another burger. I hadn't finished my first one, yet.

"It's not. It's a ballad in the eighties hair band tradition. It's like trying to turn a football player into a ballet dancer. It can be done, but not without a lot of hard work."

Sandy laughed. "I took ballet classes in high school when I thought I would be a wide receiver. Coach said they helped with agility. They weren't bad until my arms, legs, and feet grew crazy fast and the rest of me didn't. I looked like some sort of freak made from two separate bodies with long arms and legs and a small torso."

I wasn't sure why, but that cracked me up.

Chapter Eight

Sandy

I laughed as the memory of how ridiculous I looked back in high school popped into my head. Mom couldn't buy jeans fast enough for me. I wore high waters for months and got made fun of until I started working out like it was my job. The ones who bullied me shut their mouths pretty fucking quick midway through my junior year.

"Ha, ha. I will have you know, I looked extra hot in a leotard," I responded as we both continued to laugh at me taking ballet classes.

After Skyler finally calmed enough to speak, he grinned. "I'm sure you did. Anyway, I'll clean up. Thank you for cooking dinner." He stood and began gathering the dishes, so I did the same.

We carried everything upstairs, and that dumbwaiter idea stuck in my mind. I made a mental note to check into it on Monday, along with a possible balcony off the kitchen.

We were cleaning together, and I was at a loss for what to say. I didn't want him to go to bed or return to work because I enjoyed his company. "You wanna watch a movie?"

I was drying the dishes as Skyler washed instead of stacking them in the dishwasher. I didn't ask why, nor did I protest. After he cleaned them, I rinsed, dried, and put them away. It was a glimpse into what domestic bliss must be like, and I was shocked it didn't make me want to run out of the house like my ass was on fire.

"Which movie?" Skyler dried his hands and turned to me.

"What kind do you like?"

Aside from sports, I didn't watch much television, but maybe we could sit and watch a movie together? What was the harm?

"Not surprisingly, I like musicals. I also like scary movies and mysteries. How about you?" Skyler folded the towel and put it over the bar by the sink before he turned to me and crossed his arms.

"How about a thriller. I've got all kinds of streaming shit. We can see if there's something we want to watch." I turned off the lights except those above the cabinets and led the way downstairs to the media room in the basement.

I flipped on the recessed lights around the perimeter of the large room where my home gym was set up. There was a pinball machine, a pool table, and a big-screen television, but my theater room was through the door to the left of the stairs. I'd wanted one like it when I lived in Chicago so I could review game film, but I never got around to making it happen.

My house in San Jose was everything I'd dreamed about while playing. I had to lose my fucking job to get what I wanted, but the one thing I'd never wanted was to enjoy it alone.

I took Skyler through the game room/gym and into the deep maroon-and-black media room. I turned on the lights so he could see the setup—four large black theater chairs in the front row with a long couch behind it. A projector from the ceiling was directed at an eight-foot screen on the far wall.

It was everything I used to dream about having yet rarely ever used because I didn't like sitting in there by myself. What was it they said—be careful what you wish for?

I handed the remote to Skyler and sat in one of the theater chairs. He walked around the room, taking in the décor of offset lighting, movie reels, old film canisters, and vintage movie posters. It was the only room in the house I had remodeled after I moved in. I was proud of it.

Skyler sat to my left and turned on the projector, scrolling through the selections. I couldn't take my eyes off him.

"You must spend a lot of time down here. You've got a lot of great choices." He was so fucking cute it wasn't funny.

"Not really. I've sort of fucked around doing nothing since I got released from the Breeze. I've been at loose ends, unsure what to do with my time." That was a goddamn understatement, and why couldn't I control my goddamn mouth?

"I'd guess it was a shock that you were let go. I mean, you didn't do anything any other football player hasn't done in the history of the game."

Apparently, Skyler had done his homework. "True, but my problem was that I tried to do it with a guy—an undercover cop—and I have a morals clause in my contract that every player on the team violates at one time or another. Unfortunately, I believe I was made the example because I'm gay."

Skyler turned sideways in the chair to face me, so I kicked back the recliner and turned on my side to face him. "Ask if you want to know."

"Have you ever had anyone who was important to you besides your family?"

I exhaled. "No. I never let myself give a damn about any of the hookups, and the night it all went to hell, that's all I was trying to do was hook up. The guys I've been with served a purpose: for me to blow off some steam. I made sure they knew that's all it was for me. It wasn't meant to be permanent."

"I'm sorry that happened to you. I'm not out at school because West Peoria is a conservative town in a conservative Midwestern state. I don't date. I mean, some of my friends know—well, a couple of them—I'm gay. It should be a lot easier, shouldn't it?" Skyler stared into my eyes, empathy dripping off him. *Why the fuck did he have to be so nice?*

"It should indeed. So, what do you want to watch?" I was done talking for the night. I'd said a hell of a lot more than I ever intended.

I took the remote and scrolled through the horror movies, finally settling on one that had come out a couple of years earlier. Skyler kicked back in the chair next to me, and we turned on the movie.

Aliens who tracked humans by sound. Who knew I'd be sitting with a sexy teacher in my dark media room watching such a thing?

My phone buzzed just as the doorbell rang. I opened my eyes to see a big ass, spider-looking thing on the projector screen chasing a family over a rickety-ass bridge.

I turned to my left. Skyler was also asleep, and my hand was on his thigh with his hand on top of mine, holding it in place. Time stood still. The warmth from his hand lit up every nerve ending in my body.

The doorbell rang again. When I checked my cell screen, the entry camera showed a delivery man on the porch, so I hit the mic icon. "I'll be right there."

Skyler's eyes shot open at the sound of my voice. When he glanced down at our clasped hands, he quickly released mine and pressed the button to lower the leg rest of the chair so he was sitting up, just as I was doing the same. "What happened? Who's at the door?"

He turned toward me, and I wanted to pull him over the arm of the chair and sleep for another five hours. "Your piano is here. I'll go meet the delivery guys." I hopped up and stretched before running up the stairs.

"Delivery for Skyler Ashe," a young guy announced when the sun blinded me as I opened the door. Two other guys were standing next to a delivery truck in the driveway.

"He's here. Come on in. It's going in there." I pointed toward the mostly empty formal living room where the piano would look incredible.

There was an ivory couch, a black-and-ivory leather chair, and a gold-and-glass cocktail table near a black-and-gold marble fireplace against the far wall. On the other side of the large room was a huge picture window that let in a lot of light and nothing else. It was the perfect spot for a grand piano to be placed, and I hoped it was a good place for Skyler to be creative.

The handsome teacher entered the living room, and when the movers brought in the gleaming black instrument with one leg on one wheeled cart and three legs on another, he got a dreamy expression on his face.

Skyler hurried forward to watch the three men assemble the magnificent beast. When the delivery men seemed a bit baffled regarding how to connect the foot pedals, Skyler slid under it and used their tools to do the job. When he slid out from under the grand piano, his grin was as bright as a spotlight.

The crew leader handed over a clipboard, and I signed it. "What about tuning it?" I had no idea if they did it or if we needed to find someone to do it so Skyler could use it for writing his music. Seemed like it was important.

"Oh, that's okay. May I borrow this? I'll return the tools with the piano. I can tune it myself. Thank you, guys." Skyler reached into his pocket and handed the lead delivery man some money before they gathered their equipment, and I walked them out.

I closed the door and locked it, turning to see Skyler had lifted the large top and propped it on the arm from inside the piano. He raised the cover and touched a key, cringing a little. "That'll take some work."

"Before you get started, do you have time for some coffee or breakfast?"

He chuckled. "That would be great. I need a shower and a change of clothes too."

I chuckled and walked by him on my way to the kitchen to start the coffee maker when Skyler touched my arm. "Thank you for dinner and the movie last night. I had a really nice time."

God, my lips wanted to take his, but it seemed we had an unspoken agreement not to push things between us. It was probably for the best. He lived in Illinois, and it sounded like he had a job he loved. It was best to let any thoughts of hooking up fade into the back of my brain, never to be heard from again.

I returned from my run Tuesday morning to find two young guys in the living room with Skyler, one sitting on my couch and the other in the chair while Skyler played the piano he'd tuned on Monday with the deliverers' borrowed tools. There was a music composition book on the bench next to him.

"Hello." I glanced between my guests, waiting for someone to explain what was happening.

Skyler stood and gently pushed back the bench. "Sandy, you remember my brother, River. This is JD Horn, Ripper's son. JD plays bass like his father. We're trying to figure out the guitar bridge. JD, this is Sandy—"

"Kensington. Wow, man, nice to meet you." JD stepped forward to shake my hand. I'd seen River at Hope's rescue farm, but I hadn't met him. I shook his hand, too.

I was sweaty and smelly, so I headed toward the stairs. "I'll get out of your way."

"Thank you, Sandy. We'll try not to disturb you." Skyler's big sage-green eyes met mine, and he smiled. I sighed. The moment was...jeez. I had to stop thinking like that.

I went downstairs and did some free weight reps since I didn't have anyone to spot me on the bench—not that I ever did. My mind was all over the place, and the likelihood I'd end up hurting myself or maybe even choking on the weight bar was high.

I hadn't put on music for fear of interrupting them, nor had I put in earbuds because I was nosy and wanted to hear what was happening upstairs. The sound of the piano carried easily throughout the basement, making me smile involuntarily.

The song Skyler was playing was the original version of 'Bury Me', which was growing on me, especially since I knew the meaning behind the song. Then, there was a loud, aggressive guitar chord that stopped abruptly. The same chord was repeated twice more.

I knew nothing about music, but it sounded cool. The piano played softly again, and someone began to sing. I stopped my curls immediately because the voice was beautiful.

Bury Me

You said I'm cold you think I'm mean You claim when I'm with you, you still feel unseen

But you don't know How hard I try To be the man who walks Through life by your side

The singing stopped, and there was a muted conversation I couldn't exactly pick up. Were they talking about me? How did JD know my name? Why was I such a fucking idiot?

All very good questions for which I had no answers.

Chapter Nine

Skyler

"Those riffs are great but make them a little rougher in contrast to the melody. Make it like they're breaking into the song uninvited." I turned to JD. "Let's double the tempo on the chorus, okay? River, let's take it from the top."

Having the two of them there to flesh out the song was perfect. When River called me, I hesitated to agree for him to come over to introduce me to JD. The song wasn't ready for their collab, but I could hear in River's voice that he was excited to get involved. Heck, he was Regal's other son, so it wasn't my place to not hear his suggestions.

Sandy wasn't home, so I couldn't check with him, but I didn't think he'd object. I'd heard him leave that morning while I was doing yoga in my room as the sun was coming up. I'd apologize to Sandy after the guys left if I overstepped.

I played the accompaniment for 'Bury Me' and began to sing the lyrics the way my father had on the original recording. The song started with a beautiful acoustic intro, but to change it up, I switched from acoustic guitar to piano, which would probably work for the movie because the melody could easily be manipulated for background music if the studio was interested.

The song built to a crescendo at the chorus, adding lead guitar, then a hard bass line, and finally, the drums banging in. At the chorus, everyone would go full throttle and then drop out when the second verse began. If it wasn't overdone, it would be epic.

We went through the first verse several times so I could get down the notes as we were figuring out the best way to proceed. River's choices were incredible, and he was great at altering the notes to give us options, as was JD. They were both extremely talented.

When we got to the chorus, I stopped us. "Let's take a break. You guys want something to drink?"

JD and River placed their instruments on the couch before turning off the amps. I led them into the kitchen and got the three of us some water. The two sat at the large white-and-silver island while I paced.

Something was still off. "What's missing?"

JD's phone buzzed in his pocket, so he pulled out the device, checking it before he glanced at River. "We need to get going. I gotta get to work." JD then looked at me. "Thursday?"

I nodded. Hopefully, by then, I'd figure out what was still missing.

After JD and River left, I moved their guitars to lean against the wall next to the piano so they were out of Sandy's way and went back to working on the chorus, hearing the lead guitar riffs and the bass beat in my mind. I honestly couldn't wait to get behind my dad's drum kit in the studio.

As I thought about it, I decided I should call to check up on my crazy father. I pulled my phone from my pocket and dialed Mom's number.

"Hi, honey." She sounded upbeat, which probably meant Regal was home from the hospital.

"Hi, Mom. Did Regal come home? Nobody called me, and I forgot to ask River when he was here this morning."

"Yes, he came home yesterday. Getting him to drink water was a problem, so they kept him until he could do his business. He was unhappy about it, but he wasn't following doctors' orders, so I refused to bring him home. None of the others would go get him. Not even Jeanne."

I laughed. "Sounds about right. How's he doing?" *Please don't offer for me to talk to him.*

"He's right here having lunch. Hang on." *Crap!*

Regal cleared his throat. "S-Sky?"

"Hi, Regal. How are you feeling?" I didn't want to care, but Regal Ashe lived inside me, and what kind of person would I be if I didn't? Regal had done a lot of stupid things in his life and made some supremely poor choices, but I didn't want him to die. If my mother loved him as much as I believed, there was something inside the man worth loving. Maybe someday I'd see it too.

"I'm better, Sky. Tired, but your mom and Jeanne make me walk in the morning and the evening to build up my strength. I was able to go out and sit on the patio for a bit. Hope still won't let me have a cigarette."

Mom said, "If I catch you with one, you'll eat the pack."

I couldn't hold the laugh. I remembered hearing the same thing from Mom when I was thirteen. Jenny Singer, one of the neighbors, brought her mother's cigarettes over so we could try them. We were in the front yard, and after sharing one, I puked all over the front porch. Mom saw me.

My flimsy excuse that the guys in From the Ashes smoked—though it wasn't cigarettes they were smoking—and I wanted to try one got me nowhere. Mom told me I'd have to eat the pack next time. Throwing up was enough for me to swear I'd never try it again.

"I can't imagine your doctor would be too happy about you smoking either. What's the recovery schedule like?"

"I'm out for six to eight weeks. No singing and no playing, according to my doctor. I start respiratory therapy this afternoon, twice a week. I need to build up my lungs again. I had fluid on the right one that I didn't get checked out, but they gave me meds for it." That explained why he still sounded out of breath.

"Are you going to listen to the doctors?" I already knew the answer.

Regal started laughing and then broke into a coughing fit. When he finally stopped, he asked the question I dreaded. "How's the song going?"

"Ugh. River and JD came over this morning, and we worked on it. We're trying to transition the original song into the rock world, but I'm not sure it will be what you and the band want. How sure are you about the movie studio's interest?" It was a lot of work to change an iconic song into something completely new.

"Well, I guess you understand the trouble we were having. Look, if you've got to change the melody or even the time signature, do it. Whatever you can do, Sky. This is important not just to me but to all the guys. None of us were great with money, though I think I was the worst. Now, with these doctor bills, I'll really need the cash, son."

No guilt at all. I should have known to expect it.

"I'll do my best." We ended the call, and I glanced down at the piano keys.

Something came over me, and I started playing an Elton John song. Then I moved on to Billy Joel, Queen, Michael Jackson, and Alicia Keys. I then played a song I'd written a long time ago.

I'll Find You

[verse]

I wake up aloneI go to bed the same wayI'm tired of going outI wonder where you are today?
There once was a timeI thought I'd found a true lovebut in the blink of an eyeit flew on the wings of a dove

Momma says you're out there Daddy says I'm a fool for believing such things can exist How can fate be so cruel?

[chorus]

I'll find you (yeah, I'll find you) my heart tells me to trust you're yearning for my touch Oh, I'll find you (yeah, I'll find you) and when we finally meet, you'll love me just as much

And when I find you, (when I find you) Our hearts will know we fit We've been waiting for so long It will be clear that this is it

[verse]

Our eyes will meet across a crowded room All the rest will fade away Our hearts will know they've found their other half The sparks we'll feel are here to stay

[chorus]

I'll find you (yeah, I'll find you) my heart tells me to trust that you're yearning for my touch Oh, I'll find you (yeah, I'll find you) and when we finally meet, you'll love me just as much

And when I find you, (when I find you) Our hearts will know we fit We've been waiting for each other for so long It will be clear that this is it

"Wicki-wicki-wicki. Bom-ch. Bom-bom-ch. Bada bada... this song sucks."

The loud laugh from behind me caused me to jump. I turned to see Sandy standing at the top of the stairs from the basement. He was wearing a full-size towel and drying his hair with a smaller one.

"Sounds like a top forty hit in the making. Where'd the others go?"

The hair under his navel that disappeared beneath the towel had my mouth watering. I so hoped the towel would come untucked and reveal the treasure lying beneath.

I snapped out of it and shifted my eyes up to his face to see a smirk. "They, uh, they had to go. JD works for a delivery company, and River had given him a ride over here."

"How's it going?" Sandy was holding on to each end of the hand towel that was now around his neck as he stood, feet spread shoulder-width apart. Lord almighty, I was going to die from blue balls.

"It's not. I'm still stuck, but we had some good ideas for the beginning of the song." I didn't sound optimistic, but I didn't feel it either.

Sandy was silent for a moment, head leaned back, eyes focused on the ceiling. Finally, he nodded and stared at me. "Feel like going for a hike? There's a great place not far from here, but it's about a thirteen-mile hike if you do the whole loop."

"Sure. Why not? How rugged? I haven't been hiking since last summer. I try to get enough exercise, but I may be slow." Getting outside was a great way to clear my head—or so I hoped.

"It's kind of rugged, but I've seen people run it with dogs. It takes about six hours, but it's nice, and I'll be there to carry you if I must. Or maybe you want something smaller to start out?"

Oh, I sensed a challenge. "No. I'll be fine. Let me change."

We both went upstairs, Sandy veering off toward his bedroom. I glanced over my shoulder to see the towel drop when he went into his room, his beautiful ass on display.

"Mmmm." I couldn't stop the groan if I wanted to, and when Sandy turned toward the sound, he laughed before walking out of my view.

I should have been embarrassed for openly gawking, but a body that beautiful deserved to be admired—or so I justified to myself. I went into my room and changed into shorts, socks, and the hiking boots I'd had in the closet at my mom's house in case I got to ride one of the rescue horses.

I splashed cold water on my face to try to calm my dick because Sandy did things to me that I'd never felt before. I couldn't figure out if I wanted to get away from him or crawl into his skin and live forever.

I combed my hair, which had grown a bit, though not nearly as much as it seemed Marshall Kensington wanted, and grabbed a baseball cap and sunglasses, sliding them into the neck of my West Peoria High Band tank top. I rubbed some sunscreen on my shoulders and face so they didn't burn and hurried back downstairs.

Sandy was at the counter, filling a backpack with water bottles and snacks. He was wearing a tank top, but he had a lot more muscle to show. I really needed to start building muscle in my arms and worrying about my stamina behind the drum kit. If I was going to tour with From the Ashes, I needed to be able to carry the beat for at least the length of a concert set.

"You ready?"

I nodded, not exactly sure I was making the right decision. "Anything I can carry?"

"Here." He handed me the backpack and grabbed a basket from behind the counter. I followed him downstairs and out the back door. We went around the pool deck and over to a large building that looked like a warehouse.

"What's this?" I followed him to the door, where he used a key to open it, revealing eight motor vehicles. Cars. Trucks. SUVs. Sports cars. A couple I didn't recognize. It was shocking.

"These are my babies. I started collecting them and couldn't stop." As we walked down the aisle between the two rows of expensive metal, I couldn't believe it wasn't a dream. My little Ford Escape back in West Peoria would be a play toy compared to some of these vehicles.

"They're, uh, they're nice. Do you drive them all?"

Sandy chuckled. "All except this one." He stopped at the end of the row on the left, and I glanced at the vehicle to see it was an old white Jeep Wagoneer with wood-look side panels.

"This is cool."

"It was mine while I was in high school. It had been my grandfather's, and when he passed away, he left it to me. I've hung onto it because it reminds me of good times."

I followed Sandy to a shiny SUV—a silver Yukon. It was nicer than the rental Marshall had left for me to drive. "Hop in." Sandy opened the door for me, so I did as he asked.

He closed the door, walked around to open the back door, and set the basket inside. He got in on the driver's side and started the SUV. "Ready?" Sandy wasn't a big talker, but he had an incredible smile.

"Yeah." We were both quiet for the first ten minutes we were in the SUV. I wasn't sure what to talk about with the man. I didn't know much about football—anything, really—and I wasn't sure if Sandy even wanted to talk about anything. We seemingly had nothing in common. Of course, if we didn't talk to each other, we'd never know, would we?

The drive was nice—the terrain was much different from what I was used to in Illinois. We had hills. In San Jose, they had mountains. Sandy pulled into the parking lot, and I grabbed the backpack before getting out.

He wrote on his window with a white marker before closing the door on his side and walking around the vehicle. He took the backpack from me and pulled it onto his back. "Ready?"

"What about the basket?"

Sandy smirked. "That's for after."

Chapter Ten

Sandy

We arrived at Almaden Quicksilver Park, where the trailhead was located for the Senador Mine to Mine Hill Loop. I was kicking my own ass for suggesting we hike instead of taking a naked roll in the sheets.

Skyler's scent had filled my head while we were in the SUV, and I was dying. Fresh air was good. Fresh air was necessary for me to be able to form a sentence.

I parked near the trailhead and pulled out the dry-erase marker I had in the console of the SUV. I wrote our departure and anticipated return times on the driver-side window, as recommended by the park service, before locking the vehicle.

Walking around the SUV, I took the backpack from Skyler and pulled it onto my shoulders. "Ready?"

"What about the basket?" Skyler was referring to the picnic basket I'd packed before we left the house.

"That's for after." I then headed toward the trailhead, filled out a slip with my name and license plate number, and slid it into the lockbox the rangers checked every few hours. "Let's go."

Once we got to the trail proper, I stopped and pulled two water bottles out of the backpack before we proceeded side by side. "You guys sounded great, but I only listen to music, not make it. I got the impression you weren't happy with how the session went."

Skyler smiled. "I hope it wasn't so obvious to them. River's nineteen and still trying to find himself so I don't want to discourage him in any way. JD is twenty-two, and he's a great musician, but I think he's dying to break into music, and I'm not sure this will help his career aspirations.

"I don't want to let my family down, but I'm still sort of lost about what to do with the song. I do better with marching music." He giggled, and my stomach felt like it was filled with bats. It was ridiculous that his laughter had any effect on me, much less made me feel tingly inside.

"Well, for what it's worth, you have a great singing voice. I didn't realize you were a triple threat."

"Ha! Hardly. Can't dance for heck. So, what about you? Any ideas about what you want to do going forward?" Skyler's head was on a swivel, taking in the scenery—or was he purposely avoiding looking at me.

We were just over twenty-two hundred feet in elevation, so it was a nice seventy-five degrees with little humidity. The skies were clear with miles of visibility, which was damn incredible.

"*Look!*" Skyler pointed to a little hill before scrambling for his phone to take a quick picture. It was a doe and her fawn resting on the grass.

He turned the screen toward me and grinned. "For my kids when school starts. We always have an icebreaker for the new kids joining us where we talk about what we did over the summer, and I'll have pictures to go with my story this year."

Fuck if he wasn't so damn adorable that I wanted to eat him up. Skyler was around thirty, and I was thirty-nine, which was a bit of a spread but not an insurmountable hurdle. Why was I even thinking about it?

"You like teaching?" I couldn't imagine being around teenagers all day, but Skyler had the type of personality that fit into a classroom...wearing glasses...and a sexy sweater vest... God, I wouldn't mind being the teacher's pet.

"I love teaching. It took me a while to warm up to the idea of it when I was in college because being a teacher seemed like a stretch. I had no idea I'd love it so much."

I glanced at him to see his cheeks were red.

"Good for you. I can easily see you teaching."

His blond hair glistened in the sunlight, making him look like a cover model for a hiking magazine—hell, any kind of magazine.

With the sheen of sweat on his shoulders and neck, he was sexy as fuck. I fought with myself about asking more personal questions or whether I should steel my mind not to think about him at all—which was really fucking hard with him in my home...truck...head...heart.

We climbed a hill, and there was a break in the trees where the reservoir was clearly visible. We stopped so Skyler could take a picture. "What's that body of water?"

"That's the Guadalupe Reservoir. You can fish there, but we have no fishing poles or tackle with us." I hadn't even thought about that.

"Can you swim there?" His face lit up as he turned his gaze on me.

God, the idea of skinny dipping with him had my cock hardening in the compression shorts I'd thought to wear under my basketball shorts. It damn well wasn't comfortable, but hopefully, he wouldn't notice that I could hit a home run with the bat in my pants.

"Uh"—*cough*—"no. No swimming. Not sure why."

I quickly wrestled with the backpack to unzip it and retrieve two granola bars. "Snack?"

Skyler took the cinnamon and oatmeal bar from me and walked down the hill to a large rock jutting out a bit. He climbed up and took a seat. I followed him like he had a leash on me. I sat on the other side and stared out at the beautiful sight before me.

We sat there in silence for a moment before Skyler turned to me. "Do you come out here often?"

I chuckled. "Not as much as I should. Sometimes, when I need to think, I come here. I've sat here several times trying to figure out my shit, but unfortunately, I rarely come away with good answers."

"It would be a good thinking place. It's beautiful out here. I wish I could find some answers about what to do with this stupid song. It's so freakin' frustrating."

I didn't mean to laugh, but I couldn't help myself. "Do you ever curse?" I could barely get a sentence out that didn't have an expletive.

Skyler smirked. "Back in high school and college, I used to curse like a sailor. When I accepted my student teaching gig, one of the kids heard me say the F-word when I broke a piece of chalk while writing notes on a blackboard. He then said it to his grandmother when she took him to the grocery store. She dropped a can on the floor next to him and scared the crap out of him, and he dropped an F-bomb, according to his grandmother when she came to school to scold me in person. I learned my lesson and try not to curse because we never know who might be listening."

My desire to make him yell "Fuck me" was nearly overwhelming. Hearing him swear up a blue streak as I sucked his cock into my throat would be quite an achievement.

"Admirable. Not something I'll ever try, but good for you that you can do it. Shaping young minds and all." No fucking way could I ever work with kids.

We sat for a while and enjoyed the view. Finally, I finished my water and shoved the empty bottle into the backpack before climbing off the rock. "You wanna finish the loop or just head back. I think we've gone about three miles."

Skyler slid off the rock and dusted the back of his shorts, which I'd have been more than happy to do for him. He smiled at me as if he could read my thoughts. "If you don't mind, I'd like to head back. I can run five miles a day on a flat surface. These hills kicked my butt!"

I chuckled. "Yeah, hiking is an entirely different animal."

We headed back down the trail in relative silence. Skyler's phone buzzed in his pocket, so he retrieved it and read the message. "It's from your brother. He's at your house and looking for me."

I walked up behind Skyler and looked over his shoulder, a bit dazed by his scent. He smelled clean and spicy. I didn't know if it was body wash or his natural scent, but it could become addicting.

His gorgeous neck was right there, and the urge to lick it was strong. Fight as I might, one day, I was bound to give in, and I had to wonder what the fallout might be. After what I'd endured with the NFL when I was outed, it would be a walk in the park.

When we arrived back at my house, a rental car was parked in the driveway, blocking the lane leading to my garage. It could only be my inconsiderate brother.

I parked behind the black sports car and got out, walking around my SUV to grab the picnic basket we hadn't used. We'd been in too much of a hurry to return to my place after Marsh didn't respond to Skyler's text asking what he wanted.

I let us in through the back door since our boots were dusty from the trail. We both removed our shoes and went upstairs to the kitchen, where we found Marsh stuffing a sandwich into his pie hole. His garment bag and duffel were by the stairs in the foyer as though my brother was waiting for me to carry his shit upstairs. *Fat chance!*

"Marsh, help yourself to something to eat." The sarcasm was thick.

"Thanks, big brother. I assumed that's how you'd feel. Skyler, how's it going? The song done?" His snide expression told me I wouldn't like where he was headed.

"Not...not yet. River and JD came over this morning, and we worked on it for a while. They had to leave, so Sandy suggested we take a break and go for a hike so I could clear my head. I'll get back to work. Good to see you, Marshall." Skyler hurried up the stairs, and when I heard the door close to the spare room, I wheeled on my brother.

"What the fuck was that?" I dropped the picnic basket on the counter and began shuttling the contents into the fridge.

"What was *what*?" *Fucking wiseass!*

"Your smartass comment about the song being done. You have no idea how hard Skyler is working on this, and you putting pressure on him isn't going to help."

Marsh wiped his mouth and picked up his plate, emptying the crumbs into the trash can and rinsing the plate before putting it in the dishwasher. He wiped his hands on a dishtowel on the rack under the cabinet and stared at me.

"What do you care?" Are you getting hot and bothered by the teacher?" Marsh picked up the empty soda can and put it in the recycling bin under the island, his face holding a smug expression.

"No, I'm not getting *hot and bothered* by the guy. I just think he's being used by you and the band, only to be shoved aside. I don't have to be in love with someone to not want to witness them getting screwed."

I reached into the fridge and grabbed a beer, popping off the cap and taking a long gulp. My mind reeled at the snarky tone in my brother's voice. I had no feelings for Skyler beyond friendship. He was a nice guy who didn't deserve to get shit on.

"His father isn't using him. Regal actually feels guilty for the way he treated Skyler when he was younger. Do you know what it took for Regal to ask the guy for his help?"

"Didn't Skyler's *mom* ask him to help? You just want to wring the guy out and then send him away. Don't you think that's a jack-off move?" I took another gulp of my beer.

"I don't get paid to care about it. I just need the song recorded to submit to the Harmon Studio before the deadline. After that, I'm just there to manage the tour. Speaking of which, I need muscle. I need someone to guard these old guys and make sure they stay out of trouble for the five appearances I've scheduled for them. Do you want a job? You can hire another guy to help you out. Your choice. The dates are all set and begin in mid-July, with breaks in between. I wanted to call it the *AARP* Tour, but Alicia put the kibosh on that. What do you think? You up for being a caregiver to a group of sixty-year-old men?"

Guard a group of past-their-prime rockers? How hard could that be?

Chapter Eleven

Skyler

Marshall was right. I was staying with Sandy because I needed to work, not to hang out and pretend as if I had a chance with the football player. I missed my simple life in Illinois.

I decided to tackle the end of the song, thinking it was better to address the middle when River and JD came over on Thursday because we needed to create a hard-rocking guitar bridge with a much better player than me. It might be best to do it at my father's recording studio so we could capture it on audio for Dusty so he could tweak it for live performances.

I was trying to conceptualize how a rock bridge would sound in the middle of the song with the first verse, chorus, and second verse written as they were. I tried a few riffs on the six-string River had loaned me, but it wasn't coming together. I was about to give up when there was a soft knock on my bedroom door.

"Come in." I put the guitar down and stood from the side of the bed, suddenly nervous when Sandy came inside and leaned against the wall by the door.

"Don't listen to Marshall. He's a pain in the ass." He crossed his arms over his broad pecs, studying me.

I smiled, my face heating at his scrutiny. "No, he's right. I'm here bothering you because I have a job to do, not for fun, and I need to get my work done so I can go home."

"Uh, I'm not so sure about when you'll get to go home. Marsh mentioned the dates for the appearances, and they don't start until mid-July." He walked over and sat on the bed, so I sat near the headboard. Based on his expression, he was about to give me some news I wouldn't be happy to hear.

"What are the dates, and where are they?"

"July twelfth and thirteenth in San Diego." He lifted his hand and read from the words on his palm. "Uh, July thirty-first in Long Beach. August tenth in Los Angeles. August thirtieth in Lincoln, then circling back to San Francisco on September sixth." He then glanced up, his eyes locking on mine to await my reaction.

I sighed, the tension in my shoulders increasing. "I can do San Diego and Long Beach, but the rest of the dates are out. I need to be back in Illinois for summer band camp, which starts on August fifth."

Just then, Marshall stuck his head into the room. "Can't someone else do it for you? We really need you on the rest of those dates. It will mean a lot to your father and mother. If these dates do well, not only will he get paid, but the studio would also weigh the reviews from the shows with more intensity when they're making their decision about the song."

More guilt. Could I ever get away from it? Why did it feel as though everything was resting on my shoulders? *Probably because it is, stupid!*

"Maybe I can fly back and forth for the other three?" I wasn't trying to be difficult. I was more than willing to work with everyone, but I couldn't let my kids down either.

"If you can afford that, I'll discuss it with the band." That made my stomach flip. I definitely didn't have the money for that kind of travel.

Like a flash, Sandy pushed his brother out the door and pulled it closed behind them. I stood from the bed and quietly approached the door to listen, but I couldn't hear anything. Cracking the door to check, I found the hallway empty. It happened so fast that I was still a little dizzy.

I tiptoed toward Sandy's bedroom at the end of the hallway. The door was closed, so I put my ear near it but still didn't hear anything. I had no idea where they'd gone or how they'd gotten away so quickly but standing in the hallway and wondering about it wasn't working on 'Bury Me'.

I returned to my room and picked up the six-string again, doing my best to focus. I had far too many things circling my mind to worry about where Marshall and Sandy had gone.

All day Wednesday, I worked on the song's ending, using the rented piano at Sandy's house. I had bits of an accompanying score floating through my head as well. If the studio picked 'Bury Me' for the movie, the music in my head would work perfectly for the rest of it, but it would need a lot of work for the action sequences to give it the depth needed to build the movie to the climax. I'd never composed a film score before, but it was somewhat exciting to consider.

Sandy had left before I got up that morning, probably not looking forward to another day of me plunking around. He'd left a note on the coffee maker that he'd be back late in the afternoon, and Marshall had gone to my mom's house to meet with the band. I hadn't called in the last couple of days to check on Regal, so guilt was rearing its ugly head, but I had a song to fix, and if I went to Mom's, she'd just ask me to repair something or clean up something. No thanks. I'd had my fill of shoveling animal feces for a long time.

I headed to the kitchen to get another cup of coffee when the landline rang. I forgot where I was for a second and picked it up. "Hello?"

"Is this Sanders Kensington?"

It was a woman's voice. Sandy had said he was gay—was outed in a very public way—but maybe he was bisexual? *It's definitely none of my business.*

"No, I'm sorry. I'm a friend and accidentally picked up the phone out of habit. I can hang up, and you can call back and leave a message if you'd prefer."

"Can you just give him my name, Kathleen Graves, and my number…?" She rattled off her number rather quickly, but I got it down.

"Will he know why you're calling?" Maybe it was rude to ask, but what if she was a bill collector? I'd tear up the message and never say a word.

"Tell Sandy I just took over the Baltimore Shuckers football team from my father, and I'd like to chat with him." Then, before I could ask her to repeat the number, she hung up.

I wrote down her message and put the pen and paper on the counter. I hoped it was good news.

I went back to the piano and turned on my phone's recording app so I could play what I'd written so far and listen back to it, and then I got lost in the music again.

What if, instead of a hard-banging guitar riff, we modeled the song after another rock band from back in the day and used an alternative instrument? Maybe a flute? Or a steel drum? It was something to consider.

When I listened to the recording later, I thought of ways to further change it and incorporate those changes into the last part of the song. I sang along to ensure the lyrics worked with the melody, and then I recorded it without the guitar break in the middle.

"Damn, that was fucking beautiful."

I quickly spun on the piano stool to see Sandy leaning against the doorway, his eyes appraising me. My face flushed with embarrassment. It was the second time he'd caught me singing, and I was *not* a great singer.

"Sorry you had to witness that again."

"On the contrary. It sounded great. Just enough like the original for people to recognize it, but new. I think it's fantastic." He turned to go back to the kitchen, so I quickly cleaned up my mess and followed him.

"I thought I could take you out for dinner tonight." I arrived behind him at the kitchen counter, where he was reading the note.

"What's this about?" He held up the pad with the note on it.

I chuckled. "Do you not know how to read?"

Thankfully, Sandy laughed with me. "Yes, though I sometimes need help with the big words." His sarcastic smile was more than I was prepared to see.

"That's all she said. I'm sorry I answered your phone. I forgot where I was for a minute and answered when it rang. She told me her name and left that message for you. I won't answer it—"

"No, no. You didn't do anything wrong. Thanks for picking up."

"It's important, then? You know her?" I was way out of line asking personal questions like that, but I couldn't keep my mouth shut.

"I don't *know* her, but I know *of* her. Kathleen Graves is the daughter of Jerry Graves, the owner of the Baltimore NFL franchise. It was recently announced that Jerry had a stroke, and Kathleen happens to be the eldest of his three children, though the younger two aren't her full siblings. I just want to know why she's calling *me*."

I understood the dynamic he'd described for the Graves family because, ironically, I had the same in my own life. It wasn't easy to accept people you didn't grow up with, but River and I had found common ground—our love of music. It took a while, but I'd come to appreciate River.

Unfortunately, our father wasn't any more supportive of River than me, so we had that in common. Fortunately, Regal Ashe's narcissistic tendencies seemed to have stopped with him.

"I can leave so you can call her back. I'll just go—"

"I have nothing to hide. Stick around." Sandy's smile had me stuck to the spot as he dialed the phone number I'd written down and put it on speakerphone.

"Ms. Graves' office. How may I help you?"

"Hello. I'm Sanders Kensington, returning Ms. Graves' call."

"One moment, please."

To her word, the familiar voice came on the line. "Sandy Kensington? I'm glad you called me back."

"Hi, Ms. Graves. How are you doing? I heard about your father's stroke. How's he doing?" Sandy sounded very empathetic, which was nice to hear.

"He's in a rehabilitation facility. Some paralysis on the right side, but none of his organs were affected. He'll need to undergo intensive therapy for a while. Hopefully, he'll recover more use on his right side so he'll be able to get around with a cane and not be confined to a wheelchair. As you might guess, it's a work in progress. How about you, Sandy? You've been off the field for a year. How are you doing?"

Sandy chuckled. "I'm holding my own. What can I do for you?" The sexy football player kept his eyes on me.

"I'm looking for a new assistant coach for the D-line and special teams. I tried to get Jackson Delacroix to come back to the game, but he's settled into a new business with his partners and says he's happier than ever. Do me a favor before you say no. Come to the minicamp in three weeks. Give me an evaluation of the draftees. I'll pay you for your time regardless of whether you're willing to discuss anything further."

Sandy glanced at me.

Was he waiting for me to say something? Offer a suggestion? I knew nothing about his business, and it wasn't for me to care what he did with his life, so I didn't know what he wanted me to say.

"You do know the reason I was released from my contract, right?"

The loud laugh was a surprise. "I do, Sandy, and I thought it was bullshit. Things won't be that way now, I promise. There's a new sheriff in town, and she's a lesbian."

Sandy's eyebrows shot into his hairline as he heard her remark. His big smile had me grinning in return.

"I'll come for the minicamp. Email the details. I fired my agent after I got let go because he didn't fight against me getting released from the team, but I can negotiate my own deal. I won't promise anything beyond the minicamp, Ms. Graves. I have another job waiting for me, but this won't interfere with it. Can you live with that?"

"For now, Sandy. I'll have my assistant send the details. Thanks for calling me back. Talk soon." The woman hung up, and I watched Sandy's face morph into shock.

"Can you fucking believe that?" He scooped me up and swung me around, which shocked *me*! As if realizing what he'd done, he quickly put me on my feet and stepped back.

The air was full of awkward apprehension, so I spoke up. "I'm so happy for you. You were a force on the field when you played. Why wouldn't she want you to work with her team?" That was really all I could add. I wasn't knowledgeable about many sports, though I knew enough about football to get by.

Teaching a marching band to support the team under the Friday night lights necessitated learning enough about the game to cue the band to play fanfare when the team scored or got a first down. During timeouts, we offered percussion accompaniments until the team took the field again. When there was a bad call, we played an out-of-tune razzamatazz, and I'd had to learn when and why to order those spontaneous moments.

"Sounds like a good opportunity if you're interested in returning to the game. Congratulations."

Sandy studied me for a minute. "I'll be accompanying you and From the Ashes on your five appearances. I'm helping Marsh be sure you guys are safe."

"Will you be able to make the last few gigs work? I'll have to figure out how to—"

"No, you won't. Marsh is being a tight ass. He wants a bigger piece of the pie, but if you give him an ultimatum, he'll come through with airfare for you," Sandy assured.

"I...I'm not good at that, Sandy. I'm not really good at confronting anyone outside of my parents. Don't worry about it. I'll figure it out. The airfare, I mean. Thanks though. I better get back to work."

Sandy chuckled. "Leave it to me."

His sexy smirk nearly did me in.

Chapter Twelve

Sandy

Skyler had been steadily recording at his father's studio with the help of his brother and JD Horn. Skyler usually came back to the house around eight, having already eaten. I was jealous, though I had no right to be.

I held my tongue from asking why he wasn't coming back earlier to eat with me. Was it because I'd picked him up and spun him after talking to Kathleen Graves? It'd been impulsive, yes, but there was nobody I'd wanted to share the news with more than Skyler.

The doorbell rang, pulling me from my pity party. I glanced at the app on my phone to see it was Marsh.

I went to open the door, having just finished showering after my workout. I was getting ready to go to the Ashe rescue farm where Skyler was recording, and I was in no mood for Marsh's surprise visit.

"What do you want?" My voice wasn't very welcoming as I stood in the middle of the doorway.

"I'm here to check on my clients. I need to know how much progress they've made so I can pass along the information to the studio. They're antsy for an update. I can stay here tonight, right, big brother?"

I sighed. "Yeah, come in. I'm just about to head over to the Ashes. Just so we're clear, you're gonna pay for Skyler's flights back and forth to the gigs. The guy's a fucking musical genius and a teacher, Marshall. He can't afford to foot the bill on his salary, can he? You want me to help with the tours? You pay for the guy to travel."

Marsh grinned. "Deal, but then I don't have to pay you, right? You're gone for the guy, aren't you?"

Was I? I could tell myself all day long that I didn't want anything more than a good hard fuck with Skyler, but there was something there, whether I wanted to acknowledge it or not.

"Oh, you're going to pay me, or I'm going back to the NFL, and you'll have to find somebody else to put up with your bullshit. Good luck with that. Skyler trusts me, and if he doesn't trust people, he can't be creative. Your little movie deal goes right down the shitter if he doesn't produce, doesn't it?"

Of anyone in the world, I knew Marsh's pressure points. I knew his ambitions, his wants, and how hard he'd fight to get it. I also knew his weaknesses and how to exploit them, not that I wanted to do that. For Skyler, though, I'd do anything I could.

"Fucking hell, Sandy. You're kidding me about this shit."

"Not at all. If you want me to organize and look out for those guys, you gotta meet my demands. I'm not going to fuck this up, but you gotta do your part." I turned to walk away and got about ten feet.

"Stop. Fucking stop, Sandy. Yes, I need your help, or Alicia's going to kill me. She's pissed things are going so slowly with this deal. I need to show her I'm the best to bring this collaboration to fruition. My career depends on this."

The desperation in Marsh's voice told me something more was up. "Why? Why does your career depend on this, Marsh?"

My brother sighed. "I...I've made some bad recommendations lately. The groups I've suggested haven't been stellar. This is my last chance, Sandy. You've gotta help me."

It was my turn to sigh. Was my brother setting me up to convince Skyler to work for nothing so he could reap more of the rewards than he wanted to admit?

I laughed. "Help you what? Manipulate Skyler into doing something? Are you trying to get the song from him to sell it to another group? Are you fucking kidding me?"

Staring at the contortions on Marshall's face pissed me off more than anything. I had to dig my nails into my palms to keep from decking my brother.

"Look, Sandy, you don't understand how this game is played."

"Are you fucking kidding me? I played a much rougher game, Marsh. You're not the player on the field. You're the puppet master, and you're not making the right choices for your team. Think about it. You have no faith in the band. You need Skyler to make this shit work, and you're trying to play hardball with him? You should be kissing his ass every step of the way.

"I've heard a lot of what he's written, and you should thank the gods every day that he's involved. The original song is good, and Skyler has only built on that. He's worked on the song, and he's been busy outlining his ideas for the score, Marsh. Don't fuck this up for either of you."

I was trying to get my little brother to see how shortsighted he was being, but I knew he was proud. Marsh wouldn't go down without a fight, but I had no problem smacking the shit out of him.

"I'm scared, Sand. I don't have other options. If I can't make this work with CEA and get From the Ashes to produce, I'm out on my ass."

I stared at my little brother. I held his gaze for a moment to see if he was being honest, and I pulled him closer. "I love you, Marsh. I'll always try to support you, but this time, you gotta look at the band's best interests. They need Skyler, and if you nickel and dime this bullshit, he'll take off and never come back to help any of you."

Marsh reached up with his index and middle fingers on each hand and wiped tears from his eyes before he nodded. "Okay. I'll give up on the idea of talking them into licensing it to another band. If you think they can pull it off, I'll give them a shot."

I nodded. "Go put your shit upstairs and change into something else. That expensive suit makes it seem like you're going to steal the eggs from under the chickens."

Marsh glanced down at his flashy suit and nodded before taking off upstairs to his room. I pulled out my phone to send a text to Skyler.

> I'm coming over to the farm, and Marsh is coming with me. Just giving you a warning. Sandy

I didn't want to scare the guy, but I wanted him to be ready. A surprise visit wouldn't help anyone at this point, especially with Skyler worrying about the song already. He needed confidence, and I'd help him find it however I could.

We pulled up to the rescue farm to see a lot of cars parked around the property. I knew three of them belonged to the residents, but the other five, not a clue.

"Oh, I guess the whole band is here. That's a good sign. Let's go." Marsh jumped out of the SUV before I even had my seatbelt off.

I hurried to follow him to the building to the right of the house—the studio, I was guessing. As we got closer, I recognized the song as Skyler's version of 'Bury Me', but the voice belting it out wasn't Skyler.

"Let's go to the booth side in case they're recording." Marsh led me around the building to a side door. He tapped on it lightly, and a man I didn't recognize opened the door.

"Hey, Ace." The two men shook hands and added a one-armed hug. Marsh stepped back. "Ace Gregory, this is my big brother, Sanders—"

"Kensington! Number 82. Nice to meet you, man. Big fan." Ace gave me the same hug. His long brown hair was in a braid at the bottom of his head, and his nails were painted red and black. He had a bit of a gut, but he looked pretty fit otherwise.

"Thanks." I turned to look through a large glass window as Ace sat back down and punched one of the zillion buttons in front of him. "Marshall's here, guys. Let's take it from the top."

Skyler was behind a massive drum kit and my dick definitely took notice. Thankfully, I hadn't tucked in my polo shirt when we left the house. At least I had a little cover as I watched a shirtless, sexy-as-fuck Skyler hold drumsticks over his head and hit them together to set a beat.

He smashed two cymbals with the sticks, one on his left and one on his right. JD began plucking out a steady baseline in time with the beat Skyler set, and then River joined them with a wild guitar riff that rang through the speaker in the room where Ace was busy adjusting the sound levels of each instrument.

Another guy was standing to the side, his head nodding in time with the air guitar he was playing. My brother couldn't take his eyes off the guy, who was younger than Skyler but probably older than River.

"Good, ain't they?"

I turned to my left to see Regal Ashe sitting on the couch behind me, tapping out a beat with his left foot. His arms were moving in time with Skyler's, his eyes closed as if he could see the music in his head.

The guitar-heavy sound softened, but the tempo didn't slow. Another guy I hadn't noticed sitting at a keyboard to Skyler's right started to play the familiar music Skyler had been playing in my living room. The guy Marsh was staring at stepped up to the microphone and the background music, except for the piano, got softer, the lead guitar playing a rhythm that blended with the keyboard's hypnotizing melody.

You say I'm cold you think I'm mean You claim when I'm with you, you always feel unseen

But you don't know How hard I try To be the man who walks Through life by your side

"I can't fucking believe Sky took our old song and made it into this." Dusty sat on the couch next to Regal, who had opened his eyes and was staring through the glass at his sons. I had no idea who the other two guys were, but together, the five of them were incredible.

"Do you not like it?" I couldn't hold my tongue. I'd still rather hear Skyler sing it while he played piano, but what I was hearing was definitely better than the original.

"Oh, God no. I love it. I had no fucking idea it could sound like this when we wrote it back then. It's phenomenal." Dusty stood and walked closer, smiling as he watched the guys playing together.

"Who's the singer?" The guy's voice soared and grew soft as he sang the rest of the first verse. On the chorus, Skyler swung the mic in front of him and sang harmony, as did JD on bass. It sounded like they'd been singing together their whole lives.

Bury Me Oh, set me free Lay me in the ground Right there beneath your feet
Without your love I have no need to breathe Have mercy on me Please have mercy on me If you ever loved me, won't you bury me

"He's Arlo's friend." Dusty pointed to the keyboard player.

"Who's Arlo?" Was I supposed to know these guys? How fucking old was I?

The guys in the room laughed as Dusty responded. "He could be any of our undisclosed son."

My heart nearly stopped before I turned to look at Regal. He was smiling like a fucking loon. "So, you might have *three* sons in there? Do Skyler and River know?"

Ace spoke up. "Nobody knows for sure who the kid belongs to 'cause he doesn't look like any of us. We all had a round with Cindy Timmons back when we were touring, but the timeline sounds like Regal is the boy's dad. Though none of us have taken the test, we all chip in to take care of him. Hell, even Ripper chips in, and he never cheated on Franny."

I almost couldn't believe my ears, but then Arlo's friend started singing another verse that sounded like a whisper.

You want to leaveAnd lock me in the pastIf you're not in my armsI don't think I can last

He won't know youHe won't love youHe won't kiss youhalf as well as me

Before the last word of the verse faded, River took over the melody with his guitar riffs and they were rocking hard. I could see the sweat flying off Skyler's hair as he slapped the heads of the drums, lost in the rhythm.

The music died down and the singer sang the chorus and final verse.

Bury meOh, set me freeLay me in the groundRight there beneath your feet
Without your loveI have no need to breatheIf you ever cared then please won't youHave mercy on me
Have mercy on me Have mercy on me and
Bury meLay me lowWithout your loveThere's nowhere else for me to go

Then came the cherry on the top. All music stopped, and they all harmonized on the final two lines of the song.

So bury me before you walk away

The silence that followed as the last note trailed off was nearly deafening. I felt the tears glide down my cheeks as a soft cymbal faded.

Chapter Thirteen

Skyler

I rested the sticks on the snare and grabbed the towel I'd tossed on the riser where Regal's massive kit was assembled, patting off the drenching sweat I'd worked up. We'd been practicing and working out the kinks in my arrangement all morning. We'd played it through five times, adjusting after each run, and finally, Ace had decided to record it so we could get feedback from the band.

I'd be lying if I didn't admit I was riding a high after playing the song with the full band. JD, River, and I had been working on disjointed parts of the song for several days, and we all agreed we needed a keyboard to round out the sound. When River mentioned it to Regal, he brought in Arlo, a cool guy two years older than River.

Arlo brought a buddy of his, and dang, that guy could belt out a song with the best of them. His name was Golden Robbins, Goldie for short. He and Arlo had grown up together. They were decent guys and added to the sound I'd hoped to create for the new iteration of the song.

I stood, stepping off the riser and bending over to stretch out the knots from sitting on the stool for so long. I grabbed my T-shirt and slid it on before I walked around the kit and gave everyone a hug. We had played hard and done a great job, but we still had a lot of work to do.

We walked into the booth where the band and Marshall were waiting, and I saw Sandy with a big smile. He even winked.

"Thoughts? Criticisms?" I eyed each of the band's original members, knowing my father couldn't keep his mouth shut. No one said a word, so Ace hit the playback, and we listened for a moment before they finally started speaking.

"The intro needs to go slower. I can't play that fast anymore." Dusty looked at me, so I nodded. When I was composing the guitar score for the intro, I wasn't sure Dusty could play at the tempo we set, but we could slow the intro down for him.

Ace stopped the playback. "Regal, man, you can't sing that high."

"We can lower it," I told my dad as he stared at Goldie.

I glanced at Ripper, who laughed. "I think what you created is perfect, Sky. I just know us old farts can't play or sing it like you boys just did."

"Wait, guys. If you're not happy with what Skyler created, we can have someone else take a crack at it. This isn't the only iteration of the song, okay?" Marsh glanced around, his face filled with panic.

Ace hit the button to continue the song, and nobody said anything until the end. I glanced over to see my father looking down at his fingers, tapping a beat on the couch cushion between his legs. I wasn't sure if that was good or not.

When Ace lowered the fader controlling the song and shifted another up, I held my breath. It was the score I'd roughed out for the soundtrack that I hadn't known was being recorded. "When did you get that?"

Regal chuckled. "I snuck in here the other day to record you guys so we old men had some idea of what you'd come up with."

There was no word from anyone regarding what they'd heard. My frustration bubbled over, and I walked out the studio door to the paddock where the miniature donkey was still roaming around, now with a cat friend on his back.

I walked to the fence and banged my head against the top fence rail. Obviously, it was a mess. "Fuck."

That deep chuckle had me turning my head. "I knew a bad boy was in there somewhere. I don't know what the problem is with the band, but I thought it was amazing. You wanna go commit a sin or two?"

I turned and rested my forehead against Sandy's broad chest as though it was natural. Surprisingly, his strong arms wrapped around me like steel bands. He kissed the top of my head, and the tears came, which I couldn't stop.

"Let's go get drunk, teach." Without waiting for another word, Sandy picked me up and tossed me over his shoulder, causing me to giggle, which I hadn't done since I was a kid.

He carried me out to his SUV, opened the door, and plopped my butt in the passenger seat before he opened the console and pulled out a box of tissues. After buckling my seatbelt, he lifted my chin with his index finger, plucking two tissues from the box and patting my eyes. "Beautiful, you did an exemplary job, and if those folks are too dumb or old to hear it, then fuck them." He kissed my forehead and closed the door, amazing me again.

Sandy backed out of the parking spot, spun the wheel like an Indy car driver, and once he made a right onto the blacktop, he took my left hand and placed it on his right thigh, covering it with his.

"We need to talk, Sky. We both have some decisions to make and maybe if we talk them out together, we can help each other come to some conclusions. What do you say?"

"Okay." That was all that would come out without more tears following.

Sandy chuckled again, driving back to San Jose and pulling into the parking lot of a place called Cash Bar. "Is this your spot?"

Sandy turned to me. "I've been here a time or two. This place has pool and an old-school tavern feel. I think you'll like it if you give it a chance, teach."

I unbuckled my seatbelt, blew my nose, and exited the SUV. Sandy caught up to me and put his hand on my neck as he guided me toward the door. The guy was incredible, and I fell for him just a little harder.

We ordered drinks—me a lemon drop cocktail with a sugar and salt rim, and Sandy got a Greyhound. I wasn't a goodie-goodie. I'd gone to bars with the folks on my softball team, and we teachers had a Friday night out twice a year—before the Christmas break and the end of the school year. I'd missed the last happy hour to come waste my time in Cupertino, and I'd almost regret it if I wasn't sitting in a booth across from a gorgeous former football player.

"What's on your mind?"

The server delivered our drinks and a basket of popcorn. Sandy stared at me as he took a sip of his drink.

He put it on the table and cleared his throat. "The other day, I thought going back into football as a coach was exactly what I wanted. When I got fired from Chicago, I was willing to be the fucking towel boy just to stay in the game. I've been wallowing in self-pity for a goddamn year, and I'm done with it."

I took a sip of my drink as he spoke. It was delicious, and I couldn't really taste the alcohol, which was likely bad news because it would hit me like a ton of bricks when I least expected it.

"So, you're not going to the minicamp?"

"No, I'm going because I want to get a feel for the team. I'll be accompanying you guys on the road, and I'll decide after the tour what I want to do. That's the deal I'm gonna present to Kathleen, anyway. She can take it or leave it. Now, you."

"Me?" I sipped my drink, slipping my tongue out to catch the sugar and salt on my lips.

"Hmm. God, that kills me." His eyes grew heavy-lidded, though I wasn't sure why.

"Huh?"

The server returned, and Sandy ordered another round of drinks and an order of jumbo corn nuts. "They only serve snacks here, but I've got a place in mind for us to eat. So, what do you need to decide? Are you going to freak out because you don't think they liked your rewrite of 'Bury Me'? I think it's a huge upgrade, but what do I know?"

That was a great question. "I went on the road with my dad and the band a couple of times, and every night of their tours, they played the same set. No changes. No new jokes or banter. No variations whatsoever, not even when they had a high-energy crowd. That's why they got tired of touring and making music. They got complacent and started fighting. They actually broke up at one point, though they didn't announce anything because I guess they didn't think anybody cared."

As I kid, I didn't see why they fought all the time, but as an adult looking back, it was plain as day. One of the guys would suggest something—mixing up the playlist, changing an intro to a song, or playing a cover of someone else's song—and the rest of the band would pick it apart until the idea was abandoned completely.

"Would you ever consider giving up teaching to pursue performing and composing?" Sandy picked up some popcorn and sifted it into his mouth, his eyes never leaving mine. He was so bleeping sexy I had to push my palm into my dick to try to get control of it before I embarrassed myself.

"That's a hard question. I really enjoyed what we did today. I think it's the critique from the band or the fans that I hate. When my kids perform at competitions, I dread them having to listen to the judges' remarks. I want them to enjoy the mere act of performing, but to keep the funding coming, we're required to participate in competitions. The school district pours all its extra money into the sports teams, so we have to get our money from donations. I wish we didn't have to compete because it's a killer to the kids' motivation if the critique is harsh."

Sandy's face spread into a kind smile. "You love those kids, don't you?"

I drained my cocktail as the server brought the next round and our jumbo corn nuts sprinkled with chili powder and cumin. They were warm and tasted delicious.

"I love my kids. They're all so excited to learn, and when I see one of them *get it*, I throw a little parade in my head. It's like a reward for me."

I'd never said those things to anyone, not even my mother. With the rock 'n roll lifestyle she lived with Regal, I wasn't sure she'd understand, and I knew Regal wouldn't get it at all. They already thought I was odd because I was gay. I was careful not to share such personal details for their judgment.

Sandy's phone rang, which reminded me I'd left mine at the studio behind the drum kit. For once, I didn't give a crap.

Sandy picked up his phone and checked the screen, chuckling to himself before he sent the call to voicemail. He glanced up and grinned. "I hope there are more teachers like you out there. I remember back in high school, I had a coach like that. He was great. He expected a lot from us, but he was diligent about giving us our props and telling us he was proud of us." Sandy slipped into a memory right there before my eyes. His sweet smile made me want to kiss him and hold him in my arms—more than usual.

I nodded. "I wish to heck Coach Sutter at West Peoria was that way. I hear him yelling at the team all the time, and it's never in praise. I want to give them all a hug, though they'd probably beat me to a pulp." We both laughed before we finished our drinks.

Sandy tossed money on the table and reached for my hand. "Let's go eat before we go home. How'd you get to your mother's place this morning?"

I'd returned the rental car Marshall had left because I wasn't using it every day, so the money was being wasted. I'd been fortunate that JD didn't live far from the rental company and was willing to pick me up and give me a ride to Cupertino.

"I returned the rental your brother left. JD lives a few miles from the rental place, so he met me there and gave me a ride out."

We walked out of the bar and got into the SUV. Sandy touched my thigh, sending hot sparks directly to my crotch. "You can use one of my cars. No need to fuck around with the rental."

He pulled onto a side street and turned around, parking the SUV in the parking lot of a steakhouse called Prime. I chuckled. "Why'd you move it?"

"I hate parking on the street, but that place doesn't have a parking lot because it's in a zoned residential neighborhood. We were in a two-hour zone, and I think it'll take us longer than forty-five minutes to eat."

We got out, and Sandy put his left hand on the back of my neck again, guiding me to the entrance. The smell when he opened the large wooden door nearly knocked me over. I didn't realize how hungry I was until that moment.

We ordered the twenty-ounce porterhouse steak to share, along with sides, and we feasted. I hadn't laughed so hard as I did through dinner as we swapped stories from our various experiences, him in football and me in teaching.

Sandy ordered a piece of chocolate cake for us to share, and we both ordered coffee. We'd switched to iced tea with the meal, so we were sober by the time we finished eating.

We got into an arm-wrestling contest at the table for the check, and finally, Sandy let me pay. The meal was delicious and the company better, so it was definitely worth the tab.

Sandy opened the door for me and waited for me to step out before he followed very closely. "We didn't really talk about what I had in mind."

We walked around the side of the building, and when we stepped into a dark spot on the way to the parking lot, Sandy spun me against the building and caged me in with his arms. "Hmm. What I wanted to talk about was *us*. What's this draw between us? Do you know, because I can't get you out of my head."

Without waiting for him to say another word, I pushed my body into his and kissed him, tasting the chocolate and coffee that we'd just enjoyed. Sandy pushed me against the building again and pressed his body to mine, lips to toes.

Our tongues battled in his mouth, then mine, as my arms wrapped around his broad shoulders for balance. It wasn't just our first kiss. It was the most amazing kiss I'd ever had.

Chapter Fourteen

Sandy

Our make-out session was interrupted by the clearing of a throat as a couple walked by on the way to the parking lot. I wanted to dismember the dude, but maybe it would be better if we took it home.

It was a nice evening, low eighties. "How about we go home and take a swim?" Skyler's unexpected request put all kinds of naughty ideas in my head.

"Swimwear *optional*?" I cocked an eyebrow at him.

"Your call. You own the pool."

Releasing my hold on him, I led him around the building to the parking lot and over to the SUV. I opened his door, and once he was inside, I went around and got in myself. There was one thing I wanted to know. "Was this a date?"

"A-A date?" His voice was breathy, which made my cock flex against the zipper of my shorts.

I smirked, though he couldn't see it because the cab of the SUV was dark. "Well, you paid for dinner. I'm just trying to figure out what you want from me. I don't usually put out on the first date—"

"Oh gosh, I'd never expect you to... I didn't mean to make you think..." His voice trailed off, and I was sure if I flipped on the overhead light, he'd be glowing.

"You didn't let me finish. I was going to say, 'Unless I know for sure there will be a second date.'"

"A second date? You'd go out with me again?" Skyler sounded surprised.

I pulled out of the parking lot and stopped at the curb because there was a jackass behind me with his brights on. "Was this a date?"

Skyler turned toward me. "I'd like it to be."

"Are you going to ask me out again?" Now I was just needling him.

He started to nod, but then he chuckled. "Actually, you asked me out, and it was a pretty lame way to do it."

I grinned. "You're right. Let me try again. Skyler, would you go out with me tomorrow night?"

"Uh, I'll need to check my schedule." He cracked up, and I did too. Once we stopped laughing, he took my hand. "Yes, Sandy. I'd love to go out with you tomorrow night. It could be late. We have another rehearsal tomorrow. By the way, I've looked at all your cars in the garage, and I'm not driving any of them."

I got it. They were expensive cars, and really, why did I have them in the first place? To prove how much of a man I was? How successful I was? If that was how I estimated my own worth, I needed a shrink.

"Would you drive this?" I asked, tapping the steering wheel.

"It's kinda big. Much bigger than my little SUV in West Peoria." It was a large GMC SUV, but I hauled things...sometimes.

"Let's trade places, and you drive us home to get a feel for it. It's not larger than the Suburban you've been driving." I stepped out and walked around the Yukon to open his door. Skyler stepped out, and after a quick kiss, I got inside, and he closed my door, jogging around the vehicle and getting in behind the wheel.

He buckled in, as did I, and we were on our way. He was a careful driver, which I had expected, and was respectful of my Yukon. That told me a lot about him, and if I wasn't coming to want more from him than friendship, I could fall for the guy in a heartbeat after seeing the care he took with my vehicle. That thinking was a bit of a shock to my system.

"Do you want to get up and run with me in the morning?" I needed plans to get my mind off the realization settling into my thick skull. For once in my life, I wanted more with a guy than just a quick fuck.

Skyler glanced out of the corner of his eye before he grinned. "Yes, and can you help me work on my core? My back is going to kill me tomorrow, as will my arms."

"I got just the thing."

Instead of the pool, we'd sit in the hot tub, and I'd give him some mild pain relievers and a rubdown before he went to sleep. I was looking forward to it.

Once we got home, he parked in the garage, and we got out, heading toward the house. I stopped on the pool deck and set the temp for the hot tub and the jets. We went into the basement, and I undressed, draping my clothes over the Peloton in the gym.

Skyler was stuck to the spot by the treadmill, watching me. "Get your clothes off, teach."

I was down to my tan boxer briefs as he reached behind him and grabbed the back of his black T-shirt, pulling it over his head and tossing it on the floor. He toed off his sneakers and then slid down his jeans before he pulled off his socks. He wore red bikini briefs that made me want to bite my fist.

"Those... Those are nice. I didn't figure you for a bikini man." There was no hiding the boner in my own drawers.

I sighed. Trying to meet the man's eyes was nearly impossible. "Let's go." I opened the back door and grabbed a few towels from the bin on the pool deck. I pulled up the app on my phone and turned on some of the lights so we could see, and then I took his hand and led him across the patio to the spa, which was bubbling away.

Now, we were at a crossroads. To go au naturel or respect his modesty and keep the underwear on.

Fuck it.

I slid my thumbs inside the waistband of my underwear and stared at him. "Speak now or forever hold your peace."

Surprisingly, Skyler nodded really quick and mirrored my actions, sliding his thumbs between the fabric and his bare flesh. "One. Two. Three." We pushed our underwear to our ankles, and right there in front of me was his gorgeous cock.

"Uncut, huh?"

"In case you couldn't tell, Mom's a firm believer in keeping everything one was born with." And right there was the hood I couldn't wait to explore.

"Wow!" I followed his line of sight to see he was staring at my erect prick. He licked his lips. I stepped closer to him and put my palms on his cheeks—the ones up top. I'd get to the ones below in good time.

"You wanna have a sword fight?" It was an incredibly stupid joke, but honestly, I wasn't sure what to say. I was a bit tongue-tied at seeing the beautiful uncut cock between his legs. I was even more excited to see he kept a tidy hedge.

I'd started shaving my junk years ago to keep things cooler when I wore a cup on the field, and I'd kept up the practice even after I was out of football. The maintenance was quick since I'd been consistent all those years. Besides, I read somewhere that a clean slate made Sandy Junior look bigger.

"As tempting as that invitation is, I don't think I could put up much of a defense."

I stared at his face to see traces of pain, so I ignored my eager cock and stepped out of my underwear before I bent down to relieve him of his. The head of his dick brushed across my cheek, and we both moaned at the contact.

Once he stepped out of his briefs, I took his hand and led him up the two steps to the spa beside the large, curved swimming pool. I got in first and helped him down the steps before I started the jets to massage his aching body.

Mine was aching too, but for far different reasons.

He sat on the bench, and I noticed his face was bright red. "Too hot?" The temperature in the spa was only ninety-eight degrees. The evening was in the low eighties, so I thought the water felt good.

"No, uh, seeing my penis bob in the water with you sitting across from me is a bit daunting."

I shook my hand to fling water, grabbed my phone, and dimmed the lights in the spa. "How's that?"

Skyler grinned. "Better." He tilted his head back and studied the sky, so I moved around and sat closer—not enough to make him nervous, I hoped.

"You know, I didn't like you at first. My brother told me nothing about you, so I thought you were another spoiled rock star's kid. When he shoved you into my home, I wanted to beat his ass." I put my arm on the spa ledge behind Skyler's head—not touching him but wanting to.

He turned to stare at me. "You didn't like me? I mean, I'm not one of those people who thinks everyone must like them, but what did I do that made you not like me?"

I grinned and kissed his temple. "Not a damn thing. I thought you were hot immediately. I also thought you were like the stars' kids you read about in the gossip pages. I didn't want to get to know you because I assumed you'd be more trouble than you were worth."

Honesty was the best policy, right? I didn't mean to upset him, but I thought laying it all out there might be the best thing. Was I an idiot? Probably.

Skyler turned his body toward me. "You thought I would be... You judged me before you met *me*?" His voice pitched an octave higher, and I wanted to kiss him.

"It's my character flaw to prejudge people. I've been screwed over by a lot of people during my life, so I try to judge who's going to try to fuck me over before they get the chance. I apologize for it, but I'm thrilled I completely missed the mark on you." It was the god's truth.

His handsome face turned up to me, and I met his mouth with mine. The kiss started soft, just a gentle brush of flesh, but before I could take a breath, Skyler climbed into my lap and slid his tongue between my lips. My tongue didn't hesitate to come out to play.

I pulled back but didn't let him move. "I was wronger than wrong."

Skyler chuckled as he wrapped his arms around my neck. "Wronger, huh?"

"I'm a master of language. You can use that word if you'd like." We both laughed at my stupidity.

"I'm sorry if I wasn't friendly when we met. I damn well wasn't ready for someone like you to come into my life. Hell, I'm not sure if I am now, but we don't have to do more than blow off a little steam if that's all you want."

Hell, what was I saying? I'd just told myself I wanted more than that, but Skyler was leaving…eventually. Where would I be after that?

Skyler attached himself to my lips again, and I got lost in the kiss. I wanted to do so many things for him…to him…with him…but we had a bit of ground to travel, and part of that ground was— What the hell would a future for us look like?

When his hard cock grazed mine as he floated over me, I wanted to grab him and pull our cocks together in my hand and stroke us to climax…but I didn't.

"Sit on the bench and let the jets work their magic. They really do help ease the aches if you relax." I wasn't lying because when I woke up achy and stiff, I'd sit in the spa for a while and feel much better when I got out. Truth be told, I could make him relax with a few licks—and I really wanted to.

I helped Skyler settle on the bench with his back to a jet. Once he was, I turned on some quiet background music on my phone.

"You didn't tell me what you thought of me when you saw me at the airport." Maybe I was asking him to say he was impressed. What if he wasn't?

Skyler stared at me for a minute before he smiled. "You didn't appear happy about being there, but I thought you were handsome. Honestly, I couldn't remember seeing anyone nearly as handsome."

"You're full of shit, but I'll take it as a compliment. You date much in West Peoria?"

"My number is four if that's what you're aiming to find out. Based on your pictures on the internet with those beautiful women, you've probably lost count." We both chuckled.

"Never had sex with any of them. I searched for guys to hook up with when we were on road trips because it was less likely I'd be recognized. It worked until the one time when shit went to hell." That was a fucked-up night I tried not to think about.

"What happened that night?"

It was the question I dreaded the most of anything anyone could ask me. As I stared at him, I decided it was better to get it out there, so I told him the sad story that made me sound utterly desperate and pathetic.

"And you got kicked out of football because of it? That's terrible. You didn't even get to—well, you know. Anyone since?"

I sighed. I've thought about trying to meet someone for more than a night, but I always ask myself if the person I'm speaking with is worth losing everything all over again. The answer has always been no."

Until now...

Chapter Fifteen

Skyler

Sandy and I sat in the spa for an hour, laughing and talking. We got out, wrapped ourselves in plush blue pool towels, and went inside through the gym to the bar area. "How about a nightcap?"

He listed off a few brandies and cognacs before he got to my favorite Irish whiskey. I didn't drink it often, but I drank it on occasion. I liked how it warmed me from the inside out.

A lovely crystal tumbler was placed in front of me, and then Sandy poured himself the same. He walked around the bar and sat on the stool next to me, both of us still in towels. He held up his glass and grinned. "Here's to the beginning of a beautiful friendship."

I laughed. "Plagiarizing Bogey?"

"You know that movie? I love old classics. I took a film class in college, and of course, it was included in the syllabus. Films by Decade introduced me to some amazing movies." His grin was excited, which made me excited with him.

"I know *Casablanca*. What true romantic doesn't know those famous lines and Rick's sacrifice for love. I cry at the end every time I watch it." That was no lie.

I sipped my drink, enjoying the warmth and wishing his arms were around me as they had been while we were in the spa. I should have pushed him more. Being intimate with him would have fulfilled a new fantasy that haunted me nightly.

"Have you heard from Marshall? I forgot my phone at the farm." I pulled my towel closed as I turned my stool toward him.

"Oh! What are we drinking, boys? Did we just get busy in the pool? How long does it take the filter to cycle so your jizz is out of it." I turned to see Marshall standing in the doorway to the gym.

Sandy growled a little as he turned toward his brother. "You're a dick. We didn't do anything but soak in the spa. Skyler was stiff from sitting behind a drum set all day."

Marshall walked behind the bar and poured himself a drink, leaning against the counter behind him. "What are we talking about? Where'd ya go?" Marshall's voice mimicked a sixteen-year-old girl's voice.

I chuckled, but Sandy didn't. "What did the old guys say after we left? About the song?"

"Oh, uh, they love the song, but they don't think they can pull it off, even with Skyler playing in Regal's place. So, maybe we're back to the drawing board? The others are coming back tomorrow, so I guess you better get to bed, right?" Marshall pointed to me.

I shot back the rest of my drink and gathered my clothes, taking them upstairs. Just to be a real jerk, when I got to the stairs to go up, I dropped my towel and walked slowly up the stairs with my bare butt hanging out.

I was sure my whole body was red because I was embarrassed by my own behavior, but Marshall was really plucking my last nerve.

"Son of a— Marsh, you fucking prick, go to hell." Sandy's voice carried up the stairwell behind me. The frustration in his voice made me giggle again.

A week after my walk out, I met JD, Arlo, Goldie, and River at Regal's studio. We'd taken a week off for me to re-evaluate the rewrite and make some changes to better accommodate the men in From the Ashes. We were set to record the song on Tuesday to send to the studio, and a producer was coming from San Francisco to help us out. Ace was good, but we needed a professional.

I'd been training with Sandy twice a day to work on my core, and my new constant friend was ibuprofen, antacids, and some sort of healing green tea in the mornings, followed by protein shakes and a dietary change with lots of fish, baked chicken, and green vegetables in the afternoon, along with brutal workouts and hikes.

The best thing about it was that my body was changing for the better, and the hiking, running, and yoga I practiced helped my stamina. The worst thing about it—lots of embarrassing gas.

"Okay, I had an idea about this I want to run by the guys." I handed out new sheet music for everyone, not needing one for myself. "This is the rewrite for the intro. Let's run through it before they show up, okay?"

Everyone nodded, which was a relief, and I got behind the drum kit, picking up my phone to see I had a missed call from my mom and a text asking if I wanted to stay for dinner. I shoved it in my back pocket to deal with later and picked up the sticks.

"On my count. Play from the sheets. One. Two. Three. Four." I cracked the sticks together at a much slower pace than Ace had recorded the previous week, and we played. To me, it sounded as though we were playing in slow motion.

River stopped playing, shaking his head. "It sounds like shit, no offense, Sky. It's gotta go at the harder pace we played last week. It's the only way the song works." Sadly, he was right.

The door opened, and Regal walked in without his cane. I wasn't even sure why he had it in the first place. "What the fuck was that?" Regal wasn't an eloquent speaker by any stretch.

"It was the song with a slower tempo and a few changes in the guitar riff for Dusty." It should have been obvious to a monkey, I was sure.

"Well, it sounds like shit. Play it the other way." Nobody ever said Regal was stupid—all the time.

"You guys insist on playing the song, and all of you said you couldn't play it the way I wrote it. What do you want to do about it?" I stood from the kit and walked over to him, holding out the sticks.

"No. I'll talk to the guys. I have an idea in my head. Practice it the way you wrote it. The producer Marsh hired will be here Monday. He'll record the intro to send to the studio. That'll buy us some time, I believe. I need you guys out by three, okay? I'll order you some sandwiches for lunch."

Without waiting for another word from us, Regal walked out. I glanced at everyone and shrugged. "Let's take it from the top and do it like we did last week." And we did. River changed the guitar riff, incorporating some of my changes, and it sounded even better.

I lost myself again in the music. I slapped the toms and pounded the crash cymbals until we got to the first verse. Then we all faded so Goldie's voice could be heard clearly. The kid wailed and the runs were absolutely incredible.

The rest of us came in on the chorus to harmonize with Goldie. The synergy swirling around the room was glorious...like nothing I'd ever experienced, and the feeling was heady. No wonder my father was so addicted to this life.

For an instant, I felt like a god. Could I consider giving up teaching for this?

"I text you about staying for supper. You want to?" Mom was standing at the stove stirring something in a pot that smelled incredible.

"Is that your chili?" Mom made the most incredible chili I'd ever tasted, though she didn't put meat in it.

"Kind of. Your father, River, and Jeanne are carnivores, so I took some out for me and put hamburger in it. You're welcome to stay." I grabbed a glass of water and downed it in two gulps.

"Thanks Mom, but I can't. I have stuff to do at Sandy's house. We're going out to Los Gatos to hike Mount Umunhum. Sandy goes out there to hike a lot, so I'm going along. Thanks for the invite, but I'll see you tomorrow, Mom." I kissed her cheek and left just as Jeanne came inside with groceries.

I said goodbye and walked out to Sandy's Yukon, seeing my brother carrying bags for his mom. "I'll be back in the morning at nine. Can you tell JD, Arlo, and Goldie?"

"Sure, man. Thanks for all you're doing, Sky. I know the old guys are frustrating as hell, but I think what we're doing is incredible. After we do this, would you be interested in starting a band with Arlo, Goldie, JD, and me? I think we could really make some great tunes, man."

I definitely didn't want to dissuade River from following his natural talents, nor did I want to give him false hope that I would follow Regal into music. "I think you could find a better drummer than me, Riv. Be on the lookout. You never know when you'll find someone as ambitious as you three." I mussed his long hair before he could dodge me and head inside.

Hopping into Sandy's Yukon, I headed back to San Jose. Twenty minutes later, I parked in the garage and entered through the back door. Sandy's Maserati was in the garage, so I knew he was at the house, even though I didn't see him by the pool.

The back door was unlocked, and when I opened it, something delicious caught my nose. My stomach grumbled in response to the tantalizing scent, so I followed it up the stairs and into the kitchen.

Coldplay was on the sound system, so I snatched a cherry tomato off the cutting board and walked up behind Sandy, standing on my tiptoes to kiss the side of his neck. We'd put our romantic pursuits on hold, but I wanted to get things back on track. Taking care of things in the shower wasn't how I wanted to start my day.

"Hey, teach. How was practice?" He turned around and took the small tomato, popping it into his mouth before he put my hands on his shoulders.

"Good and bad. Regal didn't like it when we slowed the tempo. It did sound like we were playing in slow motion, but I don't see us reaching any type of compromise. River asked me if I wanted to start a band with him, Arlo, Goldie, and JD. I told him to be on the lookout for another drummer."

"So, you're really not thinking about leaving teaching?"

I move my hands to rest on his pecs. "You didn't believe me?"

"I won't say that, teach. I just thought the money you could make might be a draw." Sandy kissed the tip of my nose before turning off the oven. "I baked some chicken thighs and roasted some fresh vegetables. Let's skip the hiking until tomorrow morning and go for a run. What do you think?"

"I like that idea. I wasn't really up for a long hike. A run sounds good. Let me change." I started to walk away, but Sandy grabbed my hand and pulled me back to kiss my lips.

His tongue slid along my bottom lip, and I opened to accept him inside. Our tongues met in a wild dance that had my blood racing south in a hurry. His arms wrapped around me, and thoughts of running flew out of my head.

Sandy pulled away. We were both breathing hard. I was a little dizzy, but it was in the best possible way.

The handsome football player turned me around and swatted my bottom. "Go change. Let's do this."

I hurried upstairs and went to the spare room to change out of my jeans and into a pair of shorts. I slid off my Vans and grabbed my running shoes to hurry back downstairs. The kitchen was empty, so after I tied my running shoes, I grabbed my phone to scroll through the text messages. Most of them were stupid robotic messages, but a few were on my school bulletin board page.

The first was from Ryan Frye, a trombone player in my junior high band.

> **Mr. Ashe—my grandpa gave me his old trombone. Do you know anyone who can fix it up? Thank you. Ryan Frye.**

I pecked out a response with the name and number for Mr. Monaco, a brass instrument repair technician who owned a music shop in Deer Park, outside of Chicago. The school contracted with Mr. Monaco to rent instruments to the students in my classes. He was a very nice man and would do right by Ryan.

The next one was from the school administrator asking which teachers wanted to relocate their classrooms, which didn't apply to me because the band room was the band room, and I couldn't relocate.

The third message was from one of the guys in the jazz band I sponsored: Petey Ritter.

> **Mr. Ashe—when will you be back from vacation? I mowed your lawn today, and I was hoping to get paid. I hate to ask, but I had to pawn my guitar and need to get it out. Talk soon? Petey.**

"Shoot." I'd forgotten about paying Petey.

"What's wrong?" Sandy stepped closer to me and moved my longer bangs off my forehead. His other hand came from behind his back, and he put a headband around my neck before pushing it over my forehead to keep my bangs out of my eyes.

"Thank you. That was very sweet of you."

He tossed a drugstore bag on the counter and grinned. "What has you saying words that aren't anywhere close to curse words?"

I chuckled. "I have a student who cuts my grass. He's had some family issues in the past, and I helped by letting him stay with me for a few weeks. I'm just finding out he had to pawn his guitar for some reason. He wants to know when I can pay him so he can get it out."

"How much do you pay him to cut your grass? How much grass do you have?" Sandy rubbed the back of his fingers over my nipple, sending a shiver over my skin, the tease.

I pulled away, a shy smile taking over my face. "You're trying to get me all riled up, aren't you?"

Sandy ignored my accusation. "Can you Venmo the kid?"

"I'll have to ask him. I'd really like to know why he pawned his guitar in the first place, but I don't know if it's my place to ask. He lives with his grandmother who is really sweet but not in the best health. She has diabetes. Maybe I'll call Mrs. Brownlee, the secretary at school, to see if she knows anything. She always seems to know the gossip around town."

Sandy nodded and patted my shoulder. "Ready?" He put the house key in a little pocket inside his shorts, and the two of us were off.

Chapter Sixteen

Sandy

Has there ever been a documented case of a man dying from blue balls? I'd never heard of one, and I was pretty sure if there was one, it would have definitely been on the news. Men around the world would have been pointing at girlfriends, wives, and boyfriends, saying, "I told you so." That would have been a headline around the globe, no doubt.

I hadn't taken so many cold showers since I was a teenager, but every time I looked at Skyler Ashe, I couldn't help imagining him on his knees in front of me or bent over the arm of the couch in the theater room. My cock went from zero to one-twenty in the blink of an eye.

I was drowning in guilt about all the dirty dreams I'd had about Skyler since he was dropped into my life—*thank you, Marshall*. I was petrified to make a move on the guy. I knew beyond a doubt that if we started doing more than kissing, I'd get my heart shattered when he returned to West Peoria.

I had hoped the lure of the money he could earn might tempt him away from his teaching job and keep him in Cali where I could see him and maybe start something with him because my stupid brain kept telling me he was *the one*. That elusive unicorn I'd been searching for in every gay club and bathhouse I'd snuck into during college and my football career. The last time I tried that...

Skyler was determined to go back to his teaching job, and I didn't believe I stood a chance in hell of getting him to change his mind. For both our sakes, I determined we should keep things on the friend level, which meant no more kissing, hugging, or flirting. It might be too late, but I needed to protect my heart.

After we returned to the house from our six-mile run, I handed Skyler the extra key I had made for him to use while I was on the East Coast for a week. I really needed the time away from him before I completely lost the fight to save myself from the pain of watching him leave.

He was a nice guy, and I didn't believe he'd do anything to intentionally hurt me, but it didn't mean it wouldn't happen. After the too-recent rejection by my mother and father, I knew I wasn't ready to have my heart ripped out and stomped on again.

"I'm going to shower. I'll be back, and then we can eat something. Are you going to need to work more, or do you have time to watch a movie?" *Damn, my big mouth!*

I'd planned to slowly pull back from our interactions until I left on Friday for Baltimore. Hopefully, by the time I returned in the middle of June, Sky would be busy planning for the small tour and probably have moved back to his mom's place. That was my hope, anyway.

"I could watch a movie. Do you want to eat inside or outside? I'll set the table."

"Outside is great. Thanks." I didn't wait for him to ask me anything else.

I ran upstairs and into my bedroom, stripping my sweaty clothes as I went. I turned on the water and stepped into the large shower, standing directly under the ice-cold spray.

Had I been stupid enough to think it would be easy to shut off the feelings I was already starting to feel for Skyler? I should have my head examined.

I adjusted the temperature of the water to a mildly cool spray after my dick deflated and began to retreat into my pelvic cavity. Quickly washing my hair, I reminded myself I needed a haircut. I determined it was a bad idea to watch a movie with Skyler because being alone in the dark with the handsome teacher was entirely too tempting for my fragile resolve.

Kathleen Graves had emailed the team playbook, and I needed to study that instead of watching a movie, anyway. That would be a great excuse that wasn't a bald-faced lie.

Once I finished in the shower, I did a touchup shave on my face and then got dressed to go downstairs to eat. I decided to turn on some music louder than usual, making it more difficult to carry on a conversation.

We made our plates and headed outside, both of us opting for water with our meal. We sat at opposite ends of the table, and I wolfed down my food as though I hadn't eaten in days.

I finished my dinner in record time and gulped down the rest of my water. "I forgot I need to familiarize myself with the playbook for the Shuckers. Just put the dishes in the sink when you finish eating. I'll load the dishwasher before I go to bed."

I wanted to kick my own ass for leaving him stunned and sitting at the table alone, but I'd been enough of an asshole to him that it shouldn't be a surprise I'd do something so thoughtless.

I hurried up to my room and grabbed my laptop from my nightstand, booting it up and opening the PDF I'd received from the Shuckers front office. As I read through the document, it was like being in a time machine.

Since high school, I'd been studying plays and committing things to memory. Plays, routes, and strategies for sacking the other team's QB. They were divine inspiration to me.

I knew in my heart I couldn't have put as much energy into anything else as I had football, which was why I was a shell of myself from two years ago without the outlet. I hadn't given any thought to what I'd do after football because I never believed I'd leave the field. That was shortsighted on my part, but with this chance with the Shuckers, maybe there was more life left in this old dog.

The week progressed with little contact between Skyler and me. I didn't suggest we go hiking, though I suspected Skyler had gone on his own. We didn't run together, and I opted to run while Skyler was practicing with the new and old bands. We'd taken to leaving notes on the kitchen island in case information needed to be conveyed to the other.

I packed my bag on Thursday night, having booked a non-stop flight from San Jose airport on Friday morning that would get me to Baltimore in time to check into my hotel, eat, and get the lay of the land. I was scheduled to meet at the front office at M&T Stadium on Monday, then head out to the Under Armor Performance Center, the site for the Shuckers minicamp, on Tuesday. I wanted to be rested and ready, not jet lagged.

Thursday night as I dozed at the late hour of nine o'clock, my laptop still on my thighs, my phone pinged on the nightstand. I could hear splashing in the pool, so I got up and went to my bedroom window to see someone in the water, though the lights weren't on.

I pulled on a pair of shorts, grabbed my phone, and rushed down the stairs as quickly as possible without tripping. When I got to the back door, I found it unlocked, so I hurried out onto the pool deck to see the tiki torches burning at the end of the patio as Skyler swam laps in the dark pool.

After pushing the button on my phone for the pool app, I turned on the lights, which caught his attention immediately. He stopped and wiped the water from his face as he turned in my direction.

"Why didn't you ask me to turn on the pool lights? There's a box by the back door where you can adjust the temperature, turn the lights on and off, and turn on the jets in the spa." I was shouting, but he'd scared the fuck out of me.

"Don't worry about it. I'm leaving tomorrow. No need for me to know anything about your place. Sorry I inconvenienced you." Skyer returned to swimming laps, and I stood dumbstruck, watching him.

I was a fucking douche for how I'd spoken to him, but as I'd reasoned in my pea brain, I was in a no-win situation. My heart was already aching from the pained expression I'd seen on his face when he caught sight of me on the pool deck. I had to forget it if I wanted to survive.

Without another word, I stalked back into the house, glancing at my phone as I went upstairs. There was a text from Marshall that I didn't give a shit about, but I opened it anyway.

> **Sandy—what did you do to my drummer? He's moody and difficult to deal with, according to Hope. Did you fuck him, or did you fuck him over? Marsh**

I wanted to tell my little brother to go fuck himself, but instead...

> **I've been getting ready for a trip to the East Coast. I'm sorry if my babysitting wasn't good enough for your spoiled rock star. We'll talk when I get back. I'm not guarding your band, either. I'll be busy with a new job.**

I turned off my phone and laptop before crawling into bed. I heard the security system beep when Skyler came inside, and I listened to his bedroom door snick closed. Something told me that would likely be the last thing I said to Skyer Ashe for the rest of my life.

Friday morning, I got up, showered, dressed, and went downstairs for coffee before I drove to the airport for my flight. There was a note on the counter, next to the key

I'd given Skyler last week. Another stake of pain drove through my heart. I couldn't bear to read the note—because it was longer than a sentence—so I folded it and shoved it into the pocket of my athletic pants.

Coffee in a to-go mug, I went out to the garage to find the SUV in its spot. How the fuck did Skyler get to the farm?

The door to the garage had a code to enter, which I'd given to Skyler when we'd agreed that he would drive the Yukon. I opened the SUV door to find the keys tucked into the sun visor, as I did for all my vehicles. *Another stake in my heart.*

I went to the Cadillac CT5 at the end by the garage door, tossing my suitcase, garment bag, and messenger bag in the trunk. Part of me chose to leave the Yukon in case Skyler needed it, though I was pretty sure he'd never ask me for anything again.

When I arrived at the San Jose airport, I valet parked the car and went inside. After suffering the long line at the discount airline's kiosk, I checked my suitcase and garment bag and went to the gate area, taking a seat away from everyone.

I reached into my pocket and pulled out my phone and the note Skyler had left, preparing to slice and dice the rest of my heart.

> Sandy—
>
> Here's the house key. I got a rideshare to take me to my mother's house. Thank you for letting me stay with you. I'm sorry I became a burden.
>
> I strongly urge you to change the codes for the garage and the back door. I won't use them, but I'd prefer not to be accused if someone should break in.
>
> I'm not sure what I did or said that turned you off to the point you couldn't even be in the same room with me, but I'll apologize because it was never my intention. I wish you only the best.
>
> Skyler

My heart was in my throat as my eyes began to sting. This was all my fault because I was the idiot in this scenario. Making sure I didn't get hurt hadn't worked, and now, I'd hurt us both.

I picked up a rental at the airport and followed the directions on my GPS to the hotel where I'd previously stayed when the Breeze was in Baltimore for a game against the Shuckers. I went to my room to drop my bags, rescuing my suit from the garment bag because I had to go to the stadium to meet with Kathleen Graves before the three-day camp began on Tuesday.

I had planned to go out for dinner but decided to stay in and get room service instead. I couldn't imagine sitting in a restaurant on a Friday night, seeing all the happy couples on a date night while I sat alone.

I'd had two official dates with Skyler, the second one at my house the night after the blow-up at his father's studio. We'd gone on a short hike through the hills behind my place and then shared a huge steak salad he'd made for us. We ended up laying on a double lounger by my pool, looking at the stars to find shapes and trying to convince the other to see them as well. It was a night unlike anything I'd ever done, and I would never forget it.

Saturday, I went to Camden Yards, which was only a few blocks from my hotel, buying tickets to sit in the bleachers and watch a baseball game. I grabbed a baseball hat from the team store and sat at the end of the top row by myself. I watched the people more than I watched the game.

Doing things alone would be a hard adjustment after those few great times with Skyler. Things between us had ended before they really got started.

On Saturday evening, when I was on my way back to the hotel, my phone rang. It was an unknown number with a Baltimore area code, so I answered.

"Hi, Sandy. It's Kathleen Graves. I wanted to ask if you'd like to come to the house for brunch tomorrow. My wife's a great cook, and I think it would be easier if our first meeting was in a more informal setting."

Hell, it sounded good to me. "Sure. Uh, what time?"

"Can you hang on a sec?" The line went quiet, so I waited, pacing my hotel room.

A minute later… "Sandy? You there?"

"Yes, Ms. Graves." The room was too small to get a worthwhile pace in, but I was nervous. I didn't want to fuck anything up. Taking the coaching job with Baltimore might be my only salvation after Skyler returned to West Peoria.

"First, call me Kat. My very grouchy pregnant wife just reamed me out for not inviting you to stay with us. Why don't you pack up your stuff and bring it along? We only live about a mile from the training center. Come out about noon. Again, I'm sorry for not thinking of this, but that's why I call Lynette my better half. See you tomorrow." The phone went dead.

The woman didn't wait for me to answer, leading me to believe it was more of an order than an invitation. Obviously, she was a ball buster, but I had no problem working for a woman or being friends with them. I didn't have any female friends because the women I went out with were disappointed when I didn't call them again. I never told them I was gay for fear of it getting leaked when I didn't sleep with them. I'd probably missed the possibility of having a good friend because of my behavior.

Sunday morning, I packed up, checked out, and followed the directions Kat had sent me. I was at a stoplight when my phone rang. I glanced down at the screen to see it was Marshall, so I hit the Bluetooth button on the steering wheel to answer.

"Yeah, Marsh."

"Where the hell are you?" He was agitated, and that made me grin.

"Baltimore. Actually, I'm in Owings Mills. I'm meeting a woman about a job."

"What the fuck happened with Skyler Ashe? The kid has lost all focus, and we're about ready to pull the plug on the whole project and let the old men record the song as best as they can. I know you had to do or say something. What job are you looking into? I was planning to pay you for security, jackass."

God, I was a fucking tool.

"Look, nothing happened, okay? We only kissed a couple of times, which didn't do anything for me. Nothing against him. He's just not my type, and I never told him he had to leave or not use my SUV. Tell him he's welcome to stay and the keys are where he left them. I didn't change any of the codes, though I probably should. It would keep you out." It was the least I could do after I remembered Skyler would be staying with his mom and sleeping on a couch. Nobody wanted to do that.

"So, what's this job?" Jackass didn't even ask how I was doing.

"Defensive line and special teams coach for the Baltimore Shuckers. I'm headed to my new boss's house now for brunch. Minicamp starts on Tuesday. I'll be back home on Friday to tie up loose ends before I report to training camp in August."

Why I was making it sound as though it was a done deal, I wasn't sure, but he'd pass along the information, and then things would be settled between Skyler and me.

Maybe it wouldn't be as messy as I'd anticipated?

Chapter Seventeen

Skyler

I couldn't keep the beat worth a fuck. It was like my goddamn brain had completely shut down, and I couldn't remember a fucking change JD, River, Goldie, Arlo and I had decided on Friday. Try as I might, my mind wouldn't let go of what had happened with Sandy-fucking-Kensington earlier in the week, and it was a huge distraction I didn't need. And now I was swearing like a sailor.

What had I done to make the man hate my guts? One minute, we were talking about whether we should eat inside or out by the pool, and the next, Sandy wasn't speaking to me at all. He'd completely pulled away from me, making sure never to be in the same room as me, the son of a bitch.

All my decorum had flown out the window when Sandy basically dismissed me, and I didn't give a shit. I'd tried to be a good person, and where the hell had that gotten me?

I desperately needed to get myself back on track before I tanked the whole project. I glanced around the studio to see everyone staring at me. The new producer Marshall brought from Frisco was in the booth looking at me like I was off my goddamn rocker.

I held my sticks in the air. "Sorry, guys. Let's start at the beginning. One. Two. Three. Four." I came down on the crash cymbals with both sticks and began pounding out the tempo we'd agreed to on Friday. Everyone fell in line with me, and we were off to a good start. I was glad the engineer was recording the introduction.

Just before Goldie began to sing the first verse, Marsh's voice came over the speaker. "Hang on, guys."

Marshall was in the booth with Casey Springer, the sound engineer and producer he had hired from San Francisco. I hoped to hell the work we'd done wasn't for nothing.

Marsh entered the studio with a big smile. "That was great, guys. Let's do it once more for Casey to get a backup track, and then, Skyler, would you consent to giving me five minutes of the score you've written? I want to include it in the package we're sending to Harmon Studio."

I nodded as Regal came into the room with all the members of From the Ashes. There was a guy with him carrying a bunch of photography gear. "This is it." Regal gestured with his hand to the studio.

"This will work. I'll set up after they finish." The guy nodded, left his equipment, and walked out through the front door of the recording studio.

"What's going on?" I directed my gaze to Regal. It would be just like him to change things up at the last minute.

"We need a press package to go with the recordings, so we're going to borrow your instruments after you do the second recording and Cokely is going to take some shots." I sighed, looking down at the shorts and tank top I was wearing. I glanced around to see none of us younger guys were dressed for anything of the sort.

Marshall noticed us looking around. "Don't worry. We won't need your picture. Just the band."

It was a bit of a relief, but then again, it made me aware that it wasn't fair to the other guys for my father's band to take credit for all the hard work we'd put in to give the movie studio what it wanted. Was this the right thing to do? I really wanted to talk to JD, Arlo, Goldie, and River without the band or Marshall around.

"Give us a minute. Guys, let's take a walk." I followed the group outside and led them to the paddock, where the little donkey was busy playing with some of the disgusting goats.

Once all the humans were staring at me, I lost track of what I wanted to say. Thankfully, River seemed to read my mind.

"Okay, this is our chance to decide about the band or not." He looked at me, and I shook my head. No, I wasn't going to join them.

"Sky doesn't want to live the rock-star life, nor does he want to be famous, but I think if we find a new drummer, we can actually make some money."

JD spoke up. "My dad has a friend who runs the ski resort at Lee Canyon. Every summer they have a free concert there called Mountain Fest. Dad said they're having trouble getting acts because it's a free event. Why don't we sign up? It's next weekend on Saturday. We can leave Friday night and camp there."

Everyone nodded at his suggestion, and then they turned their eyes on me. "Fuck it. I'll play with you at Mountain Fest, but we've gotta build a playlist, and you've gotta look for another drummer. You need a band name."

The four of them stared at me. "And obviously a leader. Let's go talk this out with everyone."

We returned to the studio, but instead of picking up our instruments, we went into the booth where the band was waiting. "We need to discuss this."

"Discuss what? We figured out how to make this work. You guys will record the song for us five different ways, and then we'll use a different track for the concerts. Others have done it, so it won't be a big deal. By the time the studio figures out whether the song works or not, we'll have it worked out the way we want."

I glanced at my father and shook my head.

Marshall's face showed disbelief, as did Ace's. Ripper and Dusty looked guilty. It was inevitable that we'd get to this place where Regal would want to take credit for our work.

"Fine, but I'm not recording the soundtrack. If you guys are gonna take credit for our hard work on this, then you can write the soundtrack yourselves. Let's get the backup intro done so we can get out of here."

I sounded like a brat, but my parents had plucked my last nerve. I needed to get some control back in my life. I didn't come back to Cupertino to be treated like a child with no control over anything.

Marshall walked back into the booth while my father and the rest of the members of From the Ashes were in the studio posing for pictures. I was sitting on the couch behind Casey—a nice guy—tweaking the playback to give to Marshall. He was going to hand-deliver it to Harmon Studio before the deadline.

I scooted over so Marshall could sit next to me. "What's going on with you and my brother? He told me he's not going to provide security during the tour. I've gotta find someone because if your father and the band take the stage with a recorded track and something happens, the crowds will devour them." Marsh chuckled, and I joined him.

"Sandy has a lot on his mind. I think it was overwhelming having someone around all the time. No worries. I'll stay here with Mom and Regal until we finish this." I couldn't throw the guy under the bus. At his core, Sandy was sweet. He was thoughtful. He was generous of spirit.

After what had happened to him the previous year with getting arrested and then outed, I couldn't blame him for being guarded.

"Well, I talked to him, and he said you should stay at his place while he's gone. I figure by the time he comes back, you'll be done with this, and you two won't have to be in each other's way. I really want you to give me a sample of that score, Skyler. It's beautiful, and I think the studio deserves to hear it. It might help them decide to use the song, and that's all we really want, right?" His expression seemed sincere, so I nodded.

"I'll stay at Sandy's if you're sure he doesn't mind. The piano is there, and I can record myself playing and send you the audio file. I have my laptop with me, and it has much better software to get a decent recording than I could get on my phone."

Marshall reached into his pocket and handed me the house key. "The Yukon is outside. As soon as Casey sends me the files for the song, I'm in a Lyft and on the way to the airport."

"Thanks, Marshall. I'll be out before Sandy gets home on Friday."

"Oh, uh, he's staying a few more days. He'll be back on Monday. He's hanging out with some old football buddies next weekend." That made sense. He probably did have friends still in the NFL.

I went to the house to grab the things I'd brought over that morning. I was thankful I didn't have to share a room with River. His room was my old one, but now it looked like it had been ransacked and robbed, not that he'd ever find anything missing.

Mom was outside with the animals, but River was in his room with the speakers blaring. Obviously, my little brother was upset over what had happened earlier.

I knocked on River's door. Nothing. I opened it and saw him face down on the bed, so I went inside, turning down the speaker from his phone on the table beside the bed. He was listening to Maiden Voyage, according to the lock screen on his phone, and when I turned down the music, he flipped over and appeared ready to fight.

"Whoa! It's just me. What's wrong?" I sat on the edge of his bed and stared at him for a moment until he wiped his eyes.

"Riv, what's going on?"

"I have no job. No skills. A high school diploma that I got because I paid another kid to write my senior essay so I could graduate. Dad says I'm not very good at playing guitar and can't sing worth a damn. I hoped maybe this was my chance at finding a career, and Dad's just harpooned it by taking credit for something we've all worked hard to create." Tears leaked down his flushed cheeks, and I felt awful for him.

Staring at him, a solution came to me. "Pack a bag. Come stay with me at Sandy's house. He told Marshall I could stay there, and you can stay with me. If the others can come over, we can practice there because Sandy's gone for about ten days. You need a break from being in this house with your parents. Sandy's got a pool. It'll be a nice diversion."

River's big eyes bore into me before he swallowed. "Really?"

I patted his leg. "Yeah. I'm going to go talk to Marsh about something. I'll be right back." I grabbed my duffel and carried it to the Yukon with me, stowing it in the back seat before I walked to the studio and looked in through the window to see Marsh was in the booth with Casey.

I hurried around the building and opened the door to the booth. Casey was wearing headphones as he worked, so I snapped my fingers. When Marsh turned around, I motioned for him to come outside, hoping to enlist his assistance.

When Marsh got outside, I closed the door. "Can I talk to you about something?"

"Sure. What's up?" Marsh looked around for a second. "Where's everyone else?"

"Well, River's packing. He's going to stay with me at Sandy's. JD, Arlo, and Goldie went home, but Riv's going to call them and ask them to come to the house so we can work on the rest of the song, and Mom and Jeanne are probably at the barn. Look, I need to borrow Sandy's Yukon. The guys and I are going on a little teambuilding trip next weekend. I think it'll help bring us close enough to finish the song." First, the cursing, and now I was lying.

"You think? Well, if it'll benefit the song, sure. I'll tell Sandy I gave my permission for you to drive his SUV to—?"

"The mountains. We'll be doing a little hiking."

Marsh stared at me and smirked. "Where are you really going?"

I nervously looked around, finally seeing there was no way I could pull it off. "Okay, we're going to Nevada. We're going to Lee Canyon's Mountain Fest to debut their band and play the song as a cover song, with nobody knowing it's being considered for a movie. I think I'll have to substitute the drum kit for a djembe because we don't have a way to haul everything, or maybe we'll do it acoustically. I want to see an audience reaction to the remake to know if we're on the right track."

"Damn, Skyler! That's a magnificent idea. Does the band know?" Marsh's face morphed from worried to excited in the blink of an eye. He then turned his gaze toward the studio where From the Ashes was having a photo session.

"No. We see we're not going to get credit for the work, but I owe it to those guys to play it at least once for an audience, and while it will be a free event, I want them to get a taste of what it feels like to perform live. If they can find a drummer, Marsh, you might have a new band to manage that's on the way in, not the way out...literally. Are you going to rat us out to Regal and the band?"

I hoped not. I wanted to help the guys perform the song we'd worked so hard to create at least once. When *they* could adsorb the applause for their hard work, not just From the Ashes, who couldn't play the song as we performed it, as they'd admitted.

Marsh stared at me for a minute. "You think those guys would sign with me? They'd be my first clients that I got on my own."

I grinned at him. "If you don't rat us out, I'll make sure they give you the first chance at representing the best new band since From the Ashes."

"I'll be back on Thursday. Work your asses off while I'm gone, please. I'm going with you to Nevada, and we'll do this right."

That was how we got our first gig—or rather, that was how Accidental Fire got its first gig.

"You know Mr. Brightside?" JD asked, his eyes settling on me. We were all sitting in the fancy living room at Sandy's house.

Goldie's dad, Kenny Robbins, offered to loan us some equipment he'd saved for sentimental reasons when he used to play in a garage band before he went to college to become an accountant. I was truly grateful, as were the other guys.

Goldie had explained to his father what we were doing, and Kenny agreed to come with us to run the soundboard while we played at the festival. Through his connections, the band had been given a prime spot on Saturday evening. For a first-time band, it was a coup.

I'd also taken River with me to smuggle my drum kit out of my mom's barn and clean it up, so we were a fully functional band. I planned to donate it to the drummer they found. I wanted those guys to succeed in the worst way.

We all nodded that we knew the song, and I hit a crash cymbal for two beats before River began playing the notes at the beginning. Goldie started singing the first verse, JD jumped in, matching my beat, and Arlo's talented fingers skittered across the keyboard to support the melody.

Playing along with the band at the subtle level required through the verse, I was enjoying myself, and after we got through the song once, we decided we could fake it and moved on. We gave the same treatment to a couple more covers, only stopping when the doorbell rang.

I hurried to the door to see a man who had to be Goldie's dad standing there with another man I didn't know. "You must be Skyler Ashe. I'm Goldie's dad, Kenny, and this is a friend of mine. Reuben Chase from Murder of Crows. I do his taxes. I told him about the band's plan to play at Mountain Fest, and he agreed to come along to offer some advice. May we come in?"

Murder of Crows? I wasn't familiar with them or their music. The guy appeared to be the epitome of a rocker, so how could I doubt him?

Maybe he had some suggestions that the band could use to reach the next level? To find their big break?

We headed into the living room, and the band members went wild over seeing Reuben Chase. It was heartening to see Goldie hug his dad. The two were obviously close, and I was envious.

Kenny had not only come out to support his son, but he'd brought help. I knew in my heart Regal would never be so selfless.

"Okay, boys, play me what you have." I moved to the drum kit, and we played an old Guns & Roses song in a stripped-down version. I loved the song, and Reuben quietly sang along. When we finished playing, Reuben stepped forward with a few tips.

"I love it. You're not trying to sound like the band, which is a great idea. I've played Mountain Fest before, and you get a forty-five-minute set. What else do you have?"

Reuben stuck around, and we worked out five songs, not playing 'Bury Me' for him. That would be our surprise for the crowd. When Reuben, Kenny, Goldie, and Arlo left, I looked at River and JD. "What do we think?"

It was their band. I'd get Marshall to help them find a drummer, but man, I loved what they had going. If they were my jazz band, they'd get an *A*.

Friday morning, Marshall arrived at Sandy's house as I was just returning from my run. I'd kept up the hard-push routine to build my core because I was still committed to traveling with From the Ashes for their mini-tour to get the song out.

I didn't like the idea of not really playing the song as we'd agreed on when we were in the recording studio at my mother's farm. I planned to talk to the members of From the Ashes about leaving out the drums when we recorded the songs for the tour. I could keep up with the track if that was what they wanted to do, though I'd always say it was a bad idea.

"I cleaned up my old drum kit my mom had at the farm, and I'll happily donate it to the band. It's a small set, but I think it'll be perfect for what we plan to do at Mountain Fest. Goldie's dad has been kind enough to give us the rest of the electronics we'll need for the gig, so that's a plus, and he's agreed to run the soundboard." Marsh was helping himself to the muffins I'd bought at the store the previous day.

With his mouth full, Marsh mumbled, "Kenny Robbins? How do you guys know Kenny Robbins? And his tie to Reuben Chase?"

We weren't trying to hide the fact that Goldie's dad was helping us out, but I hadn't exactly checked in with

Marsh while he was in LA. Marsh didn't need to know everything.

"The band wants their shot at success, and I want to give it to them. If that's not something you're interested in, or if you believe it's in conflict with your contract with From the Ashes, we'll figure out something else. We're not without our own resources, Marsh."

I kind of sounded like an asshole, but I had a mission to protect my younger counterparts. I liked Marshall, but I didn't necessarily trust him. Plus, not asking about Sandy was draining most of my resolve.

Marsh stared at me. "Fine. I won't push. I've rented a van for all the instruments and gear. Goldie, can you drive it? I've invited a stylist friend to come fix you guys up. Nothing drastic, just a little refreshing here and there. Call the boys and tell them to bring a few outfits to choose from for what they'll wear on stage. You only get one chance to make a first impression."

The man was right, but I was still leery. Marsh had threatened me with a makeover early on, and I was still worried about what he meant.

Chapter Eighteen

Sandy

I was in the office at the Shuckers stadium to meet the staff. I'd spent the weekend with Kat, her wife, Lynette, and Lynette's little brother, Hardy Boyer. He was a nice guy, likely early twenties, with long blond hair and blue eyes that reminded me too much of someone I knew, not as intimately as I'd hoped. Hardy was also a musician, which was ironic since I was avoiding one myself.

My phone pinged, and I pulled it from my jacket pocket to see it was the front door camera at my house. I pulled up the feed to see Marsh coming inside. I hit the mic. "Motherfucker don't wreck my house. Call me tomorrow."

Marsh flipped me the bird, which made me laugh. I could count on him to put me in my place every time.

After I shoved my phone into my pocket, Kat walked out of her office with a big smile. "Come on in, Sandy."

Following Kat into the large room that faced the playing field, I felt a jolt of energy slide down my spine. Being on that patch of grass excited me, even if I wasn't mowing down the offensive line.

Scanning the distance to the goalpost, I glanced through the glass wall at my right to see a large conference room where I saw sneers from the eleven men sitting around a rectangular glass table, which quickly deflated my dreams of returning to the game. It was easy to see I wasn't welcome.

I was the gay guy—or the *out* gay guy—in the room, and it didn't seem as though the folks on her staff liked me. Forget that they didn't know me. They'd already pre-judged me, which wasn't a shock at all.

Kat—or rather, the head woman in charge—walked to her chair at the end of the table. She stared at her staff, and

I could see she wasn't thrilled with the faces looking back at her.

"Wipe those looks off your faces before I fire all your asses. I'm sure I can go to the closest gay club and find folks who can do a better job than you without knowing a goddamn thing about football."

The head coach smirked. "Sorry, boss. You didn't tell us who was coming in. We didn't know it was a jailbird." I took a deep breath and didn't react. It wasn't worth it.

Kathleen started laughing, her eyes fixed on the men at the table, who all joined her in laughter—though I was pretty sure it was out of fear, not because they thought the situation was funny.

The boss stared at Tiny Sloane, a former linebacker from Tennessee State, back when I was just starting at Fresno as a baby defensive tackle. "Hi, Tiny." I knew the man—who didn't? He was an All-American during his college years.

"Sandy, man, how are you? What have you been doing since you left the Breeze?"

His comment made me laugh. "What do you think?"

Kathleen cleared her throat. "I strongly urge all of you to leave your preconceived notions at the door. Sandy will be joining us tomorrow at minicamp to assess the new talent. Last year, the team was a wildcard going into the playoffs, and we didn't get into the postseason. None of you have any room for judgment since you were my father's advisers. We're starting over, and if any of you won't abide by my decisions, get your asses out of my chairs."

Each man in the room looked around, and I finally got it. There were no women in the front office, which had to be the way Jerry Graves ran the organization. It was easy to see Kathleen wouldn't be a continuation of the previous regime.

None of them moved, so Kathleen smiled. "Okay, let's give Sandy an overview of the roster."

Each coach went through the exercise, explaining their veteran players' weaknesses and strengths, and then, the team scout explained the draft picks and what they brought to the team. They had until the end of the preseason to trim their playing roster from sixty-five players to fifty-three, and I could see the coaches already had their favorites and were willing to fight to keep them. I wished to hell I'd had someone fighting for me back when I was still in the game.

We went out for drinks and dinner at a restaurant near the stadium after meeting all afternoon. Kathleen left after drinks to get home, and I told her I'd take a cab to her place after dinner. The other coaches weren't rude, but they weren't exactly warm and welcoming.

I exited the cab at the incredible house Kat and Lynette had welcomed me into. The sound of drumming caught my attention immediately. I knocked on the front door and laughed when Lynette opened the door. She laughed as she held her hands up like a megaphone so I could hear.

"I'm so sorry. When Hardy's pissed, he beats the hell out of his drum set downstairs. We've hired someone to soundproof his room down there, but the guy's a little backed up on another job and can't get here until next week. Again, we're sorry."

I chuckled, thinking about my drummer. I missed him more than I could even articulate. He was fucking talented, and it was ironic to be in a house where I heard the familiar beats. It made me miss the man I dreamed about every night even more.

"I happen to be in love with a drummer, so this is nothing new. How old is Hardy?" I was shouting too, and Lynette and I both laughed.

Suddenly, the sound stopped, and Lynette smiled. "He's twenty. He's trying to find himself because our parents kicked him out. I'm not sure what to do for him, but we're trying to love him through it."

"For your sake, I hope it gets better soon. I'm going to go for a run if you don't mind." I needed time away to try to get my shit together.

"Go. I'd go with you just to enjoy the peace and quiet." She rubbed her baby bump, and we both laughed again. "There's cold bottled water in the fridge in the hall linen closet." I nodded as I went upstairs to change.

I checked my video feed at the house to see my drummer had returned...with his brother and the other bandmates. Did it piss me off? Not really. I was glad they were making use of the house. I only wished I was there to see them in person.

Tuesday morning, I drove my rental to the practice field, ready to work. Unfortunately, the other defensive coaches and head coach weren't ready to work with me. All my questions went unanswered, and by the lunch break, I was ready to walk.

I held my tongue but made notes on a team iPad that would go directly to Kat. There were a few players who weren't keen to have me as a coach and didn't want to accept any suggestions I had. I laughed at their stupidity. Maybe I wasn't the guy they wanted, but I knew the game. I'd played it for a long time.

Wednesday, I got the defensive line together and tried to explain a play we'd done when I was in high school. The players looked at me as if I'd lost my mind.

"No shit. In a four-four-two formation, have your defenders fade back at the snap to maintain the backline. Midfielders come around, two on each side for the attack, and your forwards come up the middle for the sack."

Not one face appeared to believe me, so I stepped back to let them decide what to do. The defensive line spoke in the huddle until the offense clapped and took the line. I was ready to walk off the sideline and pack up my shit when I heard the count and the snap.

I turned back to see the defense had run my play, and they'd taken down the QB as gently as possible. It was satisfying to watch, but I was still pissed they hadn't given me the courtesy of acknowledging I knew my shit when I explained the play.

We ran patterns for two more hours, and I tried to coach the defensive line, but they didn't respect me, and I knew it would never work. Once the head coach sent us to the locker room, I went upstairs to the office where Kathleen had been watching the practice out the huge windows that faced the field.

"They won't respect or respond to me."

"Give it time, Sandy. Show them you're up for the job. Don't let them intimidate you. Show them you're not willing to put up with their bullshit." Kathleen believed her advice could fix everything, but I knew football players.

Kathleen was right that they would laugh at someone they didn't respect, but her team—and her coaches—were still trying to learn how to handle that they all now worked for a lesbian female owner. Maybe once they got the hang of that, they'd be accepting of a coach or player who was queer. Today wasn't that day.

Thursday evening, after the end of the minicamp, I returned to Kathleen and Lynette's home. When I walked through the back door, I saw Hardy sitting behind his drum kit as a video of Led Zepplin played on a big-screen television. He began playing along with the song as he closed his eyes.

That look was all too familiar to me from when I'd watched Skyler behind the drums in his father's studio. It was more beautiful than anything I'd ever seen. I immediately knew what I had to do, and I had to do it fast.

I went upstairs to my room and quickly threw my things in my bags. I changed into a pair of jeans, rebooked my flight from Friday morning to the next flight out of Baltimore to San Jose, and carried all my things downstairs, leaving them at the door.

Noises from the kitchen caught my attention, so I followed them to say my goodbyes. Kat sorted the mail by the trash bin while Lynette moved something around a skillet. Lynette glanced up first. "Dinner will be ready in about half an hour. Feel free to grab a beer from the fridge."

Kat glanced up and studied me for a moment. "Sweetheart, I don't believe Sandy will be staying for dinner."

I nodded. "Thanks so much, ladies, for your hospitality, but I need to get back to California. I've got a man who doesn't know how much he needs me yet. I plan to make sure he does very soon."

Kat smiled. "Let me see you out."

I hugged Lynette and followed Kat to the front door. She pulled up the handle on my suitcase while I grabbed my garment bag. I'd left my messenger bag in the SUV. We went to the back of my rental, and I opened the tailgate. Once everything was inside, I turned to the woman.

"I wish you the best of luck. I don't think your coaching staff is in a place to accept another queer person among their ranks. I'd strongly urge you to hire a diversity coach and make one of your offensive coaches go both ways with special teams and the defensive line until you can find a good replacement." We both laughed at my choice of words, but Kat nodded.

"I brought you here because I respected you as a player, and I was sure you would be a big asset to the coaching staff. I also hoped that if the coaches and players saw a gay man could do everything they could, they might see me as a competent leader. I'm sorry if I inconvenienced you."

"Naw, you didn't inconvenience me at all. It gave me the chance to sort out my head, so thanks for the mini vacation. Please call me when the baby comes. I wish you and Lynette the best of luck with everything." I hugged Kat and thanked her again before leaving.

I made the flight because the security officers let me take my luggage through to check at the gate, and once I settled into my seat on the plane, I shoved my earbuds in and turned on some soothing music. In about five hours, I'd be back home, where I could clean up the mess I'd made before running away.

When I arrived home at eleven that evening, the house was dark. I parked in the garage and unloaded my crap from the car. The Yukon was parked in its spot, so when I walked by, I touched the hood to feel it was warm, which was a relief. That meant Skyler had been driving it.

When I came out of the garage, I noticed the pool lights were on, so I went to the back gate to let myself in, seeing Marsh sitting in the spa with Arlo and Goldie, the three of them drinking my beer and laughing.

I glanced around to see River wrapped in two towels, sitting at the patio table with an acoustic guitar on his lap as he studied a paper in front of him. I walked to the spa first. "Where's Skyler?"

Marshall started laughing. "You made good time, big brother."

"That's not an answer to my question."

Arlo spoke up. "He's inside at the piano. He's working out some bars so we can play an old song at Mountain Fest." At least he had the good sense to answer me without giving me bullshit like my brother.

I hurried through the basement, dropping my luggage and running up the stairs. I could hear the piano tinkling as I reached the main floor, so I stopped to listen. It was a Lifehouse song I remembered from high school: "Hanging by a Moment." It was damn appropriate since that was exactly what I was doing.

I took a deep breath and walked through the house to the entrance of the living room. There, at the rented piano, sat Skyler. He was using the light from the porch to scribble something onto a paper next to him, seeming to concentrate very hard on the task at hand.

"I'm glad you came back," I said into the semi-darkness.

Skyler jumped at the sound, his head snapping in my direction. I stepped farther into the room, flipping on the lights over the fireplace. I turned to stare at his handsome face, now illuminated by the soft light in the room.

"I thought you weren't back until Monday."

My brother was an asshole, but at least he'd done me a favor by giving Skyler bad information so he'd stick around. "Marsh had no idea when I was coming back. He needed you to keep working, so he lied. I'll have to thank him for that."

"I can leave. I mean, we can leave. We're all leaving tomorrow anyway. Sorry for—"

I rushed over to the piano, pulling Skyler up from the bench. "You have nothing to be sorry for, so stop that. I've been thinking about you every waking minute and dreaming about you every night. I can't stop. You've gotten into my heart, Sky, and I don't want you out."

Skyler's shocked face made me smile as he struggled to speak. "I— I thought you didn't want me. I thought you weren't attracted to me and I was bothering you."

"Oh, you bother me all right. Not in the way you're thinking though. Hang on to your hat, Sky. I've fallen in love with you." I kept my gaze on him, hoping to gauge his reaction to my confession.

I didn't expect him to pull away. "Fuck you."

I completely lost it. I laughed so hard at how quickly those harsh words came out of his mouth. I braced my hands on my knees to keep me upright, and I completely lost my shit.

"What's so damn funny?"

After a minute, I stood upright and used the neck of my T-shirt to dry my eyes from laughing so hard. Skyler had his hands on his hips, staring at me in disbelief.

"I'm sorry, but hearing those words out of your mouth caught me by surprise. What happened to Mr. You Never Know Who's Listening?" Now, I was deflecting the pain knocking on my heart's door because it seemed he was rejecting me. That would never do.

"You made me feel"—he crossed his arms over his chest—"like I wasn't worth your time." His face was so vulnerable it ripped at my heart.

"I'm sorry. I panicked because I've never felt this way about another human, much less a guy who breezed into my life just a minute ago. I had no idea how to handle it, so I fucked it up, like usual."

I figured I had nothing to lose at this point. If he didn't want me, there was nothing to fight for. If he did but was hurt because of my stupidity, I'd make sure he knew he was the most important person in the world to me, bar none.

Chapter Nineteen

Skyler

"Well, you sure as fuck handled it wrong." I gave a defiant nod and adjusted the piano bench to get back to work.

Sandy laughed again, but this time, he moved my composition notebook and sat on the bench next to me before gently placing his left hand on my right cheek, turning my face toward him. "You're right. I did. Give me a chance to make it up to you, okay? What about this festival Arlo mentioned? Where is it?"

I moved away from his touch. "It's in Nevada outside Las Vegas. We're driving there tomorrow and camping overnight somewhere. We play on Saturday afternoon at two." Why was I telling him anything? Was I really going to give him a second chance?

"Who's *we*?" I couldn't begin to figure out what his expression meant. Was he jealous?

"Me and the guys—River, Arlo, Goldie, and JD. They've chosen a band name, Accidental Fire. I'm only playing with them until they find a new drummer."

Sandy grinned. "So, you're not going on the road with a band?"

"Nope. Not permanently."

"Why is Marsh still here?"

I chuckled. "You mean, why is he back? He's going with us to Vegas. Goldie's dad, Kenny, is letting us borrow some equipment he has from when he played in a band. We're picking up a rental van tomorrow, and uh, I was going to drive your Yukon. Goldie's going to drive the van."

Sandy laughed. "*Fuck no!* We're not sleeping on the fucking ground. We're staying at a hotel, and Marsh is going to pay for it. I'm too old and banged up to sleep in a tent."

I chuckled. "I don't think we even have tents. Sleeping bags, but no tents, and who invited you?"

Sandy kissed the side of my neck. "Good god, we'll get bit by snakes or some shit. Nope, there's gotta be a motel or someplace out there where we can safely sleep. I'll find it. By the way—I'll be your security, so I'll be going along with or without an invitation. No worries. I'll handle everything. You still need to work on this?" He pointed to the stave notebook on top of the piano.

I glanced at the sheet music he'd moved from the bench to the top of the piano. "No. I got through what we need. I should get them to come inside so we can go through it a couple of times. Riv is supposed to be working on his part out by the pool."

"He was doing just that when I came in. Where's everyone sleeping?" Sandy glanced around, seeing his living room was littered with instruments. I'd put together my drum kit on the other side of the piano so I could at least practice while they were trying to figure out their parts.

"I'm in the room I used before. Marsh is in his room, and the rest are sleeping in the media room."

Sandy nodded. "I'll go get them. Be right back."

I watched the man walk away, and I was in shock. Did I have a stroke?

Is Sandy really in love with me?

It was extremely hot when we arrived at the campsite Sandy found for us after talking to someone at the ski resort. The desk clerk told him the resort was booked for the weekend because there was also a mountain biking event. The clerk explained there was an alternative to the resort, so Sandy forced Marshall to call the owners to make a reservation—using his corporate credit card.

We would be staying in four camping trailers set up in a semi-circle about ten miles from the sight of the festival. Our equipment was in the rented van that Goldie and Marshall had driven to the site, and everyone was excited about what would happen on Saturday.

"I'll room with JD," River announced.

Sandy stepped forward and put his hand on my shoulder. "Sky and I'll room together. Somebody gets a trailer to themselves."

Without waiting for me to respond, Sandy went to the SUV and unloaded everyone's bags, carrying mine and his to the trailer on the end. I glanced toward Marshall to see his smirk before he turned to the lead singer. "Goldie, you and I can share, and Arlo, you get one to yourself."

"Good. I need to practice on that keyboard because it's smaller than I'm used to, and I need to record some elaborations to use during our performance. This way, I won't disturb anyone."

Arlo went to the van and opened the back, pulling out the smaller keyboard. River had gone to our parents' house and liberated the old one I'd had as a kid from the back of the studio without getting caught by Regal. My little brother was sneakier than I'd been when I was his age.

"Okay, that's settled. The caretaker should be here in an hour to set up for dinner. The guy's name is Errol, and he's going to bring supplies. I thought we could have an old-fashioned cookout—you know, hot dogs on sticks, s'mores, the whole nine yards," Marshall told us.

I glanced at Sandy to see a snarl. "What?" The man's mood swings were killing me.

Sandy started after Marsh, who ran away, his arms fluttering as he ran through the brush, laughing loudly the whole time. A minute later, Sandy came back, grinning. "He'll get lost. He has no fucking sense of direction. Anyway, gimme a minute."

Sandy pulled out his phone, quickly dialing a number. "Hey, Errol. It's Sandy Kensington, Marshall's brother."

He walked to the trailer we would share and looked under a large stone in the little cactus garden. He lifted it and picked up four keyrings before he dropped the stone and returned to where we stood. Sandy held them out to show they were numbered tags corresponding to the numbers on the trailers.

"You can bring the hot dogs and stuff for s'mores, but I told my brother to order steaks for the seven of us. Uh-huh. Okay. Beer and soft drinks are fine. Thanks, Errol."

Sandy put the phone in his pocket and glanced at all of us. "Marshall is a cheap fucker. He took it upon himself to ignore what I told him to order, so I fixed it. We'll have dinner delivered in a while. I'll go look for the idiot who took off and gather some firewood so we can have a fire in the pit. Tomorrow night, we're going to Vegas after the festival, and we'll drive home on Sunday. How's that?"

The younger guys clapped, though I wasn't sure what River had to clap about. He wasn't twenty-one, so casinos were out for him.

There were places we could go that didn't involve gambling, and there were a lot of fantastic restaurants. I'd gone to Vegas with Regal and the band once, and Dusty had taken me places where I could have fun. I would always be grateful to him, and I'd do the same for my brother.

An hour later, an older model Ford Explorer traversed the gravel road to the campsite. A man and woman stepped out of the vehicle and looked around. They both went to the back of their SUV and unloaded coolers, neither speaking to anyone—or each other.

Sandy exited our trailer and walked to the group, so I followed him. I'd been sitting at the picnic table working on a new song with River's acoustic guitar while Sandy had gone inside to get the mosquito repellent he'd brought along.

The previous night, after the band and I played through the Lifehouse song I'd reworked to adapt to our abilities, Sandy had escorted me to my bedroom door, kissed my cheek, and wished me goodnight.

Standing there, I was a moment away from inviting him into my bed. I was surprised I'd resisted the urge because there was still a lot to sort through before we embarked on a physical relationship.

I wasn't a friends-with-benefits kind of guy. I needed more commitment before I could hop into bed with someone. Honestly, though, the temptation to be with Sandy was strong.

"Errol, Karen, this is JD, River, and Arlo. Marshall and Goldie are collecting more firewood, and that's my guy, Skyler. Everyone, these are our hosts, Errol and Karen Donner."

Everyone exchanged glances, but of course, River couldn't keep his mouth shut. "Wait, are we actually guests of the *Donner* party?"

My little brother was a funny guy. He sounded like one of my high school kids, and I couldn't hold the laugh. He had Regal's sense of humor.

Everyone laughed, and Mr. and Mrs. Donner made the rounds to greet and shake hands with us. They were very pleasant, and I was glad they were our hosts.

After the fire was at a low blaze, Mrs. Donner put the steaks on a wire rack they'd brought and warmed pre-baked russet potatoes in the coals. Ten minutes later, dinner was served, and the food was delicious.

After everyone had their fill, we helped the Donners clean up and thanked them for the incredible meal. Once they were gone, Marsh opened the cooler and handed out beers. I started to complain about him offering beer to River, who was a minor, but my little brother held up his hand.

"Thanks, but I don't drink. I've seen what alcohol can do to people, and I've found other ways to blow off steam."

I was truly proud of him until he pulled out a joint and sparked it. He took in a large draw before passing it to JD, who matched River's draw.

"No smoking before the show. I don't care what you do tonight, but if you're going on stage with me, you won't be high. That's it." I stood from the picnic table and went to the trailer I was sharing with Sandy.

As I walked through the small camping trailer, I immediately noticed there was only one bedroom. Obviously, Sandy intended for us to share the queen-size bed at the back. Was that what I really wanted to do?

We all sat around the little campfire, made s'mores with the things the Donners had left for us, and sang some old campfire songs—well, all of us except Goldie. His voice needed to be saved for the concert the next afternoon.

If the band got more gigs, Goldie needed to develop a routine for taking care of his instrument, much as we all took care of ours by tuning the piano, replacing drumheads, and tightening guitar strings. He was young, and his vocal cords were healthy, but with the type of music they planned to perform, his vocal cords could become strained and damaged. He was too good of a singer for that to happen.

I accompanied the campfire songs using River's guitar. We had a great time, and just before midnight, I called it a night. I made Marshall take the cooler of beer with him because JD was enjoying it a lot, and to give his best performance the next day, he needed a clear head.

Sandy and I went inside the trailer, and I stopped to stare at him. "There's only one bed in here."

He smirked at me, damn him, and I hated to say it was adorable. His eyes got big, and he stared at me through his lashes, feigning innocence. "Really? I didn't look around, but I guess you're right. Whatever will we do?"

Just then, there was a knock on the door. Sandy opened it and started to step out when I glanced around him to see Marshall. "Can you show me how to put together the other bed? I remember Dad's friend, Edmond, had that camper and the table and benches made into another bed we had to share when Mom and Dad took us camping that one time. Thank god we only had to do that nonsense once."

I stepped in front of Sandy, chuckling. "Yes, Sandy, show us how the table and chairs create another bed." He grumbled and began putting together the one in our trailer and then went to help Marsh with his.

As I studied the bed, I knew Sandy wouldn't be able to sleep on it comfortably, so I went to the little closet and found an extra set of sheets and a couple of pillows, making up the bed for myself. I quickly undressed, deciding to shower in the morning so Sandy could shower before bed. I could be reasonable.

When he returned to the trailer, I heard him mumble, "Fucking hell. Goddamn you, Marshall." I was resting on my left side with my back to the door so he couldn't see me smiling at his discomfort.

"You awake?" I stayed perfectly still, though it was hard.

"I'm killing you, Marsh."

Sandy stomped off to the back of the trailer—about twenty feet away. I could hear him cursing Marshall as he brushed his teeth, so when he got into the shower, I slipped out of my makeshift bed and into Sandy's.

Call me what you want, but Sandy was a gorgeous man who had professed his love for me. I hoped it wasn't his less-than-stellar attempt at getting in my pants. I was in love with him too, and I'd tell him—after I was certain he wasn't playing me. It was horrible to put a condition on my love, but I still wasn't confident we were on equal footing.

As they say, time would tell.

Chapter Twenty

Sandy

I turned the water to *icicle* and stepped under the spray. In less than a minute, my dick was officially inside my gut, with my balls tucked up there next to it for company. After I dried off and pulled on a pair of sleep shorts, I exited the bathroom and turned off the lights. It was too dark to see anything inside the trailer, so I felt my way to the bedroom, running smack into the door because I didn't remember closing it when I left the room.

Folding my jeans from earlier, I shoved my dirty clothes into the duffel and sat on the bed with my phone in my hands. There was a message from Marshall that we were expected at the resort by ten for a sound check, so I set my alarm for eight and stretched out on top of the bed covers.

"How was your shower?"

I was off that fucking bed like I'd been shot. I flipped the wall switch for some light, seeing a gorgeous sight. Skyler was in my bed without a shirt. I hoped to fuck he was there because he was planning to give me another chance, not because he'd decided he wanted the better bed.

"You scared the shit out of me. What's wrong? You want me to crowd into that shitty little bed?" I flipped off the overhead light and walked to the switch next to the bed, flipping on some small pendant lights so I could see him.

I sat on the side of the bed, my foot under my ass with my right leg on the floor. "I'll sleep out there if it's too uncomfortable for you."

"Really? You would do that for me? Do you get off on pain?" Skyler was grinning as his beautiful golden-brown eyes sparkled in the dim light.

"Hmm. Not whips and shit, but I like being fucked hard. I'm not a stranger to a little role-playing, and I give a hell of a blowjob—or so I've been told." None of that was a lie.

Skyler grinned. "You're not a dedicated top?"

It was my turn to grin. "I like to feel the burn on occasion. How about you?"

"I told you my number was four. Two topping and two bottoming. Equal opportunity."

"Oh, I'm glad to hear that. So, am I sleeping on that horrible fucking plywood bed out there?" My thumb and index finger were slowly dragging the sheet off him. Our gazes locked for a moment, but when he felt the graze of cotton over his skin, he glanced down, and the sexiest smile bloomed on his face. When I glanced down to see his hooded erection peeking out, my cock kicked into overdrive.

"May I sleep here...with you?"

I smiled because he was a teacher, through and through, with his proper grammar. I found it hot as hell and slid off my shorts to climb in next to him.

"Do you believe I love you? That I want to be here to support you?" Having his trust was important to me.

"I do. I want you to be with me during this new adventure. I don't know how the guys will react to performing for an audience, and I need you to be there to support all of us."

"I wouldn't be anywhere else, Sky."

I pulled him on top of me and kissed him with all the love I had inside me. "You wanna flip for it?"

Skyler laughed. "I'd like you inside me. Are you okay with that?"

I couldn't get a breath as I looked into his eyes. "More than. I need to get up unless you have condoms and lube nearby. I want to kiss the fuck out of you, but let's take care of the formalities first, okay?"

"I don't have either of those things. I didn't expect you to come back until Monday, and I certainly didn't plan to have sex with anyone else."

Those words lit up my soul. "I have what we need. I hoped to hell we'd have sex, Sky, but if you're not ready for that step, I'll wait for you. I mean it when I say I'll put in the work it takes to earn your trust."

That beautiful man nodded and leaned forward to seal his mouth over mine. I slid my tongue between his lips, and my balls finally descended from their hiding place after the cold shower.

I hummed in satisfaction at the tangling of tongues. The sensation was absolutely everything I needed, but I wanted to hear him talk. I wanted to know his thoughts.

I pulled away and looked into his sparkling eyes. "God, I wanna suck your cock." The words tumbled out of my mouth before I could stop them, but his foreskin had haunted me since I first saw it that night in the spa.

Skyler crawled up my body, raking his hard-on over my hypersensitive skin, taunting me. I pulled him up until his hooded dick was close and raised my head to take it inside my eager mouth.

"*Oh god!*" Skyler's moan had me pulling him to sit on my chest. He rested his hands on the wall and timidly thrust forward.

"Come on, teach, fuck my mouth."

My tongue licked the slit of the mushroom head as it made an appearance. I nibbled the foreskin, circling my tongue around it to slide it down to get to the sensitive skin beneath the rim.

"That feels fucking incredible." Skyler began thrusting more aggressively, and I loved it. His cock hit the back of my throat, gagging me a little, and Skyler pulled out. "Are you okay?"

I stared at the beautiful meat in front of me with a drop of precum on the tip that I snagged with my tongue. "I wondered if you cursed when you got off. Now I know. Let's try it again. Gimme."

Skyler was hesitant to move, so I flipped us so his head was at the foot of the bed, and I pounced on that thick cock. I took it all in one gulp and relaxed my throat so the head was right where I wanted it. I swallowed around it and eased off, only to repeat the move.

After the third time, strong hands wrapped in my hair and held tight, so I kept him in my mouth and began bobbing up and down before taking hold of his throbbing dick and working the foreskin up to nibble on the tip before I went down to the root again.

"I'm not going to la—" His cock became steel hard and hot just before his body stiffened and he coated my tongue with cum. As he rolled through the aftershocks, I gave my own erection three quick strokes before I blew all over the sheet.

I continued to mouth his softening cock until he pulled away. I fell flat on the bed, my face buried under his armpit. He smelled—I licked him—and tasted delicious everywhere.

After a moment to catch my breath, I sat up to see the man was out cold. I tried not to take offense, but I hoped it was because I'd sucked the life out of him.

Chuckling, I moved off the bed and lifted Skyler to position him at the head of the bed again before I climbed in with him and turned off the light. I wrapped my left arm around him and tucked him into me before pulling the sheet over us and joining him in dreamland.

"Check. Check one-two."

I was standing to the right of the stage for the sound check. Goldie was at his microphone in the front while Skyler was adjusting his drum set. It wasn't the same one I'd seen in Regal's recording studio. *Where'd he get those?*

People were milling around the perimeter of the stage, working hard to set up booths with crafts, games, and lots of different food. The delicious circulating scents caused my stomach to growl like an angry dog.

I didn't see anyone who appeared to be lurking around the area while the guys were on the stage, so I walked over to a stand to grab an iced tea and a snack. After the band played, I would suggest to them that we grab something to eat at the festival before driving to Vegas.

I approached a food truck and got in line, scrolling through shit on my phone as I waited for my turn in line. "Can I help you?" Looking up, I saw I was next in line, so I stepped closer.

"I'll take an unsweet tea if you've got it ready. Oh, and a churro, please." The woman at the window nodded before she walked away.

When she returned, she brought a large green solo cup with the food truck's name on the front. "Bring it back for a refill at half price." She handed it to me along with a hot sugar-and-cinnamon churro wrapped in wax paper.

After quickly tapping my phone to pay and leave a tip, I grinned at her. "Thanks. I will."

"Hey, did you get that for me?" I turned to see Marsh behind me.

"Who's with the band?"

"They're back at the van. You were nowhere to be found when we finished the sound check. I see now that you'll protect them until you're hungry."

I turned to see another band on the stage. "When did they leave? They were still on stage."

"Man, you're a shitty bodyguard. They finished a few minutes ago. Skyler looked for you, but apparently, he didn't know food was more important than his safety. I took them back to the van and said I'd come find you."

I glanced at the stage again. "Where's their equipment?"

"The drum kit and the keyboard are on a wheeled platform behind the backdrop, along with a few other bands' equipment that takes a bit longer to assemble. The guys have their instruments with them. We didn't have time to hire roadies, so you'll have to help us load up. I've got a guy in Vegas I want you to meet tomorrow before we fly home, so don't get stinking drunk tonight."

Marsh broke off most of my churro and grabbed my tea from my hand, walking away. I hurried to follow him because I wanted to know more about this *guy* he wanted me to meet.

We arrived at the van where the band sat in the camp chairs they'd brought along—all except Skyler, who was talking to a woman and a man near my Yukon. They were all smiling, so I slowly approached them to see if Skyler knew them.

"I'm doing this as a favor to my little brother. I have no desire to get on board with this circus." Sky looked over his shoulder and motioned me to join him.

"Miriam, Leon, this is a friend of mine, Sandy Kensington. Sandy, these are the Brownlees from Peoria. Miriam is the school secretary at West Peoria High."

I extended my hand to shake both of theirs. They seemed friendly, so my nerves calmed. "Nice to meet you both."

"I thought I saw Skyler on the stage, but I had to come back here to double-check. This is such a funny coincidence. We're driving to Seattle for a family reunion next week, and we saw an advertisement for this festival while we were in Vegas. We thought we'd check it out because it looked fun. I never imagined I'd see Mr. Ashe here behind a drum set." Her fond gaze at Skyler touched my heart.

"Is anyone at school aware that Mr. Ashe plays drums?" I grinned as Skyler punched my shoulder.

Mrs. Brownlee giggled. "They will be when I post this to the school bulletin board." She held up her phone and showed me a video of Skyler lost in the music as they played a minute of 'Mr. Brightside' for the soundcheck.

A few people were watching as Mrs. Brownlee's video scanned the crowd, but they seemed interested in the band. I saw several phones aimed toward the stage.

"Miriam, I really don't—"

"Oh no, you don't, Skyler. I think your students should see this. It will be good for them to know Mr. Ashe is a rock star."

I laughed with Mrs. Brownlee while Skyler's face turned bright red. It was cute, so I pulled my phone from my pocket and took his picture. I was sure he was about to tell me to fuck off before he remembered Mrs. Brownlee was there.

"Guys, you need to go change. The desk clerk in the resort told me you're free to use the employee locker room to get ready to go on, so let's get to it. The first act, The Earl Webb Family Band, has already started their set. You're up next." Marsh stuck his head around the side of my Yukon, motioning to Skyler.

"We'll get out of your way, Skyler. This is very exciting. I'm going to put the performance up on the bulletin board, so I'd say check it in a couple of days. I'm sure the kids will have plenty of questions for you."

Mrs. Brownlee hugged Skyler and her husband shook his hand before they left. Marshall walked over to me. "How'd they get back here?"

I shrugged. "No clue. She said they just came over. Is there someone monitoring people coming and going through the gate? They don't give out badges to show who's allowed back here?"

"I noticed that too. Let's keep a closer eye on things. Let's hope all hell doesn't break loose on our watch."

"Good point." God, I was on the verge of panic. Was I up to the task of being responsible for another person's safety?

Chapter Twenty-One

Skyler

River strummed a D-major, C-major, G-major, and then an F-major7 chord, and the crowd quickly quieted. All eyes were on the band. Goldie stood in front of the mic, unmoving and, worst of all, not singing. My biggest worry was happening in slow motion.

River glanced over his shoulder at me, and I held up my index and middle fingers for him to play the chords again, so he did, and then Arlo began playing the intro on the piano as we'd worked it out before I started a soft cymbal swell on the left crash. Thankfully, Goldie snapped out of it and began to sing in his chest voice, not mimicking Jon Bon Jovi but not losing the song's familiar melody.

We picked up the pace when we got to the verse…and we were off. Accidental Fire was playing their first professional gig, though they weren't getting paid. Nevertheless, I knew they would remember it for the rest of their lives.

Was using such a famous Bon Jovi song a little arrogant for their first performance? The four of them had gone round and round about it until finally, River had held up his hand. "Look, if we play it well and don't stray too far from the original melody, I think it shows confidence. Let's not have anyone introduce us when we take the stage. We'll sing the first song, then one of us can introduce the rest when—or if—the applause dies down."

I'd wanted to laugh, but I hadn't. They needed to work out who would be the leader of their band because it wouldn't be me. I had a life I wanted to get back to, and unlike my father, I had no desire to live that hard-partying lifestyle. Someone needed to take the helm, which was a detail they needed to figure out for themselves.

After changing the set list five times, a leader had finally surfaced. Arlo had held up his hand one night during rehearsal and said, "Let's start with Bon Jovi because it's not too gritty for Goldie, and then we can rock out on 'Mr. Brightside.' We'll end with 'Bury Me.' How's that sound?"

As the last guitar note faded on the breeze, I rolled the cymbal and then quieted it. The audience had grown to a few hundred people, which was surprising, and when they began clapping, Goldie looked back at his bandmates, a huge grin overtaking his face. It was a golden moment.

Arlo stood from the piano bench and moved his mic stand up. "Good afternoon! We're Accidental Fire! We'd love to play another one for you!"

The crowd hooted and hollered, which was a real thrill, and we moved on from there. We played the set list, and when it came time to start 'Bury Me,' I turned to the left to see Sandy with a big grin as he clapped. I winked at him, and he blew me a kiss.

Arlo stood and stepped from behind the piano. "Ladies and gentlemen, let me introduce you to the band. On vocals, Goldie Robbins." The crowd applauded.

"On lead guitar and vocals, River Ashe." More applause.

"On bass and vocals, JD Horn. I'm Arlo Timmons on piano, and our special guest drummer is Skyler Ashe. We're Accidental Fire!" The crowd clapped and cheered.

I didn't wait for the noise to die down. "One, two, three, four." I smacked my sticks together to tap out the beat and came down on the crash cymbals as River played a great variation on the intro he'd been practicing. It was even better than he'd played it before.

The kid was confident and even a little cocky, which boosted the music to a new level. That was exactly what River needed to step out of his shell—and out of Regal's shadow.

People took to the grass in front of the stage, dancing. It was a beautiful moment, and when the song ended, they stopped and clapped. I stepped off the riser and made my way to the front of the stage, where the guys stood, taking River's and JD's hands. They followed my lead, and we all held up our hands in solidarity and bowed together.

It was a day I'd remember for the rest of my life, more because I saw the smiles on the faces of the band and how much they were enjoying the attention. I could see they had the showbiz bug. They wanted to live a life I didn't, but I'd still support them—from afar—as much as I could.

A few people waited for us to come off the stage before they circled around us, wanting autographs and selfies. A few young women wore white T-shirts the guys eagerly signed. Unlike my brother and his friends, I refused to sign the front, so I signed the sleeves or the back. A few folks had paper, which we were happy to sign, and we took pictures until people stopped asking.

It was fun, but it only confirmed that it wasn't up my alley. By the time I got to Sandy, he was grinning from ear to ear.

"Well, what did you think?" I had a funny feeling in the pit of my stomach that I hadn't expected. Whether I liked it or not, Sandy's opinion meant a lot to me.

Sandy wrapped his strong arms around me and hugged me tightly. "You done good, teach."

That was the best compliment of the day right there. It warmed me inside to see his sincere smile and feel his lips touch my forehead. I wondered how we could create a relationship when we lived so far apart.

We decided to walk around the festival grounds and grab a bite to eat before we started for Vegas. I really wasn't surprised when I noticed River, JD, Goldie, and Arlo had picked up a few groupies, who followed them as though they had bacon in their pockets.

Sandy and I discreetly laughed as we kept an eye on them. They would totally fall in love with groupies who hung on their every word, so I made a mental note to give them a little pep talk about being safe, both emotionally and physically.

I hoped to have Dusty talk to them about his experiences touring because he'd already gone down that road and was more than familiar with what they would be facing. There would be pitfalls to avoid—and Regal's terrible life choices should be a cautionary tale for everyone.

After we ate and the guys said goodbye to the girls and one really cute young guy who had been in the group, we headed toward the Yukon and the van to load our equipment. Marsh had hired one of the guys who worked at the resort to watch the equipment while we ate, and I could have sworn Marsh slipped the guy a business card when they said goodbye.

We loaded the equipment, including my old drum kit, and I headed to one of the portable toilets situated around the venue because I'd drank a gallon of water to quench my thirst after playing in the afternoon sun.

I came out and headed straight to the large trough with soap and water to wash my hands. After rinsing, I splashed water on my face to try to rid myself of the salty grime from sweating during the performance.

The top of my hair was long enough that I'd pulled it back in the smallest ponytail known to man. It probably looked stupid, but it was out of my face, which was all I cared about when I did it.

"Hey there. You guys rocked the crowd."

I turned to see a man in a vintage Rolling Stones tongue T-shirt and well-worn jeans. He had dark hair that was artfully slicked back, a scruffy chin, and aviator sunglasses.

"Sorry, I'm hogging the water, man. Thanks." I stepped out of his way, thinking he wanted to wash his hands.

"No, uh, have you guys been playing together very long? You sounded great together. You have a great voice, as well as skills behind the kit."

I was a bit stunned, but I grinned anyway. "Um, thanks. I appreciate the compliment. I'm not a professional drummer or singer. I'm a band teacher. I'm just sitting in with my brother's band until they can find a permanent drummer."

The guy took off the sunglasses and slid the earpiece into the collar of his shirt. "I'm Michael Cruz. I'm working as a talent booker for Masterson Management, the promoters of Rocktoberfest 2024, and you guys could tear up a stage, I'm sure. Do you have an agent?"

"Yes, they do! I'm Marshall Kensington with CEA in Los Angeles. You are?"

Marsh stepped forward and extended his hand so the guy politely shook it. "Michael Cruz. I'm booking bands for Rocktoberfest in Black Rock. I'd like to submit your band for a spot on one of the side stages. Up-and-coming bands are my specialty, and I think you guys have a great sound. I love what they did with the songs, but I'm guessing they don't have original music yet. That From the Ashes song was fantastic. Your take on it was magnificent."

I was speechless. I didn't know this guy or who Masterson Management was, but even *I* had heard of Rocktoberfest. The expression on Marshall's face was one of awe. Being cloistered in my little world in West Peoria had left me unprepared for something of this magnitude. *Playing Rocktoberfest?*

"Accidental Fire playing Rocktoberfest?" Marsh's eyebrows were in his hairline.

"Masterson Management has taken over sponsorship and promotion of the festival. They have their headliners mostly settled, but they hired me to look for new bands who deserve a shot. I like your guys, Marshall. I'd like to send a sample to Easton Masterson for his consideration to play the festival if you have one."

Marshall turned to look at me, and I smirked in return. "I'm not in the band, Marsh. You need to talk to them about this."

"Wait... You're not going to play with the band if they're invited to Rocktoberfest?" Mr. Cruz studied me, his eyes as big as saucers. "Are you sure?" He raised an eyebrow in what I perceived as a challenge.

"Like I said, I'm filling in until they get a permanent drummer, and then I go back to my job that I love very much. Trust me, those guys are very talented. They'll find the perfect drummer, and I know they'll go places. I'm just a music teacher who happens to play the drums."

I wanted to distance myself from the discussion because I didn't want to get roped into playing with both bands for any reason—as I had been roped into service when I rewrote 'Bury Me.' I wouldn't let guilt work a second time.

Marsh, however, was not to be deterred. "Sky, here, is actually Regal Ashe's son. As is River." He pointed to Riv, who waved and returned to talking to the cute young guy who'd been following us around with the gaggle of groupies.

"Man! No wonder you were able to make that song sound so damn impressive. Now that I look at you, I can see the resemblance. How's your father doing? I saw in a trade rag that he'd had a heart attack. Is he gonna be okay?"

Mr. Cruz's attention was on me, but Marsh was a true agent. "Actually, From the Ashes will be doing a mini-tour in Cali this summer. Skyler is going to play with them, and Accidental Fire will be their opening act."

"We will?" River asked as he stepped up next to me. Marsh shot him a look that should have killed its target, so Riv stepped behind me, the coward.

"We'll need a little time to consider the offer if that's okay," I responded since Marsh was too busy staring at the guy's handsome face. Someone had to speak up. River wasn't saying a word because he was a teenager and wasn't sure of anything.

"Oh, of course. The festival is in October, as I'm sure you know. I need to speak with Easton as well, so I won't make any promises, but I'm very interested. Let's stay in touch, shall we?" Michael produced a business card, directing it toward me. Marsh snatched it out of his grasp before I could blink.

"Will do. Nice to meet you, Michael. Enjoy the rest of your day." Marshall then ushered us to the Yukon and the van.

Sandy was already behind the wheel with the air-conditioning blasting. He turned to me as I got into the front passenger seat. "What took so long? Who was that guy?"

I noticed he'd repositioned the Yukon's passenger-side mirror so he could see where we'd been standing as we talked with Mr. Cruz. *That's interesting.*

"He's a talent scout for a big festival in Nevada later in the year, and he's interested in the guys playing on one of the stages. I told him they needed a few days." I buckled my seatbelt and waited for the others to join us.

"Did he ask you out? Is he your type?"

The slight tremor in Sandy's voice told me he wasn't as sure of himself as he wanted me to believe. I wanted to tell him I loved him, but something held me back. I wasn't sure why, but something told me to wait.

"No. He didn't ask me out. He gave his card to your brother. He only talked about business with me." It wasn't a lie.

"A guy like that interest you?"

I didn't know how to answer him. I mean, the guy was hot, but I wasn't that damn easy. "I'm not looking, but if I met him in a bar, I might consider letting him buy me a drink."

After that, there was no more talking between us during the drive from Lee Canyon to The Strip. We pulled into the driveway of the Intercontinental Resort and Casino. It was a beautiful property—nothing I'd ever seen before because I didn't have the money to go to Vegas, nor did I have anyone to go with.

As we drove past massive resorts and casinos, there were hordes of people walking on both sides of Las Vegas Boulevard, and everyone appeared to be having a lot of fun. When I glanced to my left, I could see Sandy Kensington was an exception to the excitement running through the pedestrians we passed.

Chapter Twenty-Two

Sandy

Were my feelings hurt? Was I acting like a spoiled brat? Was this what jealousy felt like?

I was a stupid man in many ways, which I'd certainly concede to anyone. I'd never much cared what people thought of me—or so I told myself.

My father had been a huge sports fan, so I started playing football at a young age to try to get his attention and make him proud. I learned that as a member of a team, there were certain rules I needed to follow: be loyal to your team both on and off the field, brag about the girls you bang whether or not you *actually* do it, and regardless of what you see a teammate do, never rat them out—no matter how bad their actions are or who they're harming.

I'm sure my old high school teammates were pissed when word got out that I was gay. They probably mentally reviewed all our interactions back in the day and wondered if I had a hard-on for any of them. I hated to tell them, but I hadn't wanted any of them.

As I sat in the driver's seat of my SUV, I thought about some of the shit I didn't learn because I was in that jock mindset for so long. I never tried to put myself in someone else's shoes to understand their feelings. My feelings were all that mattered to me back then.

All the players on my various teams were spoiled. We got special exceptions to get out of class when we wanted, additional tutoring if we were having trouble in a subject, and nobody fucked with us in the halls, the cafeteria, or in our classes. Jock privilege was alive and well back then. Based on some of the shit I'd seen my professional teammates pull over the years, I'd say it still was.

The jealousy thing, though, was throwing me off. I didn't have to do much more than show up somewhere to get a girl's attention in high school and college. I didn't have girlfriends, though some thought they could claim the title.

In college and then again in the NFL, I snuck around and picked up guys, committing to nothing beyond a blowjob or a quick fuck in a public restroom or a dark hallway. If I needed a date for an event, my agent fixed me up with a nice young woman who wanted to be seen with a professional athlete. Some people lived for that shit, as I'd come to learn.

I couldn't remember twenty percent of their names if I tried. It was embarrassing as I thought about it as an adult. What a foolish asshole I'd been.

If another guy hit on a young woman I was with, I didn't give a damn. I'd thank them for going with me to the event, and I'd go home. No care about whether they got home okay or whether I'd been rude by letting them go off with some rando.

Why did Skyler's conversation with a good-looking guy bother me so much? The guy was smaller than me and not nearly as muscular, so I won on that point. Was that really a win?

Skyler had smiled at this Cruz guy the way I wanted him to smile at me, and the two of them seemed to be getting awfully cozy by the portable toilets, which pissed me off.

I'd sent Marsh over to investigate, knowing he'd break it up and fill me in later. Here I was, trying to make some headway with Skyler, and now, suddenly, I had to worry about other guys drawing his attention from me.

I made the left onto South Las Vegas Drive. "I reserved three suites."

"I'm guessing Marshall will want to room with Goldie again." Arlo and River high-fived while JD chuckled in the third-row seat.

"I thought Marshall was interested in Goldie, but when we were talking to Mr. Cruz, I saw something in Marshall's eyes that had me wondering if I'd misjudged." Skyler shrugged.

"Marshall? Really?"

I'd noticed my brother staring at Goldie a lot, but it hadn't occurred to me he might be interested. I hadn't bothered to inquire about my brother's personal life because I'd been wallowing in my own self-pity for the last year. Was my brother walking on the queer side of life now? Mom and Dad would have a shit fit I'd like to witness.

River sat forward and put a hand on my shoulder. "You don't get out much, do you?" That brought a laugh from all my passengers.

I glanced to my right to see Skyler grinning at me, and I was a little relieved. Maybe I needed to work on trusting him?

I pulled up to the valet and hopped out to give the guy the keys. Goldie stopped the van behind the Yukon and got out too. "What about the equipment?"

"Got it."

The valet stopped in front of me. "Welcome to the Intercontinental. Checking in?"

"Yes, and that one too." I pointed to the rented panel van behind me. "The van has music equipment, so can you park it somewhere safe?" I handed the guy a hundred-dollar bill, and he nodded.

I gave the Yukon keys to the valet, and we walked back to the van. Goldie already had the back open for us, so we all grabbed our bags and headed inside to check-in.

Marsh caught up with me pretty quickly. "You're supposed to meet Dallas St. Michael at his husband's restaurant tomorrow at ten. He's a bounty hunter, but he's worked as a bodyguard before, and I want him to give you some tips about watching out for the band while we're at venues."

"He's been security for bands?" Why did I ask?

"Begging for Trouble, who I was working with back then, was the opening band for Black Wing a couple of years ago at a charity event in Long Island. I met some guys there who've provided security for bands before, and I got their information for future reference. I called Gabe Torrente, the guy I met at the event, and he gave me the name of a colleague, Dallas St. Michael. Dallas has agreed to meet us for breakfast in the morning."

I rolled my eyes. Just what I fucking needed—my brother tagging along to annoy the fuck out of me when I was supposed to be getting tips on keeping these guys safe. Maybe I was worrying unnecessarily? Nobody had heard of them, so they should be fine. I could tackle anybody who tried to get close. That was what I did.

I went to the casino floor alone because Skyler wanted to take River to see some attractions and ride the High Roller just off The Strip. I hadn't been invited to go with them, which put me in a shitty mood.

The first bar I found had a few open stools, so I ordered a bourbon on the rocks, took a seat, and shoved a hundred bucks into a video poker machine. Five games and the money was toast, so I decided to take a walk. The casino was busy, what with it being early summer.

I slowly meandered through the ornately decorated gambling floor and sat on a couch in a cocktail lounge where a woman played piano. Many happy couples and groups were around, laughing and having a good time. I, most certainly, was not among them.

A cocktail server came by, so I ordered another drink. It seemed like a good night to get drunk.

I had a second bourbon and quickly asked for a third. It was delivered, along with a glass dish of warm nuts, which didn't hurt my feelings. I sat there, feeling sorry for myself, as I scrolled through my phone.

"Is this seat taken?" I looked up to see a beautiful woman standing in front of me. She was pointing to the couch next to me.

I glanced around the lounge to see a lot of empty seating groups, and then I took in the sight of her. She wanted more than just a seat, it seemed. "I, uh, I'm waiting for someone."

She smirked and sat anyway. "I doubt it. If you were waiting for someone, you'd be looking around for their arrival, not studying..." she leaned over to look at my phone, finding an ad for a heating wrap, "alternatives to seeing a chiropractor. How've you been since you quit football, Sandy Kensington?"

Oh shit! Did I take this woman out when I was here with the team for a game or some kind of event?

I coughed, nearly swallowing the whiskey down the wrong pipe. "Excuse me. Do we know each other?"

My unwanted guest smirked. "You don't know me, but I know you. You cost me a hundred grand in 2022 when you sacked Tanner Robertson in the last game of Denver's regular season."

I chuckled and shook my head. "Sorry."

She put her purse on the couch between us and pulled her long hair back into a ponytail, using the elastic she had around her wrist before reaching into her bag and retrieving a pair of glasses. She popped out contacts and put them into a napkin as she held her hand up for a server and slid on the glasses.

I sat forward and stared at her. "So, you bet against the Breeze? You were cheering for the Mustangs?"

My guest chuckled. "I'm a Mile High girl all the way. I'm being rude. I'm Mary Ellen Gaye." No idea who that was, but she looked as though I should.

The server stopped at our table and smiled. "Hi, love. I'll take a very dirty martini and give Mr. Kensington another of whatever he's having, please."

"Certainly, Ms. Gaye." The young woman damn near curtsied before she returned to the bar.

"I'm sorry, but I'm at a disadvantage. Should I know you?" I felt like a moron.

Ms. Gaye chuckled. "Oh, you should, but it's okay that you don't. I run Gaye Realty in Denver. My father was Ansel Gaye."

Nope. No idea. I shrugged.

"No matter. So, what's got you sitting here alone? You look like someone kicked your puppy." The server returned with our drinks, and Ms. Gaye quickly signed the check before I could object.

I wasn't tackling that one. "What brings you to Vegas, Ms. Gaye?" She was definitely glamorous. She was older than me, maybe late forties or early fifties, but the woman was gorgeous.

"I'm here for a business meeting. I just sat through an abhorrently boring pitch over dinner, and as I was returning to my room, I saw a handsome, albeit sad, man sitting alone. Once I figured out who you were, I couldn't resist bending your ear."

I chuckled. "It's nice to meet you, Ms. Gaye. I'm here with a band who played at Mountain Fest earlier today."

"And they played poorly? Are you in the band?"

That made me laugh. "No. They played very well, and no, I'm not in the band. I have absolutely no musical talent except to turn on the radio. I'm the alleged security for the band because my brother manages them."

"So, why aren't you with them if you're providing alleged security?" That thought hadn't even occurred to me.

"They're not very famous yet. After their set at the festival, they were followed around by a group of young women who wanted autographs. I was there to see that nobody got handsy. This was their first professional gig." I remembered recording Skyler as he played and sang. Based on the videos I shot, one would get the impression he was a one-man band.

"Darling, I'm of the opinion that everyone is just one step from fame. It's a matter of them realizing it themselves. Now, as I recall, you got roasted for being gay, so I'm going to guess the reason for that long face has everything to do with a man. On that, we can certainly relate."

Mary Ellen Gaye told me her heartbreaking tale of falling in love with a young man while she was attending NYU, only to lose him in a street racing accident, tearing up a few times as she told me the story.

"I lost our baby after I found out he'd been killed, and I was completely wrecked. A few years later, I married an older man—one of my father's longtime friends—who thought I would be his perfect trophy wife. Ansel discovered the guy was embezzling money from his own company, so he reported Daniel to the SEC. Daniel went to jail after taking a plea deal and giving me a nice divorce settlement. He was released on parole recently, and now I feel as though I'm being followed, but I'm sure I'm not."

We both glanced around, which was weird. I saw a few guys staring at the two of us, but neither looked like they were the kind of guys who would stalk someone.

"Anyway, what's your story?" She signaled to the server for another round, and I knew I'd have a hell of a headache in the morning. The beauty was I didn't know her, and she didn't really know me, other than I'd cost her money, so why not spill my guts?

"I'm in love with a guy unlike anyone I've ever met. I could go on and on about how great he is, but you don't care about that. The thing that's got me wrapped around the axle is that I don't think he trusts me, and I don't know how to fix that. I mean, we haven't known each other very long, but I would give up everything I have to be with him." I meant every word, though I was pretty sure I sounded like a drunken fool.

Ms. Gayle smiled. "Be careful about that. Daniel thought I felt the same way, but as I began seeing his true colors, I knew what he was after—my father's money."

I nodded. "If you met him, you'd see Skyler's not like that at all. He's a band teacher in a Midwestern town.

He teaches choir and jazz band too, and he's a musician. He doesn't want to quit his teaching job to play music professionally, though I'm sure he could succeed. I just...I love him and want to be with him, but we have a few stumbling blocks. We don't know each other very well, and we live a thousand miles apart. It feels insurmountable from where I sit."

Ms. Gaye laughed loudly. "If you love him and it turns out he loves you, none of that shit matters. I need something to soak up these martinis. Would you care to escort me?"

We went to a celebrity chef's burger place, stuffing ourselves with burgers and fries while swapping stories from our lives. I walked Mary Ellen, as she told me to call her, to her room because we were both drunk, and then I staggered to the front desk and got a room so I didn't wake River and Sky when I drunkenly stumbled into our suite. I let myself into a room one floor below our suite and fell asleep fully dressed. *Welcome to Vegas...*

Chapter Twenty-Three

Skyler

"What the hell are you doing?" The incessant pecking on my shoulder scared the hell out of me.

I turned around to see JD and Arlo, and they were cracking up at my sad covert stalking, the jerks. I was huddled beside a goldfish slot machine, watching Sandy sitting with a beautiful woman in a nearby lounge. They were laughing and talking and drinking, and I was pissed.

"I'm—what the hell are you two doing? Is River wandering around down here?"

We'd gone to a few places—Omni Mart for the trippy vibe they had. New York, New York to ride the rollercoaster and play in the arcade. We'd watched the fountains at Bellagio and eaten pizza until we were ready to bust. I'd reached my time limit without Sandy, so I took us back to the hotel and sent the guys to bed.

Once I knew everyone was tucked into their rooms for the night, I knocked on Sandy's door. When he didn't answer, I opened it to see he wasn't there, so I went looking for him. Finding him in the martini lounge in the casino, I sat at a slot machine nearby. My eyes were trained on the handsome man who had won my heart but didn't know it, and I didn't like what I was seeing.

"Riv's knocked out. Why are you down here? You said you don't gamble." JD glared at me before he turned to Arlo, who nodded.

"I don't gamble because I can't afford to, but I put in five dollars just to see what it's like. The last time I was here, I couldn't gamble because I wasn't old enough. Now, go away."

"Oh, are we having a band meeting?" I turned to see Goldie standing behind us.

When I glanced back at the lounge, Sandy and the woman were gone. "Shit."

Goldie laughed. "He went that way...with a lady." He pointed to his left toward the hallway that led to more restaurants.

"Let's go to bed. We'll be driving home tomorrow. Come on." The four of us walked toward the elevators, though I was tempted to stalk Sandy and the woman to see where they'd gone. What the hell was going on?

When I returned to our suite, I sat on the couch to wait for Sandy's return. Who was the woman, and why were they together? I wouldn't get any sleep until I knew he was back, and even then, I might not close my eyes.

Sweat rolled down my temple and into my ear. So annoying that it woke me from a sound sleep. I was boiling alive. I opened my eyes to see the sun blazing through the large picture window into the suite's common room. I hadn't closed the curtains when I stretched out on the couch the previous night, and now I regretted it.

I sat up on the couch, seeing the door to Sandy's room was still open and the bed untouched. He hadn't returned to the suite, and my heart shattered.

It was the worst possible outcome. I'd fucked up by not being honest about my feelings, and I'd lost my chance with him. I got up from the couch and went to my room to sulk.

River was still sleeping, so instead of lying down, I took a shower, trimming up some places that required a little maintenance. Checking my face, I decided to leave a five o'clock shadow and a soul patch on my chin before I pulled my hair back, gathering as much as I could to pull it away from my face.

When I stepped out of the bathroom, River was sitting against the headboard, hair like he'd been in a windstorm, with a self-satisfied grin. "I told you to ask him to come along."

I sighed. "I wanted to spend time with *you* before returning to Illinois." I wasn't ready to leave, but I had the feeling my time with the band and Sandy was coming to an end.

"You're full of shit, Sky. You're scared, aren't you? You don't know how the fuck to handle a real relationship. You're just like Regal."

I stomped across the room and grabbed River by the T-shirt. "You take that back."

River grabbed my hand and jerked it away from him. "Look at how fucked up our life is, Sky. God knows we've never been the picture-perfect family. Hell, our mothers are both fucking our father—or they were. Do you know Arlo might be our half-brother? Seems everyone in the band slept with his mother around the same time, so they don't know for sure who his father is, but all signs point to Regal."

That was a huge fucking surprise. "Does Arlo know?"

River chuckled. "Who do you think told me?"

My mouth dropped open because I had no damn idea my assumptions about Regal were true, though I should have expected something of the sort. I'd always waited for the other shoe to drop, and now it had. Why was I fucking surprised?

The ability to curb my language was slowly leaving me because I was dealing with Regal's bullshit once again. I'd thought I was prepared for it, but here I stood in shock. Did my mother know about Arlo? Would she be in shock as well, or was this yet another thing she'd kept from me so my image of Regal wasn't tarnished even more?

I released my brother's shirt and sat on the side of the bed. "How do you feel about this?"

My brother sighed. "Look, Sky, we've both known we weren't like the families we saw on TV. Our parents are different, ya know? They all have different ideas of family, and it's up to us to decide whether to follow their lead or run as far away from it as we can. I wanna follow in Regal's footsteps as far as music goes, but I won't be doing things the way he has. What about you?"

That was the question, wasn't it? What did I want for my life?

River and I met the guys at the IHOP across the street from the Intercontinental. JD, Arlo, and Goldie had gone sightseeing and souvenir shopping early that morning while River and I were being lazy. I had a lot on my mind, as did my little brother, and neither of us had felt like walking around The Strip.

We were put in a large booth, the three of them across from River and me. "Where's Marshall?"

Goldie smirked at me. "He had a breakfast meeting with some security guy and Sandy. Sandy looked really fucking rough when he stopped by our suite. He was wearing one of those cheap Las Vegas T-shirts and a pair of dress slacks. Musta been some night."

That wasn't what I wanted to hear at all. "I wouldn't know. Anyway, let's order. I wanna get home earlier rather than later. I need to talk to Marshall and Regal to find out what they've decided. If they're going to use a track for the song, Regal can pretend to play. I don't see that I'm really needed anymore."

Arlo stared at me. "You gotta play with us until we find a drummer. Marshall said we're gonna open for From the Ashes when they do those gigs this summer. This might be our big break, and then there's Rocktoberfest. Whatever our family history is, please don't fuck this up for us. Don't we deserve a shot too?"

The guy looked at the end of his rope, and if I had a heart left, it would have ached for him. He was right. He and River deserved their break, and if it depended on me to help them get it, I'd make any sacrifice I could.

"Yes, you do, and I'm sorry, I was only thinking of myself. I'll help in any way I can, guys." That was all I could say. My time would come to return home, and I would be more patient. Arlo, River, and I had no say in our parents. We needed to support each other.

River sat forward and focused solely on Goldie. "Yeah, yeah, yeah. What is going on with you and Marshall?" We all sat forward a little at that question, our eyes drilling holes in poor Goldie.

"What can I get ya, fellas? Separate checks or one big one?"

I knew these guys didn't have much cash between them, so I stepped up. "One check, please."

I'd eat Ramen when I got back home. I might never get a chance to hang with both of my brothers like this, so I'd better enjoy it while I had it.

We ordered our food, and then we all went back to eyeing Goldie. He chuckled. "Seriously? Nothing is going on. He's a big flirt, as we all noticed yesterday when he was talking to that Cruz guy. Marshall is in it for Marshall, all the way. He wants us to make him some money, and I get the impression he would sleep his way to the top if that was an option."

Goldie then turned to me. "Be very careful with Sandy. If he's anything like Marshall, he's probably a man-whore. You don't want an STI. A buddy of mine got a nasty case of syph and has been on meds for months. That shit will make you crazy and eventually kill you."

Goldie served the topic up on a silver platter. "I use protection, but I wanted to talk to you guys about that very thing. As we know, unprotected sex can lead to unexpected pregnancy." I pointed to River, Arlo, and myself. "There's also HIV, which doesn't just affect queer men. And there are any number of STIs you can get, and some of them are becoming more resistant to meds. Use a condom, please. Get tested. Be careful with your sexual health."

I made eye contact with each of them, though JD continued to stare at the table. I'd see if he wanted to talk, and the perfect time would be when we were driving back to Cupertino. Marshall and Goldie could ride with Sandy and the others. I'd drive the rented van with JD as a passenger.

I hoped JD had a more solid relationship with his father than I had with mine. Maybe being a big brother to all of them was something I could do. I could fly out to California or maybe meet them on the road somewhere if they got a recording contract and a tour. That was what I hoped for them, anyway.

"I'll drive the van back to Cali. JD, ride with me."

Sandy geared up for a protest, but Goldie tossed JD the keys, who handed them to me, and the two of us got into the vehicle.

Sandy was still wearing that stupid cheap-ass T-shirt. My curiosity was piqued. What the hell had happened the previous night? Did I really want to know?

We made our way through Vegas and finally took the ramp to I-15 South. It was about three hours to Bakersfield, where we'd get on the I-5, so there was time to talk.

"Don't ever get into a poker game, JD. You have a definite tell." I glanced in his direction to see him look at his hands.

"That's what Dad tells me."

A man of few words. I was a teacher. I could get young people to talk. "You got any brothers or sisters?"

"A younger sister. She's still in high school."

"Do you get along?" *Come on, man, give me something to work with.*

"She lives with Mom, and I'm staying with Dad until I can make some money and get my own place. Riv and I were trying to see if we could find something together, but he's having trouble saving. He does odd jobs and stuff, but he gives his money to his mom to help with whatever's going on in their lives. It's wild that your mom and Riv's mom are both in a relationship with your dad. Does that bother you?" JD started chewing on his cuticles, so I reached over and pulled his thumbnail from his teeth.

"I found out right before I got to Cupertino, and things have been going ninety miles an hour ever since. I haven't thought much about it, but I guess if a poly relationship makes my mother happy, I just need to support her. I'm not jealous or anything, and as unconventional as it seems, if it works for her, I'll keep my mouth shut.

"I'm assuming your parents divorced. I don't know Ripper as well as Dusty, but he seems like a good guy. Is it hard living with him?" We were meandering, but hopefully, he was becoming comfortable with me.

JD chuckled. "He's great most of the time, but he wasn't great when I got crabs last summer. He had a fit and gave me a lecture every day when we had to keep doing so much laundry. I used a condom, but they don't protect against crabs. I know what you mean about STIs. It's fucking embarrassing, and they itch like crazy. I had to shave off my pubes. I've kept them shaved since then."

I nodded. I hated to tell him, but... "You can still get them on other parts of your body—under your arms, on your legs, anywhere you have coarse hair."

"You can? How the fuck do you keep from getting them?"

"Don't have sex with someone who has crabs." It was the most straightforward way to explain it to him.

"How do you do that?" JD's face was scrunched in confusion, and he was biting his lip. Ripper really should have had a talk with the kid after that episode.

"Don't have sex with strangers…like groupies or randos you meet at concerts. I'm not saying all girls who go to concerts have crabs, but you don't know their sexual history."

That was something I needed to abide by as well—Sandy Kensington was a great example. He'd said he hadn't slept with women, but he wasn't specific about sleeping with other guys, not that I had a standing in his life to demand numbers from him. Was I going to be sorry for a reason other than the fact he was fucking with my head?

Chapter Twenty-Four

Sandy

I hurried back to the suite to see that River and Skyler had already packed their things and were gone. I'd overslept and woken with a horrible hangover, so the only thing I could do was get my shit together, find a clean shirt, and meet Marshall and the bounty hunter at an Italian restaurant in the casino.

I rushed to the gift shop and grabbed a cheesy T-shirt with the Las Vegas sign. I slid into the men's room and quickly washed up, pulling on the T-shirt and slicking my hair back with water. I dried my hands and hurried out to the sign that pointed to Cucina della Nonna. Thankfully, it was just around the corner.

When I arrived at the restaurant, I could see the place wasn't open, but there was a lot of activity inside. "Hello?"

A handsome guy walked out of the kitchen wearing a bonnet thing on his head. He was dressed in a chef's coat with black pants, and he had a friendly smile.

"I'm sorry, but we don't open until four. If you'd like to make a reservation, I can help you."

A larger man stepped out behind him in the same getup. "Cosa vuoi?"

"Rafael, no one speaks Italian here except you." The shorter guy giggled and the larger man laughed as well.

"If I didn't love you like a little brother, Parker, I'd fire you." The taller man definitely had an accent that I now assumed was Italian.

"You can't fire me. I'm doing you a favor. How does Dallas put up with your moodiness?" The shorter guy, Parker, giggled again.

"He likes to punish me."

That was a little more than I needed to hear. Another, even larger, man stepped out from the kitchen. "Are you Sandy Kensington?" I nodded.

"Come on back. I'm Dallas St. Michael. This is my husband, the chef, Rafael, and his business partner, Parker Colson. Marshall's already in the back having coffee."

The two chefs gave me fist bumps before returning to the kitchen. I followed Dallas through to a large wooden table to the left of the kitchen, where Marshall was sitting with another man wearing a crisp white shirt, jeans, and cowboy boots. I glanced at my brother, who shrugged.

"This is Shep Colson. He works for my cousin-in-law in New York. He's here for a visit, so Gabe asked him to sit in on this. Grab a seat. Coffee?"

"Yes, please. Mr. Colson, nice to meet you." The guy was definitely not someone I'd want to run into in a dark alley. His hair was short and brown, like a military cut. His hands were thick, as though he worked with them a lot, and he was staring at me. It made me nervous.

Colson stood and extended his hand. He wasn't as tall as me, but only by a few inches. His body was solid—he could kick my ass, I was certain. "Nice to meet you. I've seen ya play. Sorry about you leavin' the game. Take a seat."

He pulled out the chair next to him, so I sat, hoping I'd made the grade in Colson's eyes.

A young man came from the kitchen with a tray. He placed an empty cup in front of me, a carafe, sugar, sweetener, and cream in the middle of the table, and left without a word. St. Michael came out of the kitchen, laughing. He was carrying a platter, which he placed in the middle of the table. There were various breads that all smelled incredible.

"My Magic Chef's biscuits." Colson looked at St. Michael. "Does Rafe make things you love when you're at home? Parker won't make biscuits for me at home. Says if I want them, I gotta come to Blue Plate."

St. Michael laughed. "You gotta treat him right, Smokey. You've been married longer than me, but I find if I'm taking care of business at home, my bed's hot every night."

Marshall smirked in my direction, the fucker. "How about you, big brother? How's your bed?"

"Empty. How about yours?" I sneered at him, making both men laugh.

St. Michael extended his hand to Colson, who spoke first. "Marshall tells me you're going to provide security for From the Ashes and Accidental Fire while they're doing a small-venue tour this summer before they go to Rocktoberfest. I know you're a hell of a defensive tackle, but can you shoot a gun?"

I swallowed the bite of biscuit that had turned to sawdust in an instant. "I-I, uh, I have a handgun for protection and a gun permit. A couple of the guys on the team talked me into it, and I went to the shooting range a couple of times during the off-season."

"Do you have a concealed-carry license?" St. Michael asked.

"Uh, no. I don't carry it with me. I just have it in the gun safe at home in the hall closet. Is a gun necessary to provide protection for an unknown band and a geriatric one?" It all seemed silly to me.

A six-inch blade stuck in the table in front of me. My head nearly screwed off my shoulders, trying to determine where it came from. I saw St. Michael's husband standing by the kitchen door with a smirk.

St. Michael turned in his chair and laughed loudly. "Now, let's not scare the guest."

The chef came over to the table and removed the knife from where it had embedded in the table, pushing the wood down before walking around the table. St. Michael wrapped his arm around the chef's ass as the scarily sharp blade disappeared into the sleeve of the chef's smock.

"If we knew where a threat came from, we could eliminate it before it happened. Keeping someone safe requires anticipating dangerous scenarios before they happen."

The chef kissed St. Michael on his head and turned to us. "Now, what can I make you for breakfast?"

That knife trick scared the fuck out of me, but it drove home a point—I was probably horribly prepared to be a bodyguard for anyone, much less the man I loved.

"What do you think?" Marsh was riding in the passenger seat of the Yukon with me instead of Skyler being where I needed him to be. He was driving the van with JD riding shotgun.

I glanced in the rearview to see Goldie, Arlo, and River were all sound asleep. "I think you need to hire a professional. Those guys know their shit, and I'm not sure what I'd do if someone came after either band."

Marshall hissed at me. "Nobody is coming after any of them. Don't worry about it. And for god's sake, don't carry a fucking gun. You'll shoot yourself in the foot."

That was probably right. I hadn't shot my gun since I renewed my permit two years ago. I should see what I needed to do to renew it and when.

One thing kept circling my head from the breakfast conversation. It was Shepard Colson who'd spoken of meeting his husband and trying to keep him safe from a substantiated threat.

"What's a substantiated threat?" It was clear as a bell that Colson was former military—turned out, he'd been in special forces. His demeanor, word choices, and the way he'd scanned the room for threats were like a beacon.

"A substantiated threat is when you know someone is trying to harm your primary. Someone is coming for them, so you keep your gaze sharp and your mind clear for any signs. It's the unknown threats that scare the shit outta me. When you don't know they're coming or what to look for. That's when I get worried.

"I almost lost Parker because of a situation we didn't anticipate. Thankfully, my family was there to help me. It's hard for me to keep my wits about me when that man's around. I already loved him, and I missed some of the signs that we were in for a sneak attack. Thankfully, my mom had my six that day."

Shepard had gazed into the distance, and it was a few minutes before he returned to the conversation. St. Michael gave me a few tips—always station myself where I can see my primaries, which is what he called the people to be guarded.

Make note of all points of entrance and exit. When possible, have a clear view of the entire area where your primaries are waiting. Things of that sort, which I might not have given a second thought to. I knew how to scan the field to know where other players were during a play, so I was guessing it wasn't that different.

"Where'd you sleep last night?" Marsh asked as he scrolled this phone.

"I booked a room so I didn't wake River and Skyler. I met Mary Ellen Gaye last night. She lost a hundred grand because I sacked the QB of the Denver Mustangs in 2022, and she felt the need to tell me. Turned out to be a nice lady. I walked her to her room and realized I was hammered, so I got a separate room and slept it off." My head was still pounding, but it was getting better.

"Should I meet her?"

I did a doubletake at my brother. "What's your deal?"

"I'm a free agent. I can be what I wanna be." I didn't know what that meant, but I wished him the best of luck.

We stopped twice along the way to use the facilities and get something to drink. Skyler made sure he wasn't alone with me either time, which pissed me off. By the time we took the exit off the I-5, we'd driven over five hundred miles.

I was ready to get out of the fucking SUV, lock Skyler in a goddamn room, and not let him out until he fucking talked to me.

"When are you going back to LA?" I glanced at Marsh as I merged onto the 101 in Gilroy, near my place.

Marshall turned to face me. "What the hell crawled up your ass?"

I had an easy answer for that. "Nothing."

He was quiet for a minute, then he laughed. "Look, man, I have no idea what's going on between you and Skyler, but figure it out, please. This is like threading a needle with this damn song and the two bands. Clearly, what I saw and sent to Hammond Studio is exactly what they want for *Hurricane Alley*. It's got such a great beat that can be mixed up and fit the mood of the scene. I need Skyler to want to help with that, and if I gotta use you to get it, then I will."

I had no doubt he'd use whomever he needed to because that was Marshall's MO to his core. Always had been.

When we arrived at my place, Skyler was kind enough to pull the van forward so I could park in my garage behind the pool. When I turned off the motor, we all bailed out, and Goldie and Arlo perused the cars I had inside.

As I stared at the exotic vehicles, I kept asking myself again why I had them when I didn't drive them after the shine wore off. I was swamped with embarrassment at realizing I'd tried to replace living, breathing people in my life with material things others admired. God, I was an idiot.

Something occurred to me, so I turned to Marshall. "How are they getting to the gigs over the summer?" Marsh pointed to the U-Haul van Skyler had just exited.

"That won't work. They can't all fit in there with their equipment, Marsh. Where will they sleep? They'll have to stay at least one night on the road."

Yes, the dates were spaced out enough that they wouldn't have to be on the road for long periods of time, but there would be the drive to the venue, the concert, and then the drive back home. My brother had lost his fucking mind if he thought that shoving all of them in a van with their equipment was going to work.

"Look, this is my job, Sandy. I didn't come on the sidelines in Chicago and tell you how to do your damn job, so don't start telling me how to do mine." He stormed out of the garage and across the pool deck to the back door of my basement.

Skyler entered the garage and stepped in front of me. "Where's Marshall?"

My eyes left the door where Marsh had just entered and settled on the beautiful man in front of me. "Fuck Marshall. What do you need?"

Skyler's eyes grew huge before his lips thinned in anger. "He's supposed to be their manager. They need to know where to go and what to do next. Those four young men are at his mercy right now, and he's not giving them any information. Riv and I can't go back to my parents' place because Regal is going to throw a fit when he hears we debuted 'Bury Me' without their permission."

I might not know much about the music industry, but I knew about contracts because I'd worked through a few myself over my sixteen years in professional sports. "Did you or any of the boys sign anything?"

"No, but I guess they have a verbal agreement with him to represent them." Skyler's voice sounded quite concerned, and his compassion for the boys touched me deep inside.

I almost reached up to touch his face, but I didn't. "Who paid for the rental van?" I was trying to figure out if anything of value exchanged hands between the members of Accidental Fire and my brother. I loved him, but if Marshall wouldn't see reason, then I would find someone who could represent AF, and my brother could deal with telling his boss he'd fucked up again.

"Uh, Marshall reserved it, but Goldie's dad paid for it. He was the one who actually picked it up for Goldie, loaded all of the sound equipment into it, and brought it over to your place yesterday morning."

I reached for my wallet and handed Skyler about five hundred dollars. "Please find out how much it cost and pay Goldie for it. Did Marsh pay for any of the meals or anything?"

"The meal we had at the camp, the trailers we slept in, and the Suburban I used when I first got to town. We paid for our own food at the festival, and I paid for our dinner last night and breakfast this morning. He's paying for the piano at your place. Why?" Skyler's nose wrinkled a little in confusion. It took everything inside me not to kiss him.

"Because for a verbal contract to be binding, both sides must agree to the terms, and then there must be an exchange of something of value, like Marshall paying for the van. The Suburban doesn't count because it was before the new band was formed, and the piano is necessary for you to do work for From the Ashes. When it comes to the band, if he hasn't been paying their expenses, he hasn't lived up to his end of a verbal contract."

"How do you know that?"

Part of me wanted to be offended, but he had a point. I was a jock, and except for a few people in sports, we weren't exactly known to be members of Mensa.

"I've had a few contracts in my life, and when it comes to my money, I want to know all the details. You guys did an unpaid gig on Saturday, so there's nothing to get there. Also, I paid for the campground stuff, so that's covered. The equipment you're using is all yours, and the sound equipment is from Goldie's dad, right?"

Skyler nodded but held up his hand. "He has Michael Cruz's business card though. He was our connection to Rocktoberfest."

"I'll find him. Don't worry about Cruz. You and River are welcome to stay here, you know. You guys can store your equipment here, we'll return the van, and you and Riv will be my guests. It's the least I can do after my earlier fuck up. Besides, if you're here, maybe I can get you to talk to me so we can straighten things out between us." *I could fucking hope, right?*

"Is there something to straighten out between us? What would your girlfriend think about that?" His snarl told me everything I needed to know.

Bam! Out of left field, he's pissed again! I have no idea what he's talking about. "*What girlfriend?*"

"The woman you spent the night with. I waited for you to return to the suite so we could talk. You didn't come back all night." Skyler turned to storm off, but I wrapped my arm around his waist and picked him up, carrying him kicking and screaming from the garage to the pool deck.

"Where's your phone?" I wasn't a total douchebag.

He patted his pockets. "I forgot it in the van. Don't you dare—"

Splash!

When we both surfaced, I grabbed his beautiful face and held it so I could look into his gorgeous brown eyes. "There's no woman. I'm in love with you, and there won't be anyone else if there's any fucking chance I could have a future with you."

I brushed the water out of his eyes, and then he kissed me. He wrapped his arms around my neck, and his tongue slid inside my mouth, tangling with mine. I moved his legs to wrap around my waist and held him tightly. It was exactly as it should be when you love someone.

He broke the kiss, his breathing labored. "Water went up my nose, but I love you too."

This time, I attacked his mouth before a loud round of applause caught our attention. I ended the kiss, and we both looked around to find the members of Accidental Fire standing at the side of the pool, clapping.

"Thank fuck." River shook his head and picked up his backpack to carry into the house. He came out with two towels from the closet in the gym before going back inside.

"Don't mess it up," Arlo called as he grabbed his backpack.

Goldie followed Arlo inside, and JD squatted at the side of the pool. "Since you two are in love now, can I have Skyler's old bedroom?"

We stared at each other and smirked before turning to JD. "*No!*"

JD laughed as he went in through the basement entrance to follow the rest. It seemed as if I had five new roommates, only one of whom I wanted.

We climbed out of the pool and stripped down to our underwear since there were people in the house. "What are we going to do about Marshall?" Skyler was sitting on the large lounger next to me.

I chuckled. "We're not going to do anything about Marshall. He'll be leaving tonight, and then we'll figure it out tomorrow, okay?" I leaned forward and kissed Skyler's forehead.

"So, who was the woman?"

I grinned. "Her name is Mary Ellen Gaye. She wasn't my date. We sat in the lounge for a while and discussed our failures, then we kept each other upright until we got to

Burger Heaven in the food court. I walked her to her room, and then I went to the front desk and got another room where I passed out in my clothes. Do you like my fancy T-shirt?" I pointed to the seven-dollar masterpiece on the pool deck.

Skyler laughed. "Did you think to get one for me?"

I smirked. "You can have that one. Next time we go, we'll get matching ones. We'll be *that* couple."

His laugh was music to my ears.

Chapter Twenty-Five

Skyler

The band members were watching some stupid movie in Sandy's media room when I stuck my head inside. They'd had hot wings delivered, so the whole room smelled like cayenne pepper. I poked Riv in the arm and leaned forward, still in a towel and my briefs. "Who paid for those?"

River paused the movie and turned to stare over his shoulder before his nose wrinkled and he hissed. "*Shiiit!* Are you in here naked? That's disgusting."

All eyes turned to me, and I laughed. "No, dipshit. Listen, don't let Marshall pay for anything else. I'll explain it to you all tomorrow. If you need money, come talk to me, you brat." I mussed his hair and went upstairs, where Sandy had already taken our clothes.

Sandy met me at the top of the stairs with a soft bathrobe. "We can take a shower in my room, okay? Sleep in my room with me, please? I don't want to be away from you."

His sage-green eyes stared into my soul, and I was a bit speechless until my brain kicked in again. "Do you mean these things you say?"

It was hard to believe a former NFL defensive tackle could be so honest about wanting to be with me. Yes, I was generalizing based on a stereotype once again. Hearing him say these things reminded me how big a mistake I'd made the night before by thinking he'd slept with that woman. He wasn't a dumb jock. He was a man who had strong feelings and was willing to share them with me. For Sandy to say he didn't want to be apart from me? It took my breath away.

"I won't say shit I don't mean. So, shower? We can order some pizza or something after if you want. I sound like a fucking sap, but I just want to be next to you. Just want to hold you."

What the hell does one say to that? Honesty was the only answer.

"I don't say things I don't mean either. Yes, I enjoy spending time with you. Yes, I'd love to shower with you, and I thought you'd already extended an invitation for me to sleep in your bed. I love you too. What's it going to take for you to believe me?"

Sandy stared at me for a moment. "Do you really love me, or are you just saying it out of guilt?"

I wanted to laugh, but I could see he was serious. "I'd never say I loved anyone if it wasn't absolutely true."

"Okay then."

We went into the bathroom and finished undressing before getting into Sandy's huge shower. He reached up and pulled the elastic out of my hair that I'd forgotten about after he'd dragged us into the pool. "Can I wash your hair?"

It was an odd request. "Uh, sure."

He moved me under the spray as he stood in front of me, his clavicle right there for the nibbling. So I did.

Sandy's strong fingers massaged my scalp, so I closed my eyes—still nibbling—and let him have his way with my hair. I could feel his caring soul in every massage of his fingers.

"Do you like your hair with a little length?" Feeling the hum of his voice through my lips as I pressed kisses to his chest was new.

The top of my hair had been longer than the sides when I started letting it grow at Marshall's insistence. Would I keep it after I wasn't impersonating a rock star any longer? I wasn't sure.

"I like pulling it back so it doesn't flop on my forehead. None of the male teachers at school have long hair except the guy who teaches shop. I'm not sure how they'd feel about me with long hair since we attend music competitions." Everyone at the school was quite conservative, which was why I wasn't out and proud there.

"Do they have strict rules against such things?" Sandy moved me under the spray and ran his fingers through the strands to help rinse out the spicy-smelling shampoo.

"Nothing I've seen in writing, but the fact that only the shop teacher has long hair, which he wears in a braid, might mean the rest of the male teachers don't think it's a good idea. I really don't give much thought to my hair, you know." Sandy chuckled as he reached for a bottle of conditioner and pumped some in his palm before slicking it through my hair.

"Well, I like it, but I liked it when you got here, so that must mean I just like *you*. Anyway, trade me spots. Let that sit for a few minutes.

"What do you think your dad and the guys in his band will think of the song as you guys performed it yesterday? I'm sure Marsh will show it to them first thing."

He proceeded to wash his body, so I did the same—washed his body. Getting my hands all over him was an opportunity I wouldn't pass up...ever.

"He'll be pissed because they sounded incredible, but I still think they'll all like what they hear. I wonder what the studio will think?"

Sandy washed his hair as he rinsed off under the spray, so I washed myself, and then we traded places for me to rinse. As I started to step out, Sandy wrapped his arms around me and pulled me into his body. Once again, his eyes locked on mine. "I love you."

I grinned at him, both of us standing under the rainfall showerhead. "I love you too." It felt good to say it and know he wasn't just saying words to get into my pants.

Sandy ducked to kiss me, picking me up and hauling me up his long torso. His thick cock brushed against mine as I wrapped my arms around his neck. He pressed my back to the shower wall, and right then, I wanted him inside me more than anything.

"Have you been tested recently?" I bit his earlobe before I sucked on it to relieve the sting.

"Mmmm. Yeah. Back in March, when I had a physical. You?"

I released his soft lobe and kissed along the side of his jaw. "Due for one before school starts."

"I can get you an appointment with my doctor. He can probably see you on Tuesday. I'm negative for all problematic issues, and my blood pressure is perfect. I have the beginning of a cataract in my left eye, and I now have reading glasses I don't wear as often as I need to. The Players' Association has a great healthcare plan."

I giggled, which was becoming too frequent a thing, but the guy had me giddy. "How about your teeth?"

He opened his mouth wide and turned his head a little from side to side. That made me laugh again. "Nice. Am I too heavy?" I wasn't fat, but I had muscle tone, so I was heavier than I looked.

"Not too heavy at all, but I don't want to drop you. Let's take this to bed. What do you say?" He winked before he put me down, making sure I had my footing before letting go. He turned off the water, and we got out.

I quickly dried off, my hard cock not losing any steam. Sandy did a quick wipe down of himself before he grabbed the plush robes and carried them into the bedroom, tossing them on the bench at the end of the bed. He opened the drawer to the nightstand and reached for a bottle of lube and a condom, tossing both on the bed.

We turned down the bedspread and the top sheet before we climbed in, meeting in the middle. Our torsos were about the same length—his strong legs were longer than mine, explaining much of the height difference—so kissing him was much easier, and I didn't hesitate. His lips were soft and warm, and when mine touched them, I could see sparks flying behind my eyelids.

Our cocks brushed against each other as Sandy's strong hands explored my sides until he reached my nipples. I gasped as he tweaked them. "Sensitive?"

"Yes." His thumb and index finger pinched until my nipples were pebbled, and then he released them, and the rush of blood returning made me warm all over.

I was anxious to get him inside me, so I reached for the lube next to his knee. "You wanna get me ready, or do you want me to do it?"

"May I?" He held out his hand, and I gave him the lube. "Down on your front, ass in the air, please."

I laughed as I assumed the position. "Are you always so polite?"

Sandy didn't answer, only chuckled before he spread my ass cheeks, his tongue circling my rim. "*Gah!*"

His deep laugh reverberated through my body where his tongue was spearing inside me. It felt wonderful, but I had to relax to let him inside.

"Mmmm. You taste good, teach." Sandy flattened his tongue and licked my hole before he slapped my right ass cheek. The sting was sharp, but the intrusion of his tongue and the circling of his middle finger made me forget immediately.

The snick of the lube bottle had my heart speeding. Sandy drizzled a trail of lube down the trench of my ass, moving his lips to kiss the spot where he'd spanked me.

"I love seeing my handprint on your beautiful skin. We'll have to explore that more the next time."

Two fingers slid inside and scissored for a moment before they were removed. "On your back, baby."

Without hesitation, I rolled onto my back, happy to see his beautiful face. "Legs on my shoulders." I easily moved my legs up to his strong shoulders.

Sandy's beautiful sage-green eyes scanned my body, making me feel self-conscious. "What's wrong? Did you— Did you change your mind?"

"Not on your life. I just love looking at you." He then reached for the condom and opened the package, sliding it on before he moved his right hand back to my hole, circling it with his thumb as his left hand slicked the condom.

Two fingers slid inside, opening me. Sandy bent me in half as he leaned forward to kiss me again. His tongue traced my lips before mine came out to play. Our mouths teased each other before he spoke. "Tell me how much prep you want. I don't want to hurt you."

"Go for it. I'm ready." God was I ready.

Sandy positioned his cock at my entrance and pushed forward until the thick head breached me. I inhaled deeply, blew out my breath, and nodded. He slid inside the rest of the way until he bottomed out, staring into my eyes.

"One sec." I sucked in another breath and released it, the sting making my skin prickle. As it started to fade, I nodded. "Ready."

Sandy pushed back on my thighs until my feet rested on his pecks, and then his focus shifted to where he pumped his cock deep inside me. "God, that's sexy as fuck."

I had no doubt it was, though I couldn't see it. "You need to put mirrors on the ceiling so I can see too."

Sandy glanced up to the ceiling and grinned. "I'll have to check into that, teach. Wanna be on top?"

"God, yes." He held on to the condom and pulled out, flopping on his back next to me as he held up his hard cock.

I put my leg over his waist and reached around to move his cockhead where I needed it. I braced my hands on his strong chest and slowly sank down. "Fuck, this is good."

"There's that bad boy who haunts my dreams. Get us there."

I rode him. It had been so long since I'd had a good fuck, and I aggressively moved on his thick dick. The stimulation to my prostate was exactly what I needed as I raced toward my climax. Sooner than I wanted, I was on the verge of spraying his chest. "I'm almost there. You?"

Every sensation was mind-numbing—my taint rubbing against his pelvis. His strong palms rubbing my inner thighs before his thumbs caressed my balls. "Come on me, teach."

I reached behind me and tugged on his balls before his pelvis titled and he pulsed inside me. I let go with him, spraying cum all over his sparsely-haired chest. My heart was nearly pounding out of my chest as I rested on the thighs he'd raised behind my back.

"Fuck, that was good." Sandy reached for me, so I leaned forward to kiss him.

"Yeah, it was, stud." I giggled as he slid from me. If our lovemaking was that good every time, I was in for a lot of fun.

Monday morning, after spending a wonderful night in Sandy's bed, not getting much sleep, I sat at the table on the pool deck and opened my laptop to log into the West Peoria School District's Student/Teacher Bulletin Board to see what was going on with the students and my fellow faculty members.

The throwback tour started on July twelfth at Brick by Brick in San Diego. That gave all of us about two weeks to practice.

I logged into my teacher account on the platform, seeing Mrs. Brownlee had made good on her threat to put up the video of our performance. She'd tagged me in an email she'd posted to the general bulletin board, and those who saw it responded and tagged me in return.

There were lots of hearts and thumbs-ups from my middle school kids, which made me smile. I quickly gave them hearts as I went down the line. My high school kids gave typical teenager responses: *Cool*, *Go, Mr. A*, and a few *Why didn't you send us tickets?*

I gave hearts to most and a laughing emoji for the ticket comments. When I got to the end of the comments on the video, I decided to make a post

> *Hey gang! Mr. A here. I wanted to thank Mrs. Brownlee for posting the video of our performance at Mountain Fest. I enjoyed playing with a group of friends who have a new band called Accidental Fire. We'll be opening for From the Ashes at a few venues in California from the middle of July through the beginning of August. I might miss the first day of school, but I'll be back, never fear. Have a great summer, everyone! Mr. Ashe*

Finishing up my post, I put up the performance schedule and said I'd take pictures at each show for our beginning-of-the-year icebreaker. I was looking forward to sharing the photos with the kids.

I clicked over to the teacher bulletin board to see a note in my inbox from Christine Quinton, the elementary school music teacher and my assistant with the high school choir.

> *Skyler -- Petey Ritter's grandmother, Elsie, died on June 8th. Rich is back on regular patrols since school's out, and he told me about it. Petey has an older brother who's in jail, so Petey was put into foster care. Rich said he wasn't taking it well and kept asking how to get in touch with you. I'll update you when I know more. Give me a call if you have time. You've got my number. Chris*

That was troubling. I'd have to call her to see what was going on. Petey was a sweet kid who didn't seem to be able to get a break.

After logging out, I finished my coffee and went inside. Upstairs, the kitchen was busy as the bandmates got themselves breakfast. Sandy, however, was nowhere to be found.

"Anybody know where Sandy went? Where's Marshall?"

River glanced at Arlo, who was shoving a bagel in his mouth. He held up a finger, so I waited. "Marsh said we should go to your parents' house to discuss a practice schedule. He and Sandy were arguing when I came down for coffee."

"About what?" JD asked from his seat beside the large island.

"Some shit about Marsh trying to take advantage of us." Arlo turned to me. "Is this what you meant when you said not to let Marshall pay for anything?"

I poured myself a cup of coffee and stood in front of the kitchen island, leaning against the large farmhouse sink. They deserved an explanation, and it appeared up to me to give them one.

"Let me say I've never had an agent, so I'm only going on information Sandy told me. He believes his brother will try to enforce a verbal contract you don't have with him. He represents From the Ashes, and Sandy and I think he'll put their best interests ahead of yours. Sandy and I don't want to see that happen. I'm going for a run, and when I get back, we'll borrow Sandy's Yukon and go over to the farm. Clean up your mess."

I hurried upstairs and changed, pulling my hair back after slipping on my running shoes. I stepped out of the spare bedroom I'd been using and stopped to look into Sandy's room, remembering what we'd shared almost all night. I wondered if his ass was as tender as mine was this morning.

I went downstairs and headed toward the front door just as it opened. Sandy was chugging a bottle of water as sweat poured down his gorgeous body. His T-shirt was draped around his neck and his grin was a mile wide.

"You're late today," he teased. I usually got up before the sun and went for a run, but I was too lazy to move this morning, so I'd slept in and hadn't heard him leave earlier.

"Yes, well, I wonder why? Someone fucked the life out of me," I teasingly whispered in his ear.

He chuckled. "Yeah, tell me about it. I was hoping you weren't up yet."

It was my turn to grin. "You could go another round?"

"I doubt it, but I sure as hell would like to try." He kissed the side of my neck. "What's the plan for today?"

"After my run, may I borrow your Yukon? We need to go to my mother's place to meet with Marshall and From the Ashes regarding a practice schedule. We've got to hash out how they want to proceed with the song. You don't want to be a part of that."

Sandy smirked. "I really don't because I'm afraid I'd beat the life out of my own brother. Don't let him talk you into anything."

"I hate that this mess has you guys on opposite sides." I truly did hate it. I knew Sandy loved Marsh, and I didn't want to come between them.

"Teach, don't worry about me. Marsh and I have a history of fighting, I promise you. This is nothing. I don't want you to worry about it. Where *is* Marsh?"

I shrugged. "Not sure. He must have left after you went out for your run. I'll be back."

I headed out, trying to clear my thoughts as I ran so I could prepare to do battle with Regal. I hoped it wasn't necessary, but I needed to be ready. He was a cagey old dog, still as manipulative as ever. He would definitely try to take advantage of me, and if he could talk my mother into helping him, he'd likely win.

Chapter Twenty-Six

Sandy

July 13th San Diego – House of Blues

The luxury motorcoach I rented for Accidental Fire was parked behind the concert venue on Sixth Avenue. The guys and I had ridden to San Diego in it while From the Ashes had flown. It was an in-your-face look at the different stages both bands were in on their career path. At least Accidental Fire wasn't riding in a beat-up VW bus.

The band and I were sleeping on the bus, while Marsh and From the Ashes were sleeping down the street at the Westin. They'd fly home the next morning while we'd be riding back to San Jose on the bus. Based on the ride down, the guys were excited and didn't mind being cooped up for so long. I, however, had been going stir-crazy.

Things had been quite tense between both bands the previous night and were shaping up to be even worse tonight. Only Ripper spoke to the guys in Accidental Fire and had even hugged all of them before they took the stage.

"Hello, Judas."

I glanced over my shoulder to see my brother staring at me. He wore a From the Ashes T-shirt and skinny jeans that were too young for him. They looked great on Goldie and River, but Marsh was thirty-five. It was time to wear big-boy pants.

My guy was sitting behind the drum kit on the stage, waiting for the curtain to open, along with the other band members. Skyler had been working with Accidental Fire—or AF as they called themselves—on a new song. It was one of the songs Skyler had written, and I'd heard it one night months ago. I thought it was great, but my guy was less than pleased with it.

AF wasn't allowed to play 'Bury Me,' but From the Ashes wasn't capable of playing the new version. They were all at a standoff, and everyone was fucking frustrated, but none more than Marshall because he couldn't send great reviews of the song to Harmon Studio since the ones from the night before were mediocre at best, giving the old-timers props for performing at their ages.

Sky played with both bands but didn't sing with either. He didn't want his voice to set the precedent for either band's sound. When he said as much to his father, Regal decided to sing with the band and keep Sky playing drums in his place.

"Hello, asshole." I turned back to the stage. Sky had his eyes closed and was whispering something to himself. I wasn't sure if he was praying or giving himself a pep talk. I wanted to rush out there and hold him. Give him another smoldering kiss as I had before he took the stage to let him know how much I loved him. I doubted the crowd would appreciate finding me eating my boyfriend's face when the curtain opened.

"I need to talk to you, Sandy, please." The pleading in Marshall's voice had me turning my head again. It was then I noticed he seemed wired. He was fidgety and his pupils were huge. What the fuck was going on?

"What do you want, Marshall?"

We stepped away from the stage and walked over to a small alcove where we could have some privacy. "What the hell is going on with you?"

The harshness in my voice couldn't be helped. Marshall had been a complete prick for the two weeks Skyler had been practicing with From the Ashes and Accidental Fire at his mother's rescue farm.

Marsh had harassed Sky every day to sign a contract with From the Ashes, giving them not only the rewrite of 'Bury Me', but the score Skyler had written. The contract had an exclusivity clause that he wouldn't play the song with anyone other than FTA, and Skyler had refused. He'd insisted everyone sit down and hash it out, but FTA refused.

"Please, please, convince Skyler to sign the contract. He'll be compensated for the work he's done, and he'll assign his rights to his father. Skyler and Accidental Fire performed the song without permission at Mountain Fest, and those videos are circulating widely and the identity of the song has shifted from Regal and the guys to Accidental Fire. Alicia is having a fit, so please talk to Skyler."

I shook my head. "You were fucking there, and you were pushing them to perform it so you could get reviews on the song to send to the studio, Marsh. I heard you say it. You thought at the time you'd signed a new client, but you didn't want to compensate them for anything because you're only looking out for yourself. Where did the values that Mom and Dad instilled in us go?"

Was it dirty pool to remind him of how we grew up with two of the most conservative people on the fucking planet? Maybe, but I had skin in the game, and I would fight for Skyler as long as I breathed in air.

"One. Two. One-two-three-four."

Skyler was tapping out the beat to a New Radicals song they were starting with instead of their old set list, and when Arlo began playing the intro with him, I saw the crowd bobbing their heads in time to the beat.

When the band harmonized on the chorus, the audience stood from their seats and began singing along and dancing. I turned to Marshall. "You can't deny that those young men are talented. Come on, Marsh. I know your boss is pressuring you but listen to them. They deserve a shot, and you have the power to give it to them."

"Sandy, Skyler is an incredible musician with a real talent. Without him, those kids are just another garage band hoping to stumble into a break. If Skyler doesn't commit to playing with Accidental Fire, they have no drummer, and therefore, they're not a band."

Something sparked in the back of my mind. "What if they got a new drummer and Sky worked with him?"

Marshall laughed. "Yeah, because drummers are falling off trees, yeah?"

Cocky prick. "What if?"

"You find a drummer the caliber of Skyler, and I'll do my best. He'll still need to play with From the Ashes until his dad can play, but I'll try to sell it."

I nodded and walked away from him, hoping I could make it work. I knew a drummer who was damn good. I just had to convince his sister to go along with it.

We were on the bus, headed back to San Jose. Sky and I were in one of the bunks, his head on my chest as he slept. I kissed his forehead as I sent a text to Kathleen Graves, the owner of the Baltimore Shuckers. Her wife's brother was a damn good drummer, from what I remembered.

I rested my head on the pillow as I listened to Goldie and River playing Skyler's song, 'I'll Find You,' acoustically. It was just the two of them, and it sounded incredible, but I loved it so much more when Sky sang it.

My phone buzzed, and I glanced at the text from Lynette Boyer Graves.

> **Hi, Sandy. Are you kidding me? You want Hardy in Cali? When and where?**

I laughed and responded.

> **Put him on a plane to San Jose with some clothes to tour with. Give me the date and time, and I'll pick him up. I've got a job for him if he wants it. Baby yet?**

She answered with a laughing emoji.

> **How much do we owe you to take him? He'll be there tomorrow. Baby coming soon! I'll be in touch.**

I thanked her and tossed my phone on the mattress beside me as we rolled toward San Jose.

The exotic car dealer was coming on Monday morning to pick up two of my cars in exchange for the bus rental, and I truly didn't give a shit that I'd sold them. We had the bus until the middle of September, and I felt it was a fair trade. The McLaren and the Ferrari weren't my favorites anyway.

I was determined to help Accidental Fire with their pursuit of making a name in the music industry. I wasn't a professional at judging bands, but these kids were so damn talented and played with so much heart that they deserved to be recognized for their hard work.

As Clancy Morse, the driver who came with the bus, pulled up my driveway. We were sitting at the tables in the front of the bus, and the guys were chattering about the review from their performance as the opening act for From the Ashes the night before. It was glowing.

Unfortunately, From the Ashes had a less-than-stellar review.

> *I was looking forward to seeing From the Ashes in concert again because they were one of my favorite bands from my teen years. And they were still a band from my teen years...*

I was pretty sure that wouldn't please Regal and the band. *Fuck 'em.*

I leaned into Skyler's ear to whisper. "I think I have a drummer for you, but you gotta decide if he'll fit with Accidental Fire. He should be here sometime on Monday. His name is Hardy Boyer, and he's twenty. What do you think?"

Skyler turned and kissed my cheek. "God, I hope so."

Monday afternoon, I drove to the airport and picked up Hardy Boyer. His hair was green, and I could imagine Kathleen Graves rolling her eyes. She was about as traditional as anyone I'd met, aside from being married to a woman. Life was filled with surprises.

"Hey, Hardy. Remember me?" I saw him coming through security, and while I didn't have Marshall's tablet, I didn't need it. I knew what the kid looked like.

"Oh, uh, yeah. How you doin'?" He was high, but that wasn't necessarily a bad thing. I knew Riv and JD smoked. Wasn't that part of the creative process? Maybe I was being a jerk and generalizing?

"I'm good. How's your sister?"

"Knocked up." *Well, isn't he pleasant?*

"You got checked bags?" I glanced at his dirty backpack and hoped to fuck he had more clothes with him.

Hardy laughed as he patted the grungy thing. "Nope. I travel light."

I nodded and headed toward the parking garage. Sky had my Yukon, so I'd brought my Porsche. I wasn't showing off, but I had a feeling the kid wouldn't be impressed anyway. His sister-in-law owned a fucking football team.

As I turned onto the road leading to my house, the phone buzzed in the cupholder. It was Skyler. I hit the Bluetooth button on the steering wheel. "Hey, babe. I've got Hardy."

"Where are you?"

"I'm almost home. What's wrong?" He sounded nervous, and that had me worried.

"Someone broke into the garage and tore up my drum kit. It's smashed to pieces." A sense of dread hit me.

"Okay, what about the rest of the equipment?" The guys always had their guitars with them. The mics, soundboard, amps, all that stuff, was stored in a big cabinet that had taken the spot where I'd parked the McLaren. I was glad they were able to use the space and grateful Ripper had made the large cabinet for them and dropped it off.

"They broke the lock on the cabinet but didn't destroy anything. The problem is, they got into your garage. They busted in the door, somehow, and we didn't hear anything."

I sighed. "We'll be there in about three minutes. I'll call the sheriff to come out so I can get a report for the insurance company."

"I'm so sorry this happened. Maybe Riv and I should get a temporary residence? You don't need this hassle." His voice was a bit shaky.

"Hang on. We're coming up the drive now." I ended the call and sped up. I parked in the circle drive in front of the house and got out, hurrying to where Skyler stood at the entrance to the garage.

"C'mere." I took him into my arms and held him as I scanned the garage for damage.

The cars were untouched, but Skyler's old drum set he used for practice at the house was in splinters in the middle of the garage. The cymbals were bent like taco shells, and the stand that held the hi-hat was twisted like a corkscrew.

I pulled out my phone as Skyler wrapped his arms around me and nuzzled his face into my chest. I called 9-1-1 and explained the problem.

"Don't touch anything, Mr. Kensington. A deputy will be out within the hour."

Skyler's phone rang as I was hanging up. He answered it and stepped away. The guys were in the garage, so I stepped closer. "Hey, don't touch anything. The sheriff's office is sending someone out to take pictures and shit for insurance."

River, Arlo, JD, and Goldie walked over to the door where I was standing, all of them looking behind me. I turned to my right to see Hardy with his backpack, staring at the damage.

"Come out here and meet Hardy Boyer. Hardy, this is River Ashe, Skyler's brother. That's JD Horn, Goldie Robbins, and Arlo Timmons. Guys, this is Hardy. He's here to audition to be your drummer, though we seem to be out of drums."

The guys stepped forward and bumped fists with Hardy, the five of them striking up a conversation about who played what. I left them to it and walked over to where Skyler was pacing.

"Yes, Mrs. Flannery. Thank you, ma'am. Give me the number, and I'll call to talk to them. Thank you again for calling me." He looked at me, and I saw the tears. "Take this down. Three-oh-nine..." He spouted off a phone number that I punched into my phone for him.

"Thanks again, Mrs. Flannery. I'll call them right away. Bye." Skyler stared at the phone for a moment.

"What's wrong?" I stepped forward for support, but I didn't touch him because I didn't know what he needed.

"Someone broke into my house and trashed it. I mean, it's a rental, and I don't have fancy things, but my neighbor, who called the police, said they dumped everything on the floor and cut up my couch."

Okay, this wasn't a coincidence. It was beginning to sound a lot like a coordinated effort, and it pissed me off immediately. A car in the driveway caught my attention. I saw an SUV with *Santa Clara Sheriff's Office* written on the side. An officer stepped out of the vehicle. I wrapped an arm around Skyler and ushered him toward the deputy.

"Mr. Kensington? I'm Deputy Sloane. You called about a break-in?"

I extended my hand. "Yes, Deputy. This is my—"

My tongue grew in my mouth to the point I couldn't speak.

Chapter Twenty-Seven

Skyler

I stared at Sandy. His face looked as if he were mimicking a fish. He didn't know what to call me, and honestly, I wasn't sure what to call him. We hadn't had a formal discussion yet.

The deputy was staring at him, which wasn't helping anything, so I spoke up. "I'm Mr. Kensington's houseguest, as are those young guys. They're a band, and I'm the older brother of some of the members. Skyler Ashe." I extended my hand, and he shook it.

"Anyway, I was having coffee on the pool deck and noticed the door looked odd. I went to get my shoes and came out to see the door was busted open and some of the band's equipment had been destroyed. We were all here last night and didn't hear anything."

Deputy Sloane pulled a pad from the back pocket of his uniform pants and a pen from his shirt pocket and began making notes. Two hours later, he'd chatted with all of us—nobody had heard anything—and he'd taken pictures.

He turned to Sandy. "You can come by the sheriff's office to pick up a copy of the report for your insurance. I'm sure sorry about this, Mr. Kensington. We don't usually get vandalism calls out here. Do you have a security system?"

"Oh! Yeah. Let's go inside, Deputy. I'll get my laptop." Sandy and the deputy went inside, with the rest of us following.

I was still trying to figure out what to do about my house. Obviously, I needed to go back to West Peoria to assess the damage. Sandy didn't seem to think it was random, but who the hell would do something like this to me?

"I'll be right back, Deputy. Sky, would you get the man something to drink?" I nodded as Sandy rushed upstairs. The bandmates all sat around the kitchen table like our own mini audience. I rolled my eyes at them.

"I just got a call that my house in West Peoria, Illinois, was broken into last night. My neighbor called the police since I'm here. I haven't called them yet."

The deputy wrote something down and looked at me. "What do you do, Mr. Ashe?"

"I'm a band and choir director for the West Peoria school district." He wrote it down.

"Do any of your students know you're gone?"

Shit! That stupid post!

"Yes. One of my colleagues happened to be at Mountain Fest outside Las Vegas, where we played, and she posted the video of our performance. I followed up and told my students about my summer plans to tour California. West Peoria is a small town. Everyone knows where everyone lives."

The deputy chuckled. "I know the feeling. Is it possible that one of your students might be upset with you over a grade, and once they learned you weren't at home, they broke in and vandalized your home? Sounds like a coincidence to me."

With his logic, I tended to agree. "That's probably right." Sandy returned with his laptop, so I excused myself downstairs to call the West Peoria police department about my break-in. I'd need information to file a claim on my renter's insurance if everything was as damaged as Mrs. Flannery had said.

Early the next morning, Sandy and I were on a flight from San Jose to Peoria International Airport. Thankfully, we were sitting in first class at Sandy's insistence. I was coming to learn Sandy could be very persistent—like when he demanded to come with me to assess the damage.

"Why don't you close your eyes? We change planes in Dallas, and we have about two hours, so we can get a decent meal there. Don't eat whatever they serve. It's just heartburn in quasi-fancy dishes." I cracked up at his comment.

I hadn't slept much, though lying next to Sandy had been a huge comfort. Marshall had left the previous evening after he returned to Sandy's house and met the nice deputy. The guy asked him a lot of questions, many I wasn't sure were necessary to help the case.

Marshall acted squirrelly, but I didn't know if that was normal, so I didn't bring it up. The footage Sandy's security system caught was dark and grainy, which pissed him off. There was one person wearing a hoodie, and they'd used a pipe of some kind to bust the garage door. The garage camera wasn't much better, but my heart broke as I watched the person smashing my drum set.

"I can't sleep until I see how bad it is. I've gone over and over it in my head, and I can't imagine any of my students doing something so stupid. I mean, grades are sort of subjective, but I'm an easy touch. I give grades based on participation, and most of my kids are great students. I used to give them all *A*s, but I got yelled at by the other teachers, so I started letting the students grade each other and then averaged it, and that was the grade assigned. None of the grades were lower than a B-minus."

Sandy squeezed my hand. "Kids are unpredictable, based on the shit I used to do when I was growing up. Everything was done on a whim when some other asshole came up with a stupid idea. Try to relax, teach. I wish you'd let me charter a plane like I wanted. We could be fucking in a bed right now."

I chuckled. "You're great in bed, but that would have been a very expensive fuck. I can't believe I let you talk me into first class."

Sandy kissed my cheek. "My dad taught Marsh and me to watch our money, which I do for the most part, but that would have been worth every penny."

He closed his eyes and was out like a light before the hot towels came.

When we landed at Peoria International Airport—no idea what international flights left from Peoria—Christine and her police officer fiancé, Rich, were there to pick us up. Sandy had wanted to rent a car, but I had my Escape parked in the garage at my house. We didn't need a rental.

I hugged Christine when we came out of security. "Thank you for picking us up, but I told you we could get a taxi or an Uber."

Rich stuck out his hand to Sandy. "Rich Sohn, Christine's fiancé. It's great to meet you. You were a hell of a tackle." *Ah, the bonding over sports has begun!*

"Sandy Kensington, Skyler's personal valet." They laughed at that because Sandy had taken my bag from me as we walked off the plane.

"Have you gone by the house?" I asked Christine as we headed toward the parking lot.

"Rich went by. It's more of a mess than damaged. The couch was trashed, for some reason, but your clothes and things in your bedroom weren't really. It's almost like they just took the things out of the drawers and put them on the floor."

Behind us, Rich and Sandy were discussing a game when Sandy played for another team before he was traded to the Breeze. They were talking over each other, so I wasn't sure how they heard what the other said, but when they high-fived, I figured they must have caught enough of it to understand.

"Do you have any thoughts on who might have done this?" Maybe I was too close to the kids to have any objectivity. I just couldn't see any of them capable of doing something so mean.

"Rich asked me the same thing, and honestly, I couldn't see any of our music students doing this. Some of the football players? You bet, but that would mean they had to even think about you, and we both know out of sight, out of mind with that crew. Oh, but Coach Sutter got fired. I forgot to send you that little morsel. Seems he got pulled over with an underaged girl in the car. She doesn't go to our school. The story is they met online, and the girl lied about her age. Anyway, he's out, and they're frantically looking for a new football coach and athletic director.

Coach Adams said he'll double for preseason training, but he also teaches science and calculus, so he can't really do much more."

We got into Rich's double-cab pickup, and he drove us to my little house in West Peoria. "We're reviewing footage of the doorbell cameras in the area to see if we can find anything, but it's summer, and a lot of kids live on your street. Brett Aames is a good cop. If there's anything to find, he'll find it. He'll be coming by later. I'll let him know you're here so he can talk to you about this. Chris and I tried to pick up a little after Brett released the scene, and I fixed the backdoor where they broke in."

"Thanks, Rich."

He pulled his truck into my driveway, and from the outside, my house looked as it had when I left it. I pulled the keys from my pocket and let us all in through the front door. The couch was completely trashed, but then again, that wasn't a great loss.

I walked into my bedroom to see some clothes stacked on my bed while other things had been returned to the hangers. "Thank you both for cleaning up."

"Like I said, it was more like they just took stuff out of the drawers and put it on the floor. Same thing with the kitchen. No broken dishes, just stacked on the counters.

The flatware and utensils had been dumped on the counters and floor, but none of it was wrecked."

Christine stepped closer to me and patted my shoulder. "Maybe one of the kids has cousins in town and thought it would be fun to cause a little chaos? They might not be in band or choir, and I think when it came time to actually do the damage, one of them felt guilty."

"Chris, let Brett talk to him about it, honey. Let's get going if we're driving to Chicago for the registry crap."

Christine turned on him like a honey badger. "I'm not the one who's demanding we register for all this fancy stuff, Richard. It's your mother—"

Sandy covered his mouth to hide a laugh, I was sure, before he looked at the crappy carpet in my bedroom. He bent down under the bed and came up with a guitar pick. "Always the musician."

I chuckled as I stared at it. It wasn't mine, but I did have some in my drawer at school. How long had it been since I'd vacuumed, anyway?

We walked Christine and Rich, who were still arguing, to the front door and thanked them for the ride again. When I closed the door, I stared at the trashed couch. "I guess I better see if I can hire someone to haul that to the dump. I probably need to go to the store too. I got rid of anything that might go bad in my fridge, but I was so busy before I left that I hadn't picked up groceries in a while. Let me call Officer Aames to see when he wants to come by, and then we can go get something to eat since we didn't eat in Dallas."

The restaurant near our gate had been too crowded to wait for a table, so we'd grabbed some granola bars from the news stand and toughed it out. I was starving, and I was sure Sandy was too.

Sandy and I went to a local brewery to grab some lunch. We each ordered a beer and some brisket sandwiches. "You eat here often?" Sandy was taking in the sights, and I was taking in Sandy.

"Not much. It's a little pricey for my teacher's salary, though we have come here for our Christmas party. They gave us a deal, and we had that private room over there." I pointed to the closed barn door near the entrance.

"I hate to ask this, but how much does a band teacher make in the middle of Illinois?"

I laughed. "A little more than forty-six. I live in a relatively cheap part of the country, so it's doable, but there are things I do for students that make money tight." I didn't go into detail. He didn't need to hear the woes of a band teacher.

"Forty-six an hour?"

I'd picked up my beer to take a sip, and I nearly spit it out at his question. "No. A year."

Sandy *did* spit out his beer, making me laugh. I grabbed napkins from the table next to us that needed to be bused and wiped up the mess.

"How— Jeez, how do people survive on that?" I could see he was being serious.

"It's not easy, and there's just me. I'm not sure how families make it. I've taken bags of groceries to colleagues' homes and left them anonymously when I hear someone's ill or having a hard time. We try to help each other when we can. That's the best part of living in a small town." It was something I loved about living in West Peoria.

"How about other LGBTQ folks? Many in town?"

"A couple of my kids have same-sex parents, but the families seem to stay to themselves. I'm not out because I don't want to become a target for those who aren't tolerant of our rainbow family. I seriously don't step outside my social circle in town, which is very small. I go to Chicago sometimes and hang out in Andersonville. There are clubs there, though I'm not really a club guy outside of Pride."

Sandy chuckled. "My former teammate has a club in Andersonville, or rather, one of his partners does. Jackson runs a gym, I believe. Anyway, do you miss having stuff nearby like in San Jose?"

"Not really. I grew up in Cupertino. It's bigger than here, but I went to college in Carbondale, and I loved it. That's part of the reason why I took the job here. I like small-town life." Sandy started to touch my shoulder but glanced around and put his hand down. It made me sad, though I knew he was doing it for my benefit, not because public affection bothered him at all.

Our food came, and I gave him the update Christine had given me about Coach Sutter being fired.

"Jesus. That's one of the dumbest things I've ever heard."

I finished my brisket sandwich and wiped my mouth. "Yeah, not the best judgment call he could have made."

We finished our beers, and Sandy reached for the check.

"Nope. My treat. Consider it another date," I said.

We went to the grocery store to pick up enough food for the couple of days we were planning to stay, and then we went back to my place. We put the groceries away, and I was exhausted.

After closing the refrigerator door, I turned to Sandy, who was folding my cloth grocery bags to put in the pantry. "Wanna take a nap?" I gave a wink for effect.

Sandy stepped closer and wrapped me in his arms. "I could take a nap." He leaned forward and flipped me over his shoulder, smacking my ass as he carried me to the bedroom.

How was I ever going to live without Sandy when my magical summer was finished?

Chapter Twenty-Eight

Sandy

Thursday morning, Skyler went to the police station to look at the footage the cops had pulled from the neighborhood cameras, so I decided to go for a run. He didn't live far from the high school, so I took off in that direction.

It was my first opportunity to get a feel for the area where he lived and worked. I hoped it would give me more insight into Skyler and whether I had a chance in hell of convincing him to stay in San Jose with me. His family was in the area, though I wasn't sure if that was a plus or not, but I knew he cared about River and now Arlo, even if the young man wasn't for sure his half-brother.

We hadn't been doing much besides spending time together and doing little repairs around his rental. I'd replaced his back door the vandals had wrecked, and Skyler had reorganized the kitchen. His friend had tried to help him out by putting things away where she would have wanted them, but my guy liked things a certain way. Who could blame him?

I ran in the direction Skyler always pointed when he referred to the school, and I was surprised to see it was as large as it was. There was a well-maintained football field with a man walking behind a broadcast spreader. He was either seeding or fertilizing, but the field looked damn good already.

I went through the gate and jogged across the field to where the man was stopped taking a drink from a metal water bottle. "Sir? Can I help you?" he asked as he stared at me.

"Are you seeding or fertilizing?" I had a lawn care service take care of my own yard because it hadn't been my priority for the last year, and I had no idea when certain maintenance needed to be performed. I didn't ask questions.

The caretaker grinned. "Seeding. We seed twice a week during the season and once a week in the off-season. We fertilize in the late fall. Are you looking for something?"

"A friend of mine teaches here, and I was just checking things out. He doesn't live too far, so I thought I'd swing by on my run. I'm Sandy Kensington." I extended my hand, and he shook it.

"Didn't you play for the Breeze?"

I chuckled. "I did. You a fan of the Breeze?"

"Nah, but my son is. We have some colorful viewing parties when we watch games where our favorites play each other. So, who's your friend who works here?"

"Skyler Ashe, the band teacher. I guess he and the band use the field a lot too."

The man, who hadn't shared his name, grinned. "You mean *when* Sutter would let the band practice. He took pride in bullying Mr. Ashe and the band and incited the players to do it as well. Skyler, though, is a true firecracker. He was diplomatic and talked to the kids about the problems with bullying right there in front of Sutter, which used to piss the man off something fierce. It was fun to watch. All the band kids respected him a lot for how he stuck up for them."

Pride swelled in my chest at hearing how great my guy was and how much people revered him. "Yeah, he is fantastic, isn't he? I'm lucky to have him in my life. You like the area? Did you grow up here?" Seemed logical that Midwesterners stayed close to where they grew up. I'd played with a few guys who returned to their Midwestern roots in the off-season.

"Grew up in Atlanta and taught school there for fifteen years. I like it here more." We chatted for a few more minutes, and then I excused myself to finish my run.

There were a lot of nice neighborhoods in little West Peoria. There were a lot of toys in yards and bikes on driveways, much like where I grew up. Marsh and I would play with other kids in the neighborhood until it was time to go in for dinner, just like kids did in many cities and towns across the country.

Letting those memories surface had me missing those times. My parents didn't want anything to do with me now, and there was nothing I could do about that, but I could figure out what was going on with Marshall and try to fix the rift between us.

I returned to Skyler's house and realized I'd locked myself out. He was still gone, so I reached for my phone in my pocket, only to remember I'd left it inside plugged into the charger. I went to the side yard that faced his neighbor's house and turned on the hose, taking a drink. I chuckled at how kids today had likely never done the same thing. Times were constantly changing.

"Hello."

Turning off the hose, I glanced over my shoulder to see a little white-haired woman wearing an apron with flowers and a ruffle around the pockets. She was carrying a tall glass with a straw sticking out of it.

"Hi there. I'm Sandy, a friend of Skyler's. You're Mrs. Flannery, right? Seems I've locked myself out." I didn't want her to think I was here to break into his home again.

"Yes, I'm Mrs. Flannery. I've seen you working around the house. Would you like a glass of lemonade?" She offered the glass to me and damned if I wasn't thirsty. I took the glass and sipped some through the metal straw, finding it sweet and tart. The perfect thirst quencher.

"This is delicious, thank you." I hadn't forgotten my manners, even with all the testosterone I'd been exposed to my whole life.

"Would you like to come up on the porch and sit for a while? I spoke to my daughter, who works at the police station, and she said they're not nearly done with Skyler. Come sit down and have some zucchini bread. I bought some beautiful zucchini at the farmers' market on Saturday."

I wanted to say I had something else to do, but I was locked out of the house, so how much could I really have to do in a pair of running shorts and a tank top? "Okay. I'd love to, but I don't want to take you away from what you were doing." That sounded polite enough.

"Oh, nonsense. Come have a seat. I'll be right back." She took the empty glass from me and walked back to her front porch, slowly climbing the steps. Her hand touched the railing, and it wobbled, causing her to almost lose her balance.

Skyler had talked about the little old lady a few of times. She'd been the person who called the police when Sky's house had been originally broken into.

"Mrs. Flannery!" I raced over to catch her before she fell and broke something.

"Thank you, dear. I've been meaning to see if I could find a handyman to come fix that, but you know, at my age, it's easy to forget some things."

Hell, I had nothing to do while I waited for Skyler to come back. "You got some tools? I'll take a look at it."

"Oh, I couldn't ask you to do that." She took my hand and pulled me into her little house, which was a mirror of Skyler's. However, her house looked like a flower garden had thrown up all over it. I didn't realize there were that many ways to use a floral print.

Mrs. Flannery took me to the kitchen, where she opened the cabinet under the sink and pointed. The top of the red metal box was wet, so I ducked to see the pipe under the garbage disposal was leaking.

"Uh-oh. Looks like you've got a leak under your garbage disposal."

"The garbage disposal? It hasn't worked in a week. How can it leak?"

Instead of trying to figure that out, I went to work on the front porch railing. "The wooden brace is split. Do you have any wood I can use to replace it?"

"There might be something in the garage. Mr. Flannery had his workshop out there. I haven't been in there since he passed away." She opened the side door of the building behind her house that was just like Skyler's, but instead of an organized space with hooks holding brooms and snow shovels as my guy had, there was crap everywhere.

Stacks of lumber of various lengths. Random pipes tossed in a corner. A plastic bucket filled with screws, nails, and washers. Tools everywhere. It looked like a raccoon had organized it after years of scavenging.

I grabbed some scraps of wood, a saw, and a handful of screws and nails, hoping I could find one that worked. I returned to her front porch to find another glass of lemonade and a plate with the zucchini bread she'd mentioned, so I went to work fixing the railing, stopping to enjoy the treat as I worked. Once that was repaired, I cleaned up the mess and took the unused wood back to the garage.

When I returned to the front porch, I picked up the glass and the empty plate—the zucchini bread had been delicious—and carried everything inside.

The cabinet under the sink was open, and everything inside was now on the counter. There, on the floor by the sink, was a bag from Lowe's. When I looked inside, I wasn't surprised to see a brand-new garbage disposal still in the box.

There was a stack of clean rags on the floor, along with a small jar of plumber's putty and a roll of plumber's tape. Pliers and a pipe wrench were nearby.

Two hours and a YouTube video I watched on Mrs. Flannery's cell phone by a self-identifying masc lesbian installing a garbage disposal later, I stood from the floor, flipped the switch, and was relieved when the disposal came to life. Mrs. Flannery had been frying chicken while I'd been working, and the smell had my stomach growling like an angry bear.

There was a knock on the door, so Mrs. Flannery went to answer it as I started replacing the things under the sink. Thankfully, I heard Skyler's voice before she found something else that needed to be done. "Is Sandy here, Mrs. Flannery?"

"Oh, yes. He's been helping me while he waited for you to come back. How was it at the police station? Did they find who did it?"

I went to the living room, where Skyler stood at the door, a smirk on his handsome face. "They're still going through the footage because nobody knows when it happened. I rang the doorbell several times, Mrs. Flannery. Is there something wrong with it?"

"Oh dear. That's right. That nice Officer Aames told me it was broken when he checked it on my cell phone. I'll need to contact someone to come look at it."

Skyler glanced up and winked at me. "I'll call a colleague who teaches computer classes at school to see if he can take a look. We'll get you fixed up."

"I don't want to put you to any trouble, Skyler. That's very sweet of you. Can you tell him I'll be going to the salon tomorrow morning? And if he comes in the afternoon, I'll make us a nice cream tea."

Mrs. Flannery packaged up some fried chicken. "Thank you, Sandy. It was kind of you to fix the front railing and install the new garbage disposal. Heat up some green beans to go with this, boys. It'll be delicious."

We both thanked her and walked across the yard to Skyler's house. He let us inside and began laughing hysterically.

"What?"

"She suckered you! She's a pro at guilting people into helping her with things around her house for free. She probably has more money than most of the folks in town, but she refuses to pay for repairs. I've been on her roof fixing shingles and reattaching her gutters more times than I can count. I had her window screens repaired, and I've been putting them up for three years now in the spring. She gets her daughter and son-in-law to take them down, clean them, and store them in her basement before they put up the storm windows in the fall."

"Now you tell me."

Sky kissed my lips gently and pulled back to look into my eyes. "I'm sorry you got roped into helping her, but she makes the best fried chicken in town. Let me heat up some green beans like she suggested." Skyler went about opening a can and pouring the contents into a bowl to microwave them while I set the table.

"How was your day, dear?" I was teasing him because I was sure it was agonizing to sit and stare at a computer screen for hours.

"I saw some footage of someone wearing a West Peoria High School hoodie and a pair of shorts running away from my house the night after I posted on the school's electronic bulletin board. Officer Aames basically told me I brought it on myself. I guess I did."

I wrapped my arms around him. "Baby, you didn't expect one of those little peckerheads to do what they did. You were trying to be a nice guy by updating your students on what you were doing on your summer vacation. There's one little bastard in every crowd who ruins things for everyone." I knew that to be true because I had been that little bastard back in the day.

The next day, while Skyler went to the police department to look at more footage, I ended up cleaning out Mrs. Flannery's garage. Lo and behold, I found an old BMW convertible under a tarp with a bunch of shit stacked around it.

Skyler and I cracked up as Mrs. Flannery acted surprised to see it, claiming she'd forgotten all about it.

July 31st Gaslamp Concert Venue, Long Beach

I stood at the side of the stage with Skyler while we waited for the guy Marshall hired to finish connecting the speakers to the sound system. "Have the guys been working with Hardy? I'm afraid you're going to drop dead with all this practice you've been doing with both bands."

I was worried about Skyler. He was having trouble sleeping. I'd found him up at all hours of the night pacing the house. River was back home with his dad and mom and Sky's mom. Arlo and Goldie were staying with Goldie's dad. JD was back home with Ripper, and Sky was with me.

He still hadn't told anyone what happened to his house in West Peoria. I'd insisted we go couch shopping, and it was supposed to be delivered when he was back home.

It was another reminder that he was going to leave sooner than I wanted, but I'd decided I'd fly home with him when he had to go back and fly out with him when he had to perform.

Hardy was staying with us at my house in San Jose. The kid stayed high most of the time, so he wasn't any trouble. He was watching SpongeBob every time I hunted him down. I didn't give a shit what he did during his off time, but we'd brought him to San Jose to play with Accidental Fire, and if he wasn't going to do that, he needed to go back to Baltimore.

"I gotta keep him from getting high so often so he can learn shit. He's a great drummer, but he's a pothead with no motivation. I'm not sure what to do about him, and I can't leave Accidental Fire high and dry."

The roadie guy finally motioned for everyone to take the stage for the sound check. Marshall was sitting at one of the tables with Regal Ashe as they waited for the kids to do their sound check before it was the older band's turn. They had brought in some unknown guy to run the soundboard, and the fucker wasn't friendly at all.

In the back of my mind, I wondered if Regal might have something to do with the break-in at my place or at Sky's place in Illinois. I had no evidence to base the theory on, but something bugged me about the guy and the way he stared at me and Skyler.

I stepped over to Marshall, who was acting all nervous again. "I'll be right back. Keep an eye out for them."

Marsh nodded, so I went out to the bus parked on the lot behind the venue on the Pacific Coast Highway. When I approached the bus, I saw Clancy, the driver, sitting in a camp chair with an e-reader and a cigar. He wasn't thrilled with the music the guys played, so he chose to sit outside and watch the bus. He did come into the venue and help me watch out for the guys during the show, and I was grateful. The guy was a fucking wall.

"Is Hardy still in there?"

Clancy laughed and flipped the ash from his cigar onto the parking lot. "I smoke one of these a day, and you know how offensive they are. I can't sit inside that bus when that kid gets his smoke on. I don't know how we'll ever get rid of that smell before we return it to Kingman." Kingman was the dealership I rented the fucker from.

"This stops now. Open it." Clancy nodded and clicked the fob to open the doors. The wall of smoke that hit me had me backing out of the bus and hacking up a lung.

"What the fuck?"

Clancy chuckled. "What the fuck, indeed." He went back to his e-reader, and I went up the steps to see Hardy Boyer sitting at one of the tables with a fucking trash can on his head as he smoked a pipe.

I picked up one of Skyler's drumsticks from the window ledge and started beating the fuck out of the can until the kid dropped the glass pipe, breaking it, and threw off the trash can.

"What the fuck you doin', man?"

I grabbed the little bastard by his shirt and jerked him up from the seat, raking his hips over the edge of the table, which probably hurt. I didn't give a shit.

"You aren't here to smoke pot and fuck around. You're here to get to know the goddamn band and learn the music. If you're not going to do that, I'll put your ass on a mother fucking Greyhound bus and send you back to Lynette. When I call Kathleen to tell her why I'm returning you by snail mail, I'm going to tell her she owes me for this fucking bus because we'll never get that goddamn skunk smell out of here."

Was I pissed? About a lot of shit, but I didn't think I was being too harsh with the guy. He needed someone to get him to see he wasn't on a holiday. He had a purpose, and if he wasn't going to live up to it, then he was off my fucking dime.

Chapter Twenty-Nine

Skyler

I walked off the stage at Gaslamp after Accidental Fire finished their four-song set. I wanted to find a bed and sleep forever, but I had the set with From the Ashes, which seemed to get longer every fucking show. I was mentally and physically exhausted.

I'd been getting text messages I hadn't told Sandy or River about. How someone got my phone number, I didn't know, but they'd threatened to burn down my house if I wasn't going to use it. I was scared shitless.

Mom wasn't really talking to me because of Regal and his bullshit, but that was fine. I was heading back to West Peoria on Monday, and Sandy was coming with me. I hoped to hell nothing happened before I got there. I loved my little bungalow.

Accidental Fire's set had been great, and I was in dire need of an energy drink, a damp towel, and a fresh shirt before I went back on the stage with From the Ashes. The good thing about playing with both bands was my biceps looked stellar, though not as good as Sandy's. I wasn't sure if they ever would, but when I wrapped my arms around Sandy's neck to kiss him, he kissed each muscle before he met my lips.

A young guy walked by with a bucket of drinks. "Hey, sorry. May I have a Green Monkey energy drink?"

"You are?" I wanted to tell him to fuck himself with that goddamn attitude, but that would be Regal's way of handling business, not mine.

"I'm the drummer, Skyler Ashe."

The guy nodded and took off. He dropped the bucket on a table behind the stage and went to the bar. I stepped into one of the dinky-ass closets they called a dressing room to freshen up.

I went to the toilet and took a piss because I'd been downing water during the performance because the fucking club was too hot. Finally, I tugged off the T-shirt I was wearing before washing my hands. I grabbed a cloth and washed my face, chest, arms, and pits.

There was a From the Ashes T-shirt hanging on a rack that I was sure was meant for me, but I wasn't wearing that just to give my father the satisfaction of having me wrapped in his brand. The longer I spent time around Regal Ashe, the more I despised the man, and my mother's submission to him upset me. I hated it, but I did respect that she was living her own life and it wasn't my business.

"Mr. Ashe, I have your drink." The young man knocked on the door, and when I opened it, he held out a tray with the drink I'd requested and a glass of ice. It was exactly what I wanted.

"Thank you. What's your name so I can tell your boss you were expeditious and polite?" Hey, I wasn't a total asshole.

"My name is Perry, Mr. Ashe. I was glad to be of service." He did this odd bowing thing before he walked away. Maybe it was part of his contract? How the fuck would I know?

I guzzled the energy drink from the glass, turning the T-shirt with the From the Ashes logo inside out. I found a pair of scissors on one of the tables and cut the arms off it, and then I reached into my back pocket and pulled out a blue bandanna, soaking it in the icy remnants of the drink before I tied it around my neck. I was ready.

I took a deep breath and walked out of the small room and down the hallway to the stage, where everyone was waiting as the adjustments were made. I'd be relieved when my family obligation was met and I was free. There was a reason I'd moved to the Midwest.

Sandy stepped up behind me and kissed my cheek as he massaged my shoulders. "You okay, teach?"

I turned my head. "I'm ready for this to be done. What are your plans for the future, Sandy?"

It wasn't ideal to ask that question at that particular moment, but I needed to know if we were headed in the same direction. I needed to know if I was more than just a summer fucking fling or if we had a real future and what it looked like.

"I'm going back to West Peoria with you. I want to be with you, Sky. We'll figure out the rest of it as we go, but we are going to make a beautiful life." A kiss on my lips sealed the deal.

"Ladies and gentlemen, From the Ashes."

Regal, Ripper, Ace, and Dusty jogged out on the stage, waving and bopping around for the crowd. I wasn't sure if it was to get themselves psyched for the performance or prove to the audience that they were still alive. I came out behind them and sat behind Regal's drum kit.

I still hated that my old kit had been smashed at Sandy's place. The cops were no closer to figuring it out than the West Peoria police were at finding who broke into my house.

I sat down on the stool, and the lights were blinding me a little, but I held the sticks in front of me and counted off. "One-two-three-four." I came down on the tom-toms instead of the crash cymbals, but Ripper, Ace, and Dusty began playing 'Man for the Job.' one of their old songs.

I kept up, but my head was foggy. We played the set, and when we got to 'Bury Me', my head spun even more. We got through the song, and as I stood to follow the band off the stage, I stumbled.

I fell off the riser and heard the crowd gasp before I threw up, which seemed endless. I tried to crawl off stage, but everything went black.

"There were small traces of cyanide in his system." I didn't know that voice.

"What the fuck is that?" I knew that voice—my Sandy.

"It's a poison. Tasteless. Odorless. It's hard to detect, and it can kill someone if enough small doses are ingested. The amount in Mr. Ashe's system wasn't enough to kill him, but it was enough to make him violently ill."

"Someone poisoned him?" Sandy sounded frantic, and I was finally able to open my eyes.

Sandy was next to me, and he appeared to be freaked out. "Baby, are you okay?" Sandy kissed my hand before he kissed my lips and brushed his thumb across my forehead.

"Yeah," I whispered.

"What in the world happened?" Sandy asked as he brushed his fingers over my hair.

"I had an energy drink between sets, and I started to feel sick while I was playing. Throwing up and passing out is all I remember."

A nurse came in and took my vitals. After she left, I turned to Sandy. "Do you think my father is involved in any of this?"

Sandy stared at me and finally exhaled. "I don't know, babe. I want to say no, but I can't deny things seem to be pointing his way. Go to sleep, okay. We'll figure this out."

I nodded and closed my eyes.

Sandy and I flew back to Illinois for a few days after I was released from the hospital so I could oversee Christine taking over the marching band camp. We'd spoken on the phone after the poisoning incident, and she'd agreed to take a stab at it. I knew my kids liked and trusted her, but I wanted them to see she had my blessing so they'd listen to her.

I had tried to track down Petey Ritter, but I hadn't had any luck. Rich knew, but he wasn't able to tell me because Petey was a minor. Hopefully, Petey would be back to school at West Peoria and I could catch up with him then.

The folks at Gaslamp had told the police they had no one on staff named Perry, and I hadn't been able to identify anyone who resembled the guy who'd brought the drink. I'd described the young man, but nobody there knew who he was.

I sat on the bleachers at the football field as Christine worked with the band. She was having difficulty articulating the instructions as I'd written them in my notebook. I walked down the stairs and onto the field, holding up my hands to silence the marching band.

They didn't know I was back and had been watching, so the cheer when I slowly walked onto the field was unexpected and made my heart smile, figuratively. It was good to know I'd been missed—and then I opened my mouth to chew them out.

"What the heck are you guys doing? This is something we learned last year." I sounded harsh, but they knew better than to jack around with the choreography we worked on every summer, and there weren't that many new kids that it should have made such a difference.

I held out my arm for Christine, who stepped closer to me. "Miss Quinton is *me*, so you need to listen to her. Now, start again." I helped Christine up on the podium I used to direct the band for halftime shows.

Christine's back straightened as she seemed to embrace the position as director, as I knew she could do. She had their attention, and they listened to her every instruction. If I ended up in San Jose with Sandy, my kids would be in good shape. Christine could handle them.

August 30th Thunder Valley Casino, Lincoln, CA

Hardy Boyer had been practicing with Accidental Fire while I'd been in Illinois with Sandy, and according to River, the guy fit in perfectly. JD had found a drum kit at a pawn shop, and they'd all kicked in money to buy it instead of using my father's kit. I gave Riv my blessing for the decision and sent some money in support.

Sandy sat next to me backstage at the casino, seemingly bored out of his mind. "You don't have to sit here, you know. You can go out on the floor and play cards or something. They're just doing a quick run-through."

"Bullshit. Last time I left you alone, some asshole tried to poison you. No way am I leaving you here alone. I have a hard time staying focused on your safety when I see you play, teach. You have my heart, you know, but I will do my damnedest to make sure you're safe. I love you, and I won't lose you."

He kissed me just as Regal walked up and stood next to us. "Isn't this cozy? Am I paying you to fuck my son?"

Sandy stood and put his finger on Regal's chest. "You're not paying me at all, you asshole. I'm here to make sure your son doesn't get killed. If I find out you had anything at all to do with this bullshit, I will fucking bury *you* where you'll never be found." It was a clever play on the words from Regal's song.

Regal turned to me. "What the fuck is he talking about?"

"Someone broke into Sandy's garage and busted up my old kit. Someone broke into my house in Illinois and vandalized it. There was the poisoning episode, and I've been getting threatening text messages that someone was going to burn my house down if I didn't return to it. Trust me, I don't want to be around you any more than you want to be around me. Get your ass behind the drums, and I'll be gone."

Marshall came running up to us from wherever he'd been hiding out. "Harmon Studio wants 'Bury Me' and your score for the movie. You beat out five other groups, and Michael Cruz confirmed that the Mastersons want Accidental Fire to play one of the side stages at Rocktoberfest."

He glanced between Regal and me. "We're sitting down tonight on the bus after the performance, and we're working this shit out. Who owns what and how much of a percentage everybody gets."

Marsh then looked at Sandy. "Since you've destroyed any confidence AF has in my ability to look out for them, you will have to act as their manager in this negotiation. I trust you can make sure they don't get screwed as you accused me of doing weeks ago."

"You bet your ass I can." With that, Marshall and my father stomped away. I could hardly wait for the show to be over. No, what I really wanted was for the whole nightmare to be over and to be back home in my bed with Sandy.

I was headed to the bus to fight over the song and soundtrack I'd worked on most of the summer. When we got back to San Jose, we were flying home so I could prepare for the new school year that began after Labor Day since I'd be in San Francisco to play at The Fillmore.

After that performance, I was out. Hardy had straightened himself up and was doing a great job with the music AF was working on, even pitching in to provide lyrics to some of the melodies Arlo was writing. They were becoming a band, and it was nice to witness.

Both bands were on the bus, along with Marshall, Sandy, and Clancy, who was there to keep things civil, I was assuming. He sat in the driver's seat, watching all of us in the rearview mirror with an authoritative eye. I wouldn't fuck with the guy, for sure.

Marsh and Regal sat across from Sandy and me, Marshall's laptop in front of him. He handed out stapled sets of pages to everyone. "Okay, here's a standard contract. We're not leaving until this is worked out, so be reasonable."

Dusty stood from his seat next to Ripper. "Before we start this bullshit, I want to announce I'm retiring for good. It's not fun anymore, and watching these kids as they work out their shit reminded me of how it used to be for us. Now, it's all about the money, and I've got enough to take me to the grave, so I quit."

I was shocked, but the expression on Regal's face told me he'd been blindsided, which gave me an idea. Sandy would probably say I was nuts, but I had everything I needed, including my football player, and the life we were making was all I wanted.

"I'm done too." Ripper stood and walked off the bus.

"Me too. It's not fun anymore." Ace was out behind him.

Tony French, who played bass and never spoke an unnecessary word, stood. "I find the draw of Montana to be more than I can resist. I'll send a forwarding address, and regarding the rewrite of 'Bury Me' and anything coming from the studio using the song, Reg, man, you can have my cut. I know I speak for the others when I say those kids did a much better job with that song than we could have done, and I believe it's best to use their version for the studio. Sky should get anything coming from the soundtrack if the studio uses it, and that's all I have to say in the matter."

I glanced at Sandy, who smirked. "I thought he was saving his voice for singing. I don't think I've heard him say more than two words the whole time I've been around." I nodded, and we both chuckled.

Sandy exhaled. "Looks like it's just you, Regal. What's it going to be?"

My father, the cocky asshole who believed he could rule the world, had just been abandoned by his band. I could only imagine the shit they'd been through with him, and as men in or near their sixties, they'd finally had enough. "Fuck it. I'll license the song to Accidental Fire, and they can record it for the movie. I want a songwriter's cut of the royalties, and I won't go after Sky for the adaptation of the soundtrack. As far as my monetary situation goes, it's my own fault, and I'll figure it out. Marshall, you're fired because we can't afford to pay you anymore, so maybe you should negotiate with those kids to represent them as a good agent should."

He stood and walked off the bus. My heart was in my throat, but relief coursed through me to the point I leaned on Sandy.

Marshall stared at me. "Okay, what about Accidental Fire? Will you guys let me represent you?"

I pointed to where the guys were sitting on a couch on the opposite side of the bus. "Talk to them. I'm not a member of the band."

I nudged Sandy, and we got off the bus to allow the band and Marshall privacy to see what they could come up with. I wished them well.

Regal walked over to where Sandy and I stood. "Look, I'm sorry I've behaved like such an asshole. I swear, I had nothing to do with any of those things you told me about earlier. You didn't tell your mom what was going on either. Why?"

I shrugged. "I see you guys twice a year. You all have your own lives, and I have mine. I talk to River on occasion, and now it seems I have another brother I didn't know about, so I'll make room for him in my life, but you, Mom, and Jeanne have enough of your own shit to work out without me piling on."

Sandy put his hand on the back of my neck. "I'm here for Sky now. We're figuring our shit out, and how dare you disrespect him by asking if you were paying for me to fuck him."

Mom, who was sitting with other significant others of the band, shot out of her seat and barreled toward us. I thought she was coming for Sandy, so I stepped in front of him. When she stepped up and slapped my father across the face, I was shocked.

"How dare you say something so disgusting, Regal. Skyler is our son, and you were absent most of his life. I had to be his mother and father. Don't you dare make a derogatory comment about him or his partner."

Mom had that hand cocked to slap him again when Clancy flew off the bus and shot around the front. There was a loud scream before Sandy ran around the bus, and like a moron, I followed.

Sandy had a pistol aimed at the guy Clancy had on the ground. I was shocked. I didn't know he carried a gun. *We'll talk about that later.*

Clancy ripped the hood off his captive's head to show a guy about River's age with dark-blond hair. He was wearing earbuds, and in his right hand—beneath Clancy's boot—was a knife.

"Who are you? What are you doing here?" Sandy's hand holding the pistol was shaking hard, so I reached over and took the gun before he accidentally shot someone. I saw the safety was on, which was good, so I put it on top of the rear tire of the bus so *I* didn't accidentally shoot someone.

"Lemme up, goddammit! I wasn't doing anything."

"Drop the knife, or I'll crush your fuckin' hand." Clancy was speaking through gritted teeth he was so angry. I wasn't surprised when the knife hit the parking lot.

When Sandy jerked the guy up, I saw it was Perry, the guy who had tried to poison me. "That's him. That's the guy who gave me the energy drink in Long Beach."

By then, we'd drawn quite a crowd, but I didn't care. "Why'd you try to kill me?"

Perry chuckled. "Kill you? I barely gave you enough to make you sick, you pussy."

"Why?" Sandy wrenched Perry's arm higher up his back, and the guy grunted in pain.

"I'm Petey's older brother. Because of you, he's in foster care until he turns eighteen next year. I was in jail when Gram died, and I couldn't get to him fast enough. He told me you'd let him stay with you until his birthday like you did when Gram was in the hospital two years ago, but you were nowhere to be found. I thought if we got you to go back to West Peoria, you could be his guardian until I can leave California when my probation finishes."

"Call the police, someone." Clancy grabbed the guy and dragged him around the side of the bus, shoving him to sit on the stairs.

I pushed my way to the front to talk to him. "Why did Petey pawn his guitar?"

Perry sighed. "To pay for my lawyer. I got caught in a drug sting in San Francisco, possession with the intent to distribute. I was just the courier, so I was given a lesser charge and sentenced to six months in jail and a year's probation because it was my first offense. I can't leave the state, so when Gram died, I couldn't be there for the funeral or to take care of Petey. Nobody would tell Petey where you were, so when that video showed up on the school's website and you posted the band's schedule, we decided to scare you into going back to West Peoria.

"Petey's staying in Peoria with a Baptist preacher and his family who are trying to beat God into him. I told him to break into your house so you'd come home to check on it, but that preacher caught him sneaking back in, and I haven't talked to him in weeks. I had to get you to go back to Illinois to check on him."

I had completely dropped the ball on Petey. This mess was all my fault.

Before I could say anything else, the police showed up, and Perry was taken into custody. Sandy and Clancy explained to the cops that Perry was planning to slash the tires on the bus and Clancy saw him in the bus's rearview mirror. They explained the other things we believed Perry had done. Sandy gave them the numbers of the other law enforcement agencies involved in San Jose regarding the drum kit, West Peoria where my house was broken into, and Long Beach where Perry poisoned me.

We all had to stay the night because it was late, so the band members went to a hotel nearby instead of going back home, and we slept on the bus. Or rather, the others slept on the bus and I sat in the booth, unable to sleep.

Clancy sacked out on the couch across from me, opening an eye to check on me every now and then. I made Sandy sleep in my bunk because he had to talk about his Glock with the police in the morning, and I wanted him sharp so he didn't end up with his sexy ass in jail.

And that was how my illustrious career as a rock star ended.

Or so I thought...

Chapter Thirty

Sandy

RocktoberfestBlack Rock, Nevada

"I can't believe I get to see this show!" Petey was standing next to me near the bus. Skyler was on the bus going over a few changes he'd made to 'Bury Me', and I was happily enjoying an adult beverage from the bar in the catering area while our new houseguest was scarfing down a massive churro that he'd picked up from a food truck nearby.

The journey to having Petey come to live with us had been a whirlwind. Skyler's friend, Rich Sohn, had investigated Perry's allegations and found them to be true—Petey was being held in the basement of the minister's home. He'd been chained to a drainpipe with only a bare bulb hanging over his head—that was turned on and off at the minister's discretion—a bucket and a Bible.

Petey was removed immediately and temporarily placed in our custody. We were living in West Peoria, so Petey was attending West Peoria High again, playing with the jazz band. What would become of him, we didn't know, but my Skyler would fight tooth and nail to see the boy had a better life than he'd had in the past.

Perry was in quite a bit of trouble, but we got him a good lawyer, and it didn't hurt that the cops found a letter on him when he was arrested that apologized to Skyler for the poison and explained the issue with Petey. We hoped the court would give him a break, but his lawyer assured us he would go to jail for some of his actions.

I didn't turn in a claim to my insurance for the busted garage door, and Sky refused to press charges for the drum kit, so the poisoning was the thing that would get him in trouble. It was a wait-and-see game at this point.

"Hey, how's it going?" I turned to see Marshall with Regal and the members of the now defunct From the Ashes.

"Really good. Skyler's going over some last-minute changes with the guys. Glad you could make it. This is Petey. He's staying with us for a while." I introduced him to everyone, and thankfully, he shook hands like a perfect gentleman.

We'd been working with him on manners. Seems Gram Elsie had had a lot of other things on her mind besides manners. As Sky had told Petey, if you wanna go anywhere in life, you need to learn to chew with your mouth closed and have a good handshake. There were many other things to teach the kid, but we were starting slow. He'd only been with us for two weeks.

"Why are we here? I knew Ripper and Franny were coming to see JD play, but Sky called yesterday and told us to get here in time for their show. It's not that we didn't want to come, but we haven't talked to you guys since San Francisco. We weren't sure they'd want us here."

Accidental Fire was taking one of the side stages at six, and Skyler had something special in mind as a tribute to his father's band. They would go down in rock history as a successful band, and one of their number one hits would be memorialized in a summer blockbuster next year, but he wanted his father's band to have one more moment of glory before the sun set on their careers. Thankfully, Easton Masterson had been great about it when Marshall approached them with the request.

We were all chatting when Michael Cruz found us. "Where's the band and Marshall?"

"Inside. They're going over the last-minute changes to the set list." I nodded my head toward Regal and company. Michael and Marshall had gotten close—apparently—so Michael knew about the surprise.

"Easton Masterson called me. They need to move Accidental Fire to the main stage. One of the bands isn't here yet. An accident has the highway closed, so they won't make it in time for their slot. If AF moves to the main stage at six, the other bands can move up an hour, and that band can play the east stage at nine. It's confusing, but I've alerted the crew to move the guys' equipment behind the main stage. They'll need to forgo a sound check over there because other bands are already playing, but we can get levels after the switch. Have them head over that way by five-thirty." With that, Michael rushed off.

The door to the bus opened and Marshall stepped off. "Was that Michael? What's going on?" I could see my brother was a ball of nerves, and I wasn't surprised at all. He knew the success of this performance was important in his career moving forward. Alicia Cordell had called him in for a come-to-Jesus meeting, and he'd straightened up his ass after that. We were still a work in progress, but we'd be fine.

"Accidental Fire has been moved to the main stage at six. It's a long explanation, but the guys need to be—" I didn't get it all out before Marshall was running in the direction Michael had gone.

Skyler came off the bus looking every bit the sexy man I loved. He hadn't cut his hair yet, and nobody at school had mentioned it. He was still on the fence about it, but he was thrilled to be back on the podium on game nights. I had volunteered to run the chains at the home games so I could watch him work, and life was purring along.

"What had Marshall running off?"

The rest of the band stepped off behind him, and everyone said hello to the members of From the Ashes. It was a bit contentious between the groups because of their less-than-stellar beginning, but things had been resolved, so it was time to move on.

"I'll only say this once, so, everyone, listen up. Accidental Fire will be playing on the main stage instead of the east stage at six. Your equipment will be moved for you, so you need to be dressed and ready to go at five-thirty."

The chatter reached epic proportions, but I herded everyone toward the catering area to grab a bite. The band didn't go on for three more hours, and hell, I was starving.

Petey was in awe of all the bands, pointing to them and telling us who they were. "That's Social Sinners over there with Embrace the Fear.

"Flightless is over there, and Grindstone is at the table next to them. Those are the guys from Warrior Black. It's so cool they all come to listen to all the bands. Oh—that's Wolf Pack. Can I ask for autographs?"

I laughed as our plates were filled with pasta, salad, and cheese bread. We went over to a large, empty table while everyone in our group started arriving with their plates.

We all ate our fill and then headed back to the bus to wait until it was time for them to head to the main stage. We pulled out more chairs and everyone sat around enjoying the atmosphere. I saw Hardy was more excited about the pot smells in the air, but he didn't go in search of it, thankfully.

A thin guy with a clipboard and a headset stopped by the front of the bus, looking at the number board on the windshield. He stepped around the side and stared at us. "I need Skyler Ashe."

River, Arlo, JD, Goldie, and Hardy started cracking up. "What did you do?" No one answered Skyler's question, so he got up and walked away with the guy.

Once they were gone, River spoke up. "We made Skyler an appointment with Tyler Kennedy. He's dating Ethan Jones from Wolf Pack, and they put out a message on the website that Tyler was doing hair and makeup for any of the band members. Sky will always be an honorary member of Accidental Fire, and we wanted to treat him."

Hope stood and walked around the table to hug the boys and thank them for thinking of Skyler in that way, which was sweet. She then came to where Petey was sitting and pulled a chair over. "Hi. I'm Hope, Skyler's mom. How do you like living with Sky and Sandy?"

"It's really great."

The two of them got lost in conversation as they tried to get to know each other. A tap on my shoulder had me standing and turning around. "Can I talk to you?"

I stood and followed Marshall around the bus. "I need to tell you something. I'm sorry I've been such a prick about everything. I love my job, but I'm still learning, and I've been so hard-headed about it. I'm going to counseling to get some help. I came out to Mom and Dad, and you can imagine how well that went."

"Yeah, I can. Well, I'm proud of you. Are you seeing Michael Cruz?"

Marsh smirked. "Yeah. He and I are thinking about throwing in together, but we haven't decided anything yet. I've been working with Franny Horn to get the band's instruments here. I had Clancy take them over to the main stage. I'm going to go over and see that everything is set up on a cart to be ready after the first song. Can you steer everyone toward the VIP section to the side of the stage when it's time?"

"Of course. You're doing a great job, Marsh. This will be a great show."

Marshall hugged me and hurried off. I felt a little sting in my eyes, but I pushed it down. I had a big surprise to pull off.

Herding the members of From the Ashes and their significant others was like herding cats. There was a lot to see, and between Petey and Hope, they were determined to see it all.

We showed our passes and were led into a VIP area with a lot of radio station contest winners and members of other bands. Murder of Crows was on the stage when we sat down, and Accidental Fire was coming after them.

Kenny Robbins made his way over to where I was standing, a big grin on his face. "Goldie's excited about this. He sent me a text that Skyler is freaking out, so maybe you should go find him. Goldie gave your name to security. I'll watch out for these folks and get the band where they need to be. Man, this takes me back."

I nodded, told Petey where I was going, and hurried over to the entrance behind the stage for the talent only. The guard looked at my pass. "You used to play—"

"For the Breeze. Yeah. I'm looking for Accidental Fire."

"Go ahead, man." He pointed to the area behind the backdrop for the band on stage. I saw Skyler and Marshall with the band, Skyler talking a mile a minute to Marsh and shaking his head.

"Thanks."

I hurried through the crowd and found my guy. "What's wrong?" He wore a white T-shirt ripped in all the right places and had a blue bandanna tied around his neck. His hair was pulled back in a bun, and there was liner around his eyes, which really made them pop.

"Look at you. They really gave you the royal treatment."

"These clowns just told me Hardy hurt his shoulder. He can't play. They want me to play in his place. I'm glad Franny got Regal's kit, but I haven't played in weeks. I can't fuck this up, Sandy."

I pulled him to the side and put my hands on his shoulders. "You've got this. It's important for the guys that this goes well, baby, and you're the best one to do it. If Hardy did hurt his shoulder, he can't go on, and you don't want to miss this tribute to From the Ashes. Now, buck up. You look smoldering hot."

Murder of Crows finished their encore and started coming off stage. Marsh grabbed my shoulder. "Go get From the Ashes now."

I honestly had no idea how I'd get them to come with me, but what Skyler had just told me about Hardy gave me an idea. I fought my way through the crowd and back to the VIP area. "Hey, From the Ashes, we need your help. The guys need you. Come with me."

Thankfully, none of them questioned me. Dusty stepped up next to me and grinned. "I worried about this. This is a larger crowd than we saw in the venues we played this summer, so I could see where they'd panic. We'll talk them down."

When we got backstage, Accidental Fire was getting ready to take the stage. Sky turned to his father and teared up. "I'm sorry for all the covert shit, but we want you guys to play with us. Your gear is over there. Regal, you sing, and I'll play."

The roadies began hustling the old guys around to get them ready, and we all heard the emcee, some radio guy. "How we doin', Black Rock?" The crowd roared.

"We have a great new band that's just making the waves. Rocktoberfest, give a warm welcome to Accidental Fire."

The guys hurried out, Sky taking the stool behind the kit, and Arlo stood behind the keyboard, mic in hand. "How's everybody doing? It's hot as fuck here, but I heard there's free water not far from the entrance, so after you listen to us, go get some while they trade setups."

Skyler held up his arms and cracked the sticks together. "One. Two. Three. Four." His arms came down on the crash cymbals, and they were off with a new song, 'Hot Tonight.' I knew it was one Arlo, JD, and River had worked on together, and it was rocking.

Sky was working hard, and I was hard watching him. After this fucking thing, I was gonna have him fuck my brains out. His eyes were closed as he played the bridge while River shredded on the guitar.

I glanced around the side of the Rocktoberfest backdrop to see a mosh pit in front of the stage and the crowd going wild. When the song ended, the applause and cheers were deafening.

Goldie walked over to the side of the stage to pick up a towel, and Marsh gave him the okay signal. He walked back to the front as he wiped his face. "Hello, Rocktoberfest! We have a treat for you guys.

"We wouldn't be a band if not for some of the best mentors in the business. Please welcome to the stage, From the Ashes." He replaced his mic and stepped back next to his bandmates while Ace, Dusty, Tony, Ripper, and last, Regal came out to rousing applause.

Regal stood at Goldie's mic, and I could see he was a little choked up. He turned around and pointed to Skyler, who counted out the slower tempo for the original song. Dusty began playing the song the way the band had played it at every venue, and Regal began to sing.

You say I'm cold you think I'm mean
You claim when I'm with you, you always feel unseen
But you don't know how hard I try to be the man who walks through life by your side

And now, you're gonna leave and rip the heart right outta me

You've found another man you think you can believe

AF accompanied them as they all sang the chorus, Regal barely able to sing through all the emotion in his throat.

'Bury Me'

Oh, set me free lay me in the ground right there beneath your feet

Without your love I have no need to breathe

Have mercy on me

Please have mercy on me

If you ever loved me, won't you bury me

As Regal's last note faded, Skyler put his arms in the air, guns blazing. "One. Two. One-two-three-four." The much faster tempo had the older guys fading back while the kids took over, playing the hell out of the song in the rewritten version. Goldie's throaty rendition fit the new version perfectly.

You want to leave and lock me in the past

If you're not in my arms I don't think I can last

He won't know you

He won't love you

He won't kiss you half as well as me

If you must go I wish you well

Before you close the door and tell me I can go straight to hell

Goldie stood next to Regal sharing the mic, and both bands sang the chorus, the older guys trying like hell to keep up.

Bury me
Oh, set me free
Lay me in the ground right there beneath your feet
Without your love I have no reason to breathe
If you ever cared then please won't you have mercy on me
Have mercy on me
Have mercy on me and
Bury me
Lay me low without your love there's nowhere else for me to go
So bury me before you walk away
Without you by my side I wouldn't want to stay.
Without your love I never ever want to stay
I just can't bear to watch you walk away

The band stopped abruptly, and Goldie handed the mic to Regal, who appeared uncertain, but he nodded and pressed the mic into Regal's hand. The crowd roared but quieted as Regal spoke first.

"This was a big surprise for us old bastards, so I want to thank Accidental Fire for their hard work. I especially want to thank my sons, Arlo on the keyboard and River on lead guitar. You're both an inspiration to me, and I'm proud of you."

I could see the guys were shocked, but they played it off. Skyler's leg was shaking as he waited.

"JD and Goldie, you guys do us proud, and last, but certainly not least, I want to thank my oldest son, the music prodigy in the family, Skyler Ashe. He rewrote the song to adapt it for a special project, and he had to deal with us cranky old farts who didn't want to change it. It was released in the nineties, and Sky brought it into the future and made it new without leaving us behind."

Regal looked at River who played the last chord again, and then he sang the ending with tears falling down his face.

So if you ever loved me won't you bury me.
Please bury me.

Skyler played the cymbal swell and then the crash, signaling the song's end. Like the first time I heard the song, I let go of a few tears. It was beautiful.

Everybody went crazy, and as they screamed and clapped, From the Ashes left the stage for the last time. Hardy then came out from the wings and took the sticks from Skyler, who was very confused, but I knew what River and the guys had done. Sky had worked so fucking hard on the song. He deserved to play it for the huge crowd.

When Sky came off the stage, I pulled him in front of me and held his sweaty body in my arms as we watched Accidental Fire soar. They sang another song they'd written, and then they sang my favorite. It was the song I would always claim as the one Sky wrote for me.

'I'll Find You'

I wake up alone I go to bed the same way
I'm tired of going out I wonder where you are today?
There once was a time I thought I'd found a true love
but in the blink of an eye it flew on the wings of a dove
Momma says you're out there Daddy says I'm a fool for
believing such things can exist
How can fate be so cruel?

[chorus]

I'll find you (yeah, I'll find you)
my heart tells me to trust you're yearning for my touch
Oh, I'll find you (yeah, I'll find you)
and when we finally meet, you'll love me just as much
And when I find you (when I find you)
Our hearts will know we fit
We've been waiting for so long it will be clear that this is it

[verse]

Our eyes will meet across a crowded room
All the rest will fade away
Our hearts will know they've found their other half

The sparks we'll feel are here to stay
[chorus]
I'll find you (yeah, I'll find you)
my heart tells me to trust that you're yearning for my touch
Oh, I'll find you (yeah, I'll find you)
and when we finally meet, you'll love me just as much
And when I find you (when I find you)
ur hearts will know we fit
We've been waiting for each other for so long
It will be clear that this is it

Sky turned to me and quietly sang a new ending.

I found you (yeah, I found you)
Our hearts know that we fit
We waited for each other for so long, and finally, this is it

We both cried then. The big football stud and his drummer-teacher partner. All it took was one smoldering look from Skyler Ashe, and that was it. Forever.

Epilogue

Skyler

West Peoria High School Gym First Pep Rally of the Season

The marching band sat in the roll-out bleachers as the students filed in. I tapped my baton against the music stand in front of me and held up my hands as I'd done many times before. "One, two, three, four."

My first-chair flutist gave a trill and then the woodwinds swelled to play the melody. The percussion came in, and then the horns. We were playing the theme for *Pink Panther*, and the kids loved it.

I glanced behind me to see Sandy and Coach James with the players behind them, ready to make their entrance. I glanced at the stage to see our principal, Mr. Hanson, shake his head, so I stopped the band and pointed to my bass drummer. He played a drumroll, and Principal Hanson announced. "Your West Peoria High School Panthers!" The players ran into the gym as the kids cheered.

Cheerleaders were flipping all over the gym floor as the team stood in two straight lines behind the principal. He motioned for the co-captains, Evan Wishnask for the offense and Curtis Johnson for the defense. Both young men stepped forward with big smiles.

"Please welcome Assistant Coach Corey James," Evan announced as Coach James ran out onto the stage and took a bow.

Curtis stepped behind the mic. "Please welcome our head coach and athletic director, Sanders Kensington."

I grinned as I held up my arms for the razzmatazz as Sandy sauntered out to the stage and shook hands with the boys.

The band stood and began playing the fight song, and the cheerleaders danced as the mascot, our own Petey Ritter, danced along with them. He'd only agreed to don the mascot outfit if he could remain anonymous. It helped him get an extracurricular on his college application.

It had been a crazy year. Sandy sold the San Jose house to Marshall and River and Arlo moved in with him. The downstairs gym was remodeled into a recording studio.

Accidental Fire signed a record deal shortly after Rocktoberfest. Hardy moved to San Jose and shared a condo with Goldie, and JD continued living with his dad.

To the best of my knowledge, Arlo and Regal never discussed whether he was Regal's son. I hoped they had the chance to do that someday, but that was between the two of them. According to River, they all got along, which was a blessing.

The fight song finished, and the band sat down. Sandy was still standing at the podium, looking all kinds of yummy. Last night, he'd had a case of nerves. He'd given interviews and soundbites to some of the most famous sports reporters in the country, but speaking to a gym full of kids made him nervous.

I'd sucked his thick cock and then fucked the nerves right out of him. As I watched him clapping for the band from the stage, he looked perfectly fine, which made me giggle as I took my seat.

"Good job, Mr. A," Christine whispered as she sat next to me in the front row. I gave her a kiss on the cheek. She'd become a great friend, and we were going to northern Illinois next weekend for her wedding to Rich Sohn.

Petey was going to stay home under Mrs. Flannery's watchful eyes. He'd taken over doing repairs and grunt work for her so Sandy and I could concentrate on things we needed at our house since we'd bought the bungalow last fall.

"I'd like to officially say hello to the students. In the summer of two thousand twenty-four, I came to West Peoria with Mr. Ashe, and I was going for a run by the football field one day when I saw a man seeding it. I stopped to speak with him for a few minutes before I went on with my run, not knowing that would become my job when I became the head coach of the Panthers."

The kids and teachers laughed, as did I. My Sandy hadn't known it was Principal James he spoke with, nor did he expect to be offered the job to coach the team after poor Coach Adams had a terrible year. He knew basketball but not so much football. Coach James helped with football and coached baseball. It all worked out wonderfully.

"Let's meet the starting lineup for the West Peoria Panthers."

Perry Ritter, Petey's brother, was still in jail for trying to poison me, but he was going to be let out on probation in December, though he couldn't leave California for three years. We planned to go to California for Christmas to see my family and Marshall, so we'd see Perry then. Marsh and Michael Cruz had joined forces and started their own talent agency, though the truth about their romantic entanglement was murky at best.

Accidental Fire was getting ready to start a US tour in May to coincide with the release of Harmon Studio's latest blockbuster, *Hurricane Alley*. The movie had been postponed for a year due to distribution issues. Sandy and I had spent June and July in Los Angeles, where I recorded the soundtrack for the movie, putting away a nice nest egg for the two of us along with the money Sandy already had. That was as much as I wanted to do with the music industry.

Accidental Fear had already factored Rocktoberfest 2025 into their tour schedule, and Sandy and I hoped to go. We'd see.

"And a big thanks to Mr. A and the band. I happen to know they've been working very hard on new marching routines for the football season, and I look forward to seeing them in person. Let's have a winning season, Panthers."

I stood as the crowd cheered and held up my arms.

"One more thing. Sky, will you marry me?" I spun to see he was on one knee with a little blue box in his hand and a worried expression on his handsome face.

Everyone knew we were a couple because we didn't keep it a secret, and surprisingly, nobody at the school had a problem with it. I was now out and proud with my handsome football coach, and it felt good.

I started running toward him, and he jumped off the stage and ran toward me. We met in the middle of the gymnasium, and Sandy dropped down on one knee again. "Will you marry me, Sky? I love you with all my heart and want to be with you for the rest of my life."

"Yes. I'd love to marry you." We hugged and shared a gentle kiss before Sandy slid the ring on my finger.

Christine stood and held up her arms, and the band played 'I'll Find You'—not really well, but as well as they could, considering it wasn't exactly written for a marching band.

It was perfect, and after the Panthers won the home opener under the coaching of Sanders Kensington, I took him home and fucked his brains out.

That night, the bed didn't smolder...it was on fire!

◻◻◻

If you enjoyed "Smolder," check out the otherbooks from Rocktoberfest 2024.

About Sam E. Kraemer

I grew up in the rural Midwest before moving to the East Coast with a dashing young man who swept me off my feet. We've now settled in the desert Southwest where I write M/M contemporary romance. I also write paranormal M/M romance under "Sam E. Kraemer writing as L.A. Kaye." I'm a firm believer that love is love, regardless of how it presents itself, and I'm proud to be a staunch ally of the LGBTQIA+ community. I have a loving, supportive family, and I feel blessed by the universe and thankful every day for all I have been given. In my heart and soul, I believe I hit the cosmic jackpot.

Cheers!

Other Books by Sam E. Kramer/L.A. Kaye

Books by Sam E. Kramer

The Lonely Heroes Complete Series

Ranger Hank
Guardian Gabe
Cowboy Shep
Hacker Lawry
Positive Raleigh
Salesman Mateo
Bachelor Hero
Orphan Duke
Noble Bruno
Avenging Kelly
Chef Rafe

On The Rocks Complete Series

Whiskey Dreams
Ima-GIN-ation
Absinthe Minded

Weighting... Complete Series

Weighting for Love
Weighting for Laughter
Weighting for a Lifetime

May/December Hearts Collection

A Wise Heart
Heart of Stone

What the H(e)art Wants

A Flaws & All Love Story
Sinners' Redemption
Forgiveness is a Virtue
Swim Coach

Love & Cowboys
For the Love of the Bull Rider
For the Love of the Lawyer
For the Love of the Broken Man

Men of Memphis Blues
Kim & Skip
Cash & Cary
Dori & Sonny

Perfect Novellas
Perfect
2 Perfect

Power Players
The Senator

Holiday Books

My Jingle Bell Heart

Georgie's Eggcellent Adventure

The Holiday Gamble

Mabry's Minor Mistake

Other Titles

When Sparks Fly

Unbreak Him

The Secrets We Whisper To The Bees

Shear Bliss

Kiss Me Stupid

Smolder

A Daddy for Christmas 2: Hermie

BOOKS by L.A. Kaye

Dearly and The Departed

Dearly & Deviant Daniel

Dearly & Vain Valentino

Dearly & Notorious Nancy

Dearly & Homeless Horace

Dearly& Threatening Thane

Dearly & Lovesick Lorraine

Dearly and The Departed Spinoffs

The Harbinger's Ball
The Harbinger's Allure
Scotty & Jay's First Hellish Adventure
Scotty & Jay's Second Hellish Adventure

Other Titles

Halston's Family Gothic - The Prologue
The Mysteries of Marblehead Manor
Mutual Obsessions

Milton Keynes UK
Ingram Content Group UK Ltd.
UKHW030858151124
451262UK00001B/79

9 798227 634931